The Whodunit Thing

Guess Who

Jo Milanne

Paperback

ISBN 978-1-7637284-8-6

Contents

PROLOGUE

The Whodunit Thing

A stand-alone novel featuring an Australian lady detective.
How Dulcy Vestige gets her man, begins with childhood aspirations and culminates in uncharted territory. This sequel expands on *three previous titles featuring characters who influence Dulcy's life from childhood through puberty to maturity.

*A FAIR CRACK
*THE PECKISH
*THE BRUISER

Also by Jo Milanne:
LEMON TANGO

Chapter 1

BEAUTY & THE TERROR

The Kiss

Dulcy Vestige and her man knew the beauty and the terror of their homeland. During their careers, they worked amongst the best and the worst of it.

Throughout her life, Dulcy upheld strict standards. Driven to get to the truth, her strait-laced attitude predisposed her to scorn wrongdoers and strive to see justice done.

The resolute young woman did what came naturally. She enlisted in the Australian Police Force straight from school. Taken under the wing of a senior mentor, DI Dougall Grimslade, spurred her ambitions for detective work.

When a main man in Dulcy Vestige's life fell from grace, her stringent ideology took a beating. Her world turned upside down. Arriving at a crossroads, sorely disillusioned, high moral ground had been abandoned. Dulcy relaxed her hard-and-fast rules to suit herself.

Boosted by a penchant for solving mysteries, Miss Vestige aspired to sleuthing from a very early age.

As a child, Dulcy spent hours hiding out in her tree house, hoping to catch a glimpse of what had been taking her sandpit toys from the backyard. She'd been rewarded to discover a rascally crow as the culprit, although the playthings were never recovered.

Dulcy's busy parents said it was her own fault for not putting her toys away. Dulcy agreed. But if she put everything away, she'd never have solved the mystery.

At times, the trap had to be baited, a ploy that came in useful later in life.

Another mystery close to home drew the young girl's interest. A crabby old widow who lived right next door, wrote a complaint to a local newspaper. Washing had disappeared from her clothesline. It had happened a few times since her guard dog died.

Dulcy crept next door and spent most of the Christmas school holidays camped out in the dead dogs disused kennel keeping watch.

After spying a big Redback spider and a web full of crawling nymphs, the child sprayed the doghouse out with insecticide. Undeterred, she lost a day waiting for the fumes to dissipate before continuing her quest to a successful conclusion. She spied the sneak thief and identified the miscreant as a woman who ran a second-hand clothing stall at a seaside flea market.

Dulcy fronted the local police station with her findings, gaining nothing. The constable on the front desk chuckled and talked down to the serious little girl. To add insult to injury, she'd been given a lollipop. Of course she took it. Why not.

Determined to get somewhere with her findings, Dulcy knocked on the severe neighbour's door. The forbidding occupant answered with a sour face.

"Whatever you're selling I don't want any." she barked.

About to have the door slammed in her face, Dulcy got in a quick response.

"I know who stole your washing."

"How would you know?"

"I saw her do it."

"So, who is she?"

"She sells clothes at the beach flea market, but I don't know her name."

"If this turns out to be true, I might forgive you."

"It is true, Missus, I promise. I told a policeman but he only laughed at me."

Dulcy admitted trespassing in the neighbour's yard and hiding out in her old doghouse.

"That's full of spiders you know." the woman said.

"Yes. I got a fright. But I sprayed them...um...I hope your poor dog didn't get bitten by a Redback."

"Nope. Brown snake. It was underneath the kennel."

"Oh."

The neighbour attended the flea market and recognised a stolen blouse she could prove absolutely to be her own. Having sewn it herself, she still had the pattern, leftover fabric and more ribbon labels printed with *Made by Me'* kept in her sewing tin for later use.

The filched item complete with the vendor's printed price tag and bespoke coat hanger, was snatched back. The seller glared as the true owner marched away. The stallholder packed up early that day, but returned to the flea market on following weekends.

The local plod was duly upbraided by the seamstress, and the case went to court. It wasn't the first time the shady dealer had fallen foul of the law. A Community Service Order came with her short prison sentence.

Appeased, the neighbour left a well-thumbed set of Enid Blyton Famous Five books beside the ladder up to Dulcy's tree house. Those very books had been the old woman's own cherished childhood favourites. A short message penned on the brown paper wrapping read: *For the little lady sleuth.*

If Dulcy needed any more encouragement to solve mysteries, those story books did the trick. She treasured the gifts and often re-read them. The little girl never again bothered the neighbour in person but posted a thank you note in her letterbox.

Ten-year-old Dulcy wrote: *I really love all the Famous Five books, thank you a million times. I am so sad your poor dog got snake bit. Those <u>durn browns</u> are the <u>wurst</u>! Sorry for hiding in the doghouse. I twig it is a sacred place because of your dearly departed. I mean the dog.*

Alone in her home, reading the childish letter, the crotchety old widow cracked a rare smile. She conceded annoying young creatures could be amusing. It caused her to think of getting another puppy, perhaps something small and suitable as a house dog. The idea cheered the lonely pensioner immensely.

At the end of high school when Dulcy and her friends reached seventeen years of age, a more serious case blipped Dulcy's radar.

For schoolies week the girlfriends shied off busier Gold Coast venues, preferring a quieter location. A ramshackle 3 bedroom cottage, had been the only roomy enough holiday rental still available in their desired beach area.

There were six single bunks, and six payers were needed to meet the expense of three weeks rent. Seven would be better but then someone would have to sleep on the sofa.

Dulcy's close knit group of friends from her senior year at the girls' grammar school, consisted of herself and four others, Pepper, Opal, Keziah and Eden.

They'd all been friends since early primary school when they formed a 'secret' club. The five girls met regularly in Dulcy's backyard tree house.

The not-so-secret club never had an official name although *The Poked Club* had been suggested using a combination of their first name initials. Their respective parents vetoed that idea. Only later did the naïve little girls realise why.

With schoolies week almost upon them, the five conferred on who else could be asked as a sixth sharer/payer. The extra person would have to be someone they all agreed upon. She must not be one of the uppity posh girls and definitely not one of the slutty ones. That criteria severely limited choices from the grammar school leavers.

At length they agreed to ask Freya Aroha, a quiet and studious loner who usually had her nose in a book. Freya never gained friends at the girls grammar, having only arrived from New Zealand during the final year. Overawed at being included, Freya agreed readily. The girl yearned to be part of a social group, despite having good reasons to keep to herself.

The five close friends drew straws for who got to share a room with Freya Aroha. Dulcy Vestige won. Or lost, depending on anyone's take on it.

Opal and Keziah shared a room and taped a sign on their door - *The OK Territory*. Pepper and Eden shared another room but couldn't come up with any good name to tape on their door.

"What about the *Peeden Territory* or the *Needpep Territory?*"
"No thanks."

Dulcy thought the door sign thing beneath her dignity, and Freya felt far too shy to offer any input. Pepper said they should combine their initials and put a sign on the front door of the cottage, perhaps something with DPOKEF for Dulcy, Pepper, Opal, Keziah, Eden and Freya.

"What about Pfoked? The P is silent." Pepper suggested, tongue in cheek.
"That would be the only time you were ever silent." Eden ribbed.

They fell about laughing but did not use that idea. It made a good start to the holiday as an ice breaker. Shy Freya actually joined in with a giggle.

The girls' holiday location accessed a surf beach via a sandy lane. The path wound through dune plants of Beach She-Oak and Coastal Banksia to emerge beside a popular public camp site. Those grounds, crowded with caravans and tents, accommodated holidaymakers and surf board riders. Sitting outdoors on pleasant summer evenings, families shared barbecues and conversation. Smoke and savoury cooking aromas often drifted up to the girls' cottage.

On a typical day, the girls went for an early dip in the surf, before sunbathing on towels. As swimwear, Pepper, Opal and Eden chose brief bikinis. Dulcy and Keziah wore less revealing one-piece racer swimsuits. Freya wore an old-fashioned shirred costume with skirted flounce, teamed with a big t-shirt and long sarong as well.

Freya only shed her all-covering sarong at the last second before entering the sea. The other girls whispered behind Freya's back, saying she was being ridiculously modest.

"If I had her fabulous figure I'd be flaunting it." Keziah said.
"Me too." Dulcy agreed.

Pepper, Opal and Eden were slim, while Keziah and Dulcy tended towards solid builds. The two more athletic girls often rued their body shapes aloud, outwardly envious of the slender set.

"At least you've both got boobs." Pepper said.
"I'd rather have a tiny waist." Keziah replied.
"Me too." Dulcy repeated her earlier wishful thinking.

In time, Dulcy trimmed down due to the demands of an exacting career, but that came about in the distant future.

For the time being, as fun loving teens, the girls enjoyed their beach getaway. Days were spent lazing, swimming and walking along the shore, inspecting pretty shells and interesting pieces of driftwood. Daily, before the sun grew too hot, they watched bronzed surfer guys riding the waves.

Among the many board riders, an interesting assortment of six youngish guys, seemed to be sharing a campsite together.

"Ooh. One each."

"That is providential."

"They've been casting an eye over us while we sunbathe, too." Pepper grinned.

"Bags the tall one if we get a chance." Dulcy jumped in.

Being slightly taller than the others, by an inch or so, Dulcy's pick was condoned, as if the boys had no say in the matter.

"I rather fancy the one with long blond hair." Pepper said.

"Oh. I was going to say him." Eden pouted.

"Fair enough, you get him. The guy with reddish hair is pretty darn cute too."

"I give long blond hair guy and the dark guy eight out of ten," Opal assessed, "but the big headband guy is exceptional. Ten out of ten for him I reckon."

"Who does that leave? Oh, the curly haired one with tattoos. I think I saw a gold earring glint as well. Bet he's a bit of a devil." Pepper said.

"Suit you then Pepper." Eden suggested.

Pepper stuck her tongue out at Eden. Everyone laughed.

"Who do you fancy, Freya?" Dulcy strove to include their timid companion.

"Oh. None of them. I would rather not get involved casually."

Freya replied primly, blushing crimson red to the very roots of her hair. They all raised eyebrows. *Was she for real?* Holiday romances were a main attraction. Dulcy made a tactful remark:

"My Mum would say you are very wise. She warned me about holiday romances."

"Mine too." Pepper said.

"And mine." Eden added.

"My Mum would be here in a shot to take me home." Keziah said.

"My Dad would not be amused either," Opal laughed. "in case you don't know Freya, my parents split and I live with my father and sisters."

Freya replied: "I don't live with my mother either. She is still in New Zealand."

This was to be a fun holiday, not a sob fest, but family dramas were ripe for gossip. While Freya had a dip in the surf, the others speculated about her.

"Maybe she has a boyfriend already? I overheard her on the phone to someone called Diddy."

"Ha ha. No. That would be her New Zealand accent. I bet she said Daddy."

"Daddy. Ooh that's childish. She might be a Daddy's girl."

"Don't be mean."

"No really. I actually saw him grab her arm and kiss her right on the lips when he dropped her off."

"So?"

"Just saying."

"Was it creepy?"

"Well everyone is different. But yeah, to me, it seemed creepy at the time. But it was also the way he grabbed her by the arm. It seemed controlling and forceful. Plus, he had a big bushy black beard."

"Yew. Gross. How could anyone want to kiss a hairy ape."

"Maybe she doesn't have any choice. Have you thought of that?"

As Freya emerged from the sea, her overly long t-shirt rode up, exposing multiple purple bruise marks on her thighs. Her glance at the others seemed guilty. Fortunately, they all wore dark sunglasses so could pretend not to notice. Freya quickly pulled the shirt down and re-wrapped her enveloping sarong. She felt sensitive and embarrassed by the bruising and did not want anyone asking about it.

Later, in private, the others came up with the thought that Freya's father might be abusing her. They spent time discussing the possibility at times when Freya was in the shower, or outside on a phone call. Her phone rang quite often and she always answered in a soft voice before hurrying outside for privacy.

"He's checking up on her I bet."

"She said her mother doesn't live with them."

"And I saw him grab her arm and kiss her on the mouth, remember."

"Then there's the bruising. No wonder she keeps herself so covered up."

"Now let's be realistic. Some fathers do innocently kiss their daughters on the mouth."

"Mine hasn't since I was a toddler. He kisses me on the forehead, if at all."

"Mine neither. I can't remember if he ever did."

"But some do. And she might have got that bruising in a number of ways."

"Sure. It's possible. I got bruised like that at gym practice."

"Does she even go to gym?"

"I've never seen her there."

"Aha. So how did she get those bruises? Are you thinking what I'm thinking?"

The adventurous 'poked club' girls decided Freya's problem needed sorting, and they were just the ones to do it. Dulcy summed up:

"We have some time and opportunity to work on Freya's situation as a project."

"A club project! We haven't done one for way too long," Keziah clapped her hands, "I'm in," she said.

"Count me in too." Opal chimed.

They made a unanimous pact to help their introverted New Zealand friend escape her bullying father.

Chapter 2

ALL THE WAY

With The Surfers

It didn't take long before the cheeky board riders made themselves known to the group of young beach belles. Their camping holiday had been great for surfing, and having some single 'women' show up, only made it better. And there were six!

"One each." Thaddeus, the tallest one observed.

"Huh. The legal brain has already arrived at a verdict."

Boone squeezed salt water out of his long blond pony tail.

"Use both hands Boone."

"Huh?"

"To count up to six." Thaddeus advised.

"The nerd is a comedian."

Thaddeus Maekris shammed slight offence, but he really liked being called a nerd. It suited his bookish law student nature.

Angus, who was a big enough bloke to get away with wearing a Hawaiian floral print headband, said:

"We should invite them over."

"For what?" Curly leered.

"Settle down Curly. You'll scare them off with all your tatts and junk jewellery."

"Junk! It isn't junk."

"Why's it going rusty then?" Jarrah replied.

"Nice try for a blackfella Jarrah. But gold doesn't rust. Dickhead."

"Get stuffed." Jarrah replied mildly.

The mates habitually insulted each other as part of their familiar camaraderie. Jarrah was okay with being called a blackfella, it's what his own people called themselves. The various ethnicities made for a fairly typical mixed bunch of Australians.

In the girls' cottage, Opal called Keziah a white girl in jest when the English girl screamed over a spider. Keziah would never dream of calling Opal a black, for fear of sounding racist. However, Keziah had no problem calling out reverse racism.

"Hey. That's racist Opal, you calling me a white girl." Keziah reprimanded.

"Why? Just stating a black and white fact. You're white. I'm black."

"You're more brown really," Keziah amended, "sort of milk coffee."

"You're just milk then. Milk sop."

"Yep. When it comes to spiders I am milk sop."

Keziah admitted to her arachnid phobia without rancour. At that point, the large Huntsman tarantula jumped towards Opal who emitted an ear-splitting shriek. Keziah leapt to the other side of the room more in reaction to Opal's scream than in her fear of the big spider.

"Now your panties are brown as well Opal. I'd say chocolate fudge."

"You're not wrong. I had a white girl moment there." Opal laughed.

"Get Dulcy. She'll know what to do."

Dulcy calmly threw a towel over the spider and shook it outside into a garden.

"Don't know what you'd do if it was actually something dangerous." Dulcy said.

"We'd get you of course." Opal laughed.

Freya, Pepper and Eden appeared on the scene to see what all the noise was about.

"Humongous tarantula." Keziah claimed.

"Nah. He wasn't that big. Wait till his daddy shows up." Dulcy said.

"Luckily one of us is a tough woman." Opal smiled.

"Yeah. My big Dad would ask my little Mum to deal with it." Pepper reckoned.

"Mine would say leave it be and let it eat bugs in the house." Eden said.

"What would your father do Freya?" Opal attempted to extract information.

"My father would probably throw a shoe at it." Freya replied.

Afterwards, in secret club discussions, it was decided Freya's dad must be the violent type for throwing a shoe at a spider. It played into expanding their theory that Freya's father abused her.

"We need more to go on. But it's beginning to look like our first impressions pan out." Dulcy said. "Poor Freya is in a terrible situation."

"I vote we tell authorities when we get home."

"What authorities?"

"Maybe child welfare? Or police? Or our headmistress even though we've finished school?"

"We could ask the head's advice anyway. She'd know where to go with it."

"For now, let's enjoy our break. Freya is safe with us. I'm going for a swim."

That morning, a mild ocean swell only rolled in half decent breakers now and then. The surfers idled offshore on their boards, bored and disgusted with waiting around, until the girls showed up.

"Here come the ladies." Thaddeus noted. "Things are looking up."

"I like the redhead." Jarrah said.

"Seriously then, that makes her a dead cert for you." David laughed.

Always popular with girls, Jarrah inevitably got his pick of any selection.

"They mightn't like any of us of course." Angus remarked.

"If they've got any taste." Thaddeus added.

"Killjoy. Of course they'll like us. I reckon they've been checking us out too."

"So do we invite them over for a fried sausage?"

"Yeah. I feel a sausage sizzle coming on." Curly said.

"Speak for yourself."

"I am."

"Guessing they're only schoolies. Better mind our manners."

"What manners."

"Exactly."

"I'm starving. Time for second breakfast."

It was as good an excuse as any to head for shore, and walk right by those six alluring 'women'. About to swim, the girls decided to lay on towels instead when they noted the surfers paddling into shore. Boards were dragged up the beach and water shaken from hair. A wide course taken back to camp took the young men very closely past the sunbathers, who studiously ignored them.

"A good day for sunbaking." David remarked as an opener.

"Oh hi."

Pepper looked up in mock surprise, as if suddenly aware six strapping bronzed board riders appeared as if by magic.

"Not too many waves at the moment." Jarrah added.

"Are you camping?" Dulcy asked although they knew the answer.

"Yep. Bivouac on the grounds." David replied.

"Bivouac?"

"Don't mind Davo, he is into everything military," Thaddeus replied, "but we've got a couple of tents and some camping stuff. So loosely speaking, it might be described as a bivouac."

"Sounds good." Opal remarked.

"How about yourselves?"

"Renting a cottage. Just up on the other side of the dunes."

"Uh huh."

"It's a quiet spot here. We're avoiding schoolies week on the Gold Coast."

"But we are actually schoolies ourselves." Dulcy added, to be precise.

"The night life is a bit quiet here though." Angus said.

"Nonexistent to be accurate." Thaddeus amended.

"Early to bed and early to rise," Keziah sighed, "supposed to make men healthy, wealthy and wise. Not sure if it applies to girls."

"Yeah all that. But anyway, we have a sausage sizzle most evenings, around a campfire." Curly dared to mention.

"Must be nice eating out in the open air."

"Yep, we go through the bread and tomato sauce like demons as long as there's a sausage in it."

"Got to love a sausage sizzle." Pepper smiled.

All twelve young people waited for some opening gambit. David stepped up.

"Say. Just a random thought. Why don't you drop by this arvo? We've got heaps of sausages and stuff."

The girls feigned complete surprise at the invitation they fully expected. Only the quiet New Zealander, Freya, held back, looking less than delighted at the prospect. Dulcy observed Freya's reticence and decided her abusive father had a lot to answer for. *Poor Freya!*

The tall lad Thaddeus had his eye on the shy girl from afar. Despite Freya's modest beachwear, he could tell she had the best figure. He admired her quiet reserve, confident his strict Greek parents would approve of a such a girl, if he were ever to bring Freya home. That long shot jumped way ahead in speculation. Tall, dark and handsome Thaddeus enjoyed popularity with the fairer sex. He'd never been turned down for a date. However, all romantic prospects were assessed according to his future in the family law firm. Any girl he partnered had to be eminently respectable to gain approval.

The group exchanged first names and the get together was set for a barbecue at the surfers' campsite. The girls supplied salads, and the guys had sausages sizzling on the hot plate over a crackling campfire, when they arrived. Countless stars twinkled in a clear sky and a light briny breeze off the ocean dissipated smoke from the barbecue. Despite the warm evening, everyone chose to sit around the fire.

Freya Aroha attempted to get out of the impromptu party. The other girls urged her to go, fibbing none of them would go without her. Fat chance of that, but the guilt trip forced the reluctant member to tag along.

During initial small talk, the girls ascertained that the campers were probably in their early twenties. The young men mentioned having to get back to work, college or university in a few weeks time. Socialising with older guys held an element of excitement for the seventeen year old school leavers. Apart from Freya, they loved being wooed by the surfers.

Thaddeus made sure to sit beside Freya. He kindly handed her two triangle folded paper napkins with her plate, as he said:

"There you go little lady. You see, not all Australians lack social graces."

"Thank you."

"So I believe you hail from Aotearoa." Thaddeus persevered.

"Yes."

"To my ear, Aotearoa sounds more mystical than New Zealand. Land of the Long White Cloud is a beautiful description of your homeland too."

Freya nodded and blushed but would not be drawn into conversation. Everyone, including Dulcy could see Thaddeus's keen interest in Freya. The girls hoped the well-mannered suitor might bring her out of her shell.

From a distance, Dulcy had opted for the tallest prospect at first, but soon changed her mind. The tallest, Thaddeus studied law so he could be good for Freya, and might even supply legal advice regarding her father.

The combination of David's attributes, a most handsome face, ready smile and toned body attracted Dulcy's keen interest. He spoke of going into the army, and she admired the discipline and civic responsibility in his choice.

"I thought about the army too." Dulcy admitted.

"So will you join up?" David asked.

David liked this down-to-earth girl. Dulcy seemed a breath of fresh air compared to his current high-maintenance ditzy girlfriend, Zelia, back home.

"Tossing up at the moment, but the police force has always been my main aim." Dulcy replied.

"That's adventurous." he said.

Dulcy's best friend Opal joined in:

"Dulcy loves solving crimes. You know, she caught her first criminal at just ten years old. The thief was an adult woman who ended up with a jail sentence."

That brought the talk around to how Dulcy managed that, impressing David with her capability and tenacity. He began glancing at her full bodied figure, and studying her facial expressions while hanging on her every word. Curly whispered an aside to Boone.

"David's hooked. Poor bugger."

"There will be hell to pay if Zelia finds out."

"For sure." Curly mimed a throat cut.

Curly, adorned with tattoos and piercings, liked the sultry Italian girl, Pepper, though he held back, his bravado all a false front. Pepper detected his interest and smiled a cheeky come on, as they only had a limited time to get together.

Boone with his long blond surfer style hair had his eye on Eden, though did not make any definite move towards her either. Slim, fair-haired Eden cast veiled peeps towards him, making them both blush as their eyes met.

Jarrah tagged the English rose Keziah early on, and he was not shy about going after her. Flattered, the quiet lass enjoyed his preferential treatment.

Angus humbly mentioned he also planned to join the police force. Opal, who had rated him a ten out of ten, commended his choice: "Wow Angus. With your sturdy build I can just see you as a policeman. I bet you work out. Your massive biceps are amazing. Would you mind if I had a little feel?"

And so began Angus's lifetime of being putty in Opal's hands.

"Angus has had it too." Curly whispered to Boone.

"Yeah I can see that. Looks like the big mug has gone all soft and mushy."

"What are you two whispering about?" Pepper asked.

"Curly said you look hot." Boone ad-libbed.

"I am hot. It's a warm evening." Pepper fanned her face.

They all began to pair off nicely, apart from Freya and Thaddeus. Freya rose to leave. Claiming fatigue and in need of an early night, she politely thanked the hosts for the barbecue. Thaddeus saw a possible chance to be alone, and offered to walk her home. The timid girl's horrified expression did not go unnoticed by Dulcy, who made an on the spot suggestion to save Freya's discomfort.

"We've got ice-cream back at the cottage, why don't we all go for dessert?"

So began a pattern for the coming days, barbecue at the bivouac and dessert at the cottage. Most of the group soon closely paired off, taking walks along the moonlit beach as separate couples. Only Thaddeus dipped out with Freya, who refused even slight overtures of friendship. Freya retired to her bedroom whenever the guys came for desserts, always pleading tiredness. The clubhouse girls talked about Freya's rude behaviour behind her back.

"She could at least be polite and join in." Pepper remarked.

"Well. That's who she is. I reckon her abusive father has made her like that."

"Sure. That makes sense. I feel really sorry for her."

"Poor thing. We really have to do something."

Within a few days, David commented on Freya's shyness to Dulcy, who explained the theory they had developed.

"Just quietly, David, we worry that she might be abused by her father."

"She is definitely introverted. Do you know the family?"

"No. Freya was brought in as a sixth to help pay the rent. She only came to our school recently so we hardly know her. She was never part of our club."

"Club?"

"Don't laugh. Five of us started a club in my tree house when we were kids. We were going to call it the *Poked* club, made up of our first initials."

"That's awful."

"I know. Our parents thought so too. It was never officially called that but we sometimes use the name facetiously."

"So what did you do at this club?"

"Mostly we ate snacks and lazed about reading books and comics."

"I used to be a comic buff as a kid. Which ones did you like?"

"My favourites were about the Canadian Mounties – I loved how they always got their man. But sometimes we took on projects as well, like looking for lost dogs."

"Sounds like it was a fun club."

"It still is. Now we're treating our concerns over Freya as a club project."

"Have you any proof that her father abuses her?"

"No. Just hints. The strongest being he was seen pulling her back into the car and kissing her on the mouth. And her mother doesn't live with them by the way."

"When was this?"

"When he dropped her off at our holiday let. And we've noticed she has some bruising, though she is careful to cover up."

"Crikey. So, I guess he will be picking her up at the end of the holiday."

"That's the arrangement."

"Maybe I'll have a friendly chat with him." David mused.

"It's only a theory, David, and we've got no real proof. I didn't see him when they arrived, but I believe he's a really big fellow."

"Angus will back me up and he's a really big fellow as well."

David considered asking Thaddeus as another back up, but the law student would most likely come up with some boring legal reason against it. Dulcy thought causing an upset wasn't a nice ending to their holiday, but they had to do something.

"Freya will be devastated to be made the centre of attention. We planned to report our suspicions to authorities immediately when we get home."

David reckoned authorities would be slow to act, and in the meantime the abusive father might take it out on Freya.

"Never fear Dulcy. I'll discuss it with Angus without telling the others. We'll work something out. At least we can be prepared for the worst, if necessary."

"Thanks David. See what happens. That can be a plan B. But we don't want to cause more trouble for Freya. Or make trouble for you guys either."

"Wouldn't it be better to stop her going home with him? I mean, could any of you offer her somewhere else to stay?"

"I should. Good thinking. My parents would understand. But Freya would have to agree. I can't just kidnap her."

"How do you feel about confronting Freya and pleading the idea of going to your place for her own safety?" David asked.

"Awkward. I scarcely know her. Pleading is not my strongest point either, to be perfectly honest."

"What if a few of us do it together. Like an intervention."

"God no! That would be too cruel. I couldn't do that to Freya."

"But if she agrees, you could whisk her away before her father gets here."

The situation came to a head sooner than expected: Freya went outdoors to answer another of her frequent phone calls. Her voice rose high enough to be heard by Eden who had been hanging towels on the clothesline. Eden reported back to the others while Freya took a shower.

"So I heard her say, 'I miss you too but I want to stay for the whole time. Yes of course there are some guys on the beach. Surfers. No please don't do that,' anyway she seemed to be having a bit of an argument." Eden said.

"Is he being an overprotective father? Or is he jealous?"

"That is the question."

"Hush. The shower just turned off. She'll be here in a sec."

Freya came out of the bathroom, red eyed. It looked as if she had been crying.

"Is anything wrong Freya?" Dulcy asked.

"I might have to go home early." she replied.

"Oh no. Why?"

"Just a thing. Anyway it won't take me long to pack. He'll be here soon."

The others were taken aback. Dulcy took the bull by the horns and ran down to the camping grounds to get David. She was unsure where it would go from there. After quickly explaining, David enlisted Angus's help, and the two strong young men followed Dulcy back to the cottage. In the meantime, Opal questioned Freya:

"Do you want to go Freya?"

"No, I don't at all. It's been lovely having this break. Just us girls together. That is, until the surfers turned up. Especially Thaddeus."

"Poor Thaddeus. He really likes you."

"He seems a nice person and his interest is flattering...but..."

Freya's comment was interrupted by the arrival of David and Angus at the same time as a car pulled up in front of the cottage. Dulcy wrung her hands in consternation. She invited Freya's father inside rather than have an argument in the street. He seemed in a hurry and declined to come in.

"I won't stay thanks. I've just come to take Freya home."

The big Maori man rumbled the words in his deep bass voice. Combined with his bushy black beard, he seemed surly and hostile. Freya came outside to meet him while everyone quaked imagining the poor girl must feel terrified. Yet Freya spoke confidently, in an annoyed tone of voice.

"I told you not to come, but you might as well come in now."

"I missed you too much. And I was worried." he replied.

They all piled into the living room.

"Freya doesn't want to go." Opal said accusingly.

"Dulcy says she can stay with her." David offered.

"What? Why?"

"Come on Freya. Sorry but we've seen the bruises. And we are just looking out for you." Dulcy replied gently.

The shy girl gaped at the group.

"Oh really! And what did you make of that?" Freya cried.

"It's pretty obvious Freya. From what we've seen you are in an abusive relationship with your father." Pepper did not mince her words.

"Oh my god!" Freya exclaimed.

David and his big friend Angus, stood prepared to confront Freya's formidable father, fully expecting his anger to boil over into violence.

"What? You all think I caused Freya's bruises?" the man shouted in alarm.

Freya appeared mortified with embarrassment. She said:

"The bruises are from my insulin injections. I am diabetic."

The others exchanged puzzled glances, unsure if Freya made that up.

"I can see by your expressions you are doubtful. Alright. I guess you might as well know the whole truth now. Didy is NOT my father. He is my husband."

"Your husband!"

The big man replied: "Yes. I am Didy Aroha. Freya is my wife and I would never hurt her."

The friends suddenly all spoke at once after being gobsmacked for a full minute. Lots of jumbled questions followed the startling announcement.

"We decided to keep my married status a secret until I finished school. We didn't want anyone making a big deal of it." Freya admitted. "It is why I chose to complete my education in Australia, instead of in New Zealand."

"And by the way, I am way to young to be Freya's father." Didy huffed.

Freya laughed at last. She went to her husband's side and kissed his hairy cheek.

"Didy is only twenty-three. I told you Didy my darling, that beard makes you look so old."

"But I thought you loved my beard. You do don't you Freya?"

Freya quoted Shakespeare:

"The course of true love never did run smooth."

"What does that mean? Are you saying my beard feels rough to you Freya?"

Freya's non-reply spoke volumes.

"Is there a barber in the town?" Didy Aroha asked.

"You could do with a haircut too." Freya smiled somewhat smugly.

"Oh dear. We are so sorry for jumping to conclusions. But you see, we had your best interests at heart, Freya." Dulcy apologised for everyone.

"We thought you were saying 'daddy' not Didy." Pepper said.

"In a New Zealand accent. Anyway, that's how it seemed." Opal added.

Didy Aroha explained: "I am named Didy after a grandfather. My mother is half Indonesian, you see."

Everyone shuffled feet, red-faced, suddenly overcome with remorse for what they'd misconstrued.

"So Didy, you have come to take Freya home before the holiday is up?"

"He worried because my blood sugar skyrocketed. My fault for over indulging on ice-cream and sausages on bread. That's why I had to avoid the desserts."

"I am afraid for Freya and I believe she needs to see her doctor." Didy said.

"Why didn't you at least tell us of your diabetes Freya?" Dulcy asked softly.

"I don't like being different. I was just trying to fit in and not seem weird. Anyway my glucose levels have gone down again now that I have avoided sweets and carbs for a few days."

"So you want to stay on?" Didy asked his young wife.

"I don't know. Now that you're here. Maybe I should go." Freya replied.

Everyone thought it a terrible shame Freya's holiday had to be curtailed after only one week.

David came up with a solution: "Didy, could you stay for the rest of the holiday, yourself?"

"There's a thought. I could. I am owed time off work."

"Then you must stay," Dulcy decided, "Didy, you can have my room with Freya, and I will sleep on the sofa."

"Wow. That is really nice of you." Didy Aroha replied. "I will shout takeaway tonight for everyone. Anything. Whatever you want. As long as it doesn't come to over fifty bucks all up." his laugh boomed through the room.

So the sofa came into use after all. Thaddeus had been enormously pleased to learn of Freya's married status. It assuaged his feelings of rejection.

"Thank goodness," he declared, "I couldn't understand how my indelible charm, impeccable manners and impressive stature failed. I thought I'd lost my mojo there for awhile."

"What mojo?" Boone teased.

"Yeah, what mojo Thad?" Jarrah laughed.

Amid all the ribbing, Dulcy kicked herself for the grand blunder. It might have been worse if David and Angus had a set-to with Didy before learning the truth. They might have been charged with assault. Dulcy would never forget the awful gaffe.

The hard lesson compelled Dulcy to check facts before jumping to conclusions and judging others.

Her diligent attention to detail would earn respect from an important associate in the future. But at this early stage, Dulcy could not foresee how her career would pan out. Her immediate concern had been to vacate the bedroom for Freya and Didy.

Dulcy packed her bags and shoved them under the sofa.

Later, walking together along the beach at dusk, David picked up on Dulcy's self-condemnation.

"It worked out well in the long run anyway, Dulcy. I reckon Freya kind of brought it on herself, but I understand why she behaved that way." he said.

"I still feel ugly." Dulcy replied. "Anyway I've relegated myself to sleeping on the couch now. Karma."

"If the couch gets too uncomfortable I'm happy to share my sleeping bag with you, and by the way, you're far from ugly." David told her.

"Cheeky thing." Dulcy smiled.

"I think you're beautiful." David said sincerely.

Serious about the sleeping bag, David took Dulcy's hand in his. Tentatively they shared a first kiss together. David led her into the darkened sand dunes.

The thrum of the ocean beat a rhythm with their heartbeats, urging them on.

Dulcy fell easily smitten with her first ever lover. David suppressed any twinge of guilt over his regular girlfriend at home. He had never considered Zelia to be a forever kind of thing anyway.

Over the next two weeks, David and Dulcy revelled in each other's company. Under the cover of darkness, they enjoyed intimate romantic episodes on the beach every night. All too soon, the holiday sped to an end. David asked if they might continue their budding relationship before he went into army training camp. Dulcy agreed readily. She had tumbled head-over-heels in love with David Dubois. Among the girls, Dulcy and Opal were particular best friends. They confided in each other about 'going all the way' - Dulcy with David and Opal with Angus.

"So we've done it now. Does this make us bad girls Opal?"

"Not really. Just doing what comes naturally. Anyway, I'm going to marry Angus." Opal smiled dreamily.

"Does Angus know about this?"

"No of course not. We only just met a couple of weeks ago."

"Um...but wouldn't marriage depend on what Angus wants?"

"He does want it. He just doesn't know it yet. And not only does he want it, I'm going to let him think it's his own idea." Opal winked.

"Okay. Apparently, for a slender willowy little sheila, you can handle that big hunk of a bloke quite well."

"I can. He weighs a ton. Talk about a beefcake. I had to be the one on top. He pretended to have no say in the matter. He even said 'eek' when I held him down and straddled him."

Opal and Dulcy shared amusement at Angus's expense. It gave Dulcy more to think about.

"Really? You go on top? I never thought of taking that position."

"Add a little spice and try it next time Dulcy. Pepper reckons riding the guy is the best way to get where you want to go."

"Pepper should know, she's made a comprehensive clinical study of it. I am definitely going to try it on David next time, but I doubt if it will scare him. It's funny, big Angus pretending to be afraid of you, Opal."

"I knew from the first time I set eyes on Angus, he is the one for me. I can't exactly explain why. What do you most like about David?"

Dulcy gave that serious thought.

"Bravery, being prepared to front up for Freya, and his career choice of the army. I imagine him as my brave soldier."

"Bravery counts with me for Angus too."

"Even though he said *eek*?"

"It seemed really cute at the time. You should have seen it! Well, perhaps not in the circumstances. Anyway, everyone can see David is absolutely besotted with you Dulcy. So how does he measures up as a lover? If it's not too rude a question."

Opal wanted to hear all the hot details. Dulcy had no prior lover to compare David with but gave it her best shot:

"I suppose I'd have to say, David is forceful." Dulcy admitted.

Opal could not envisage Dulcy taking an upper hand in the seduction, and she   instinctively knew the handsome David would be experienced.

"So Dulcy...are you saying David forced himself on you the first time?"

"Not really. I mean, I wanted him like mad. I'm besotted with him too. But he took charge. I don't know if I could have stopped him. Not that I wanted to."

"Hmmm. I see. So did the earth move for you?" Opal asked.

"What does that really mean anyway?" Dulcy wanted clarification.

"It generally means achieving an orgasm. So did you?"

"I don't know. Not sure. How can you tell?"

"Oh dear Dulcy. That means you didn't. Because you'd absolutely know it, if you did."

"I suppose you know because the earth moved for you with Angus?"

"Ooh yes. That's why I'm going to marry him. No one could be better for me."

"Did I fail then? Or can I blame David?"

"According to Pepper, it can take time. Everyone's different as well. I feel really lucky to click with Angus right off. Maybe David rushes you."

"I do feel it is over quickly. David is so eager for me, so I can't complain."

"Eager is good. Angus says he loves that about me." Opal replied dreamily.

"Now I can't wait to try your suggestion. I want to feel the earth move too."

"Yep. Do it Dulcy. I say, take the upper hand. No member of the poked club can ever call themselves wilting violets."

"Now we really are the poked club."

"Funny isn't it, we thought Freya seemed ridiculously shy and old-fashioned, but she got poked well before any of us."

"In the interests of accuracy, we can't claim to know how well she got poked."

"Dulcy! That's a very naughty comment."

"True though."

Opal and Dulcy shared a titter. Aware of transitioning into the first phase of adult life, the girls obsessed over their newfound sexual maturity. Dulcy aspired to feeling the earth move with David since Opal seemed so sure it was the ultimate thrill. The recommended novel position filled her thoughts.

Sadly, disaster struck, robbing Dulcy of any chance with David that night.

David Dubois' current girlfriend, Zelia Wild, turned up at the beach bivouac. The surprise visit had not been welcomed by anyone else, least of all David and Dulcy. Zelia arrived just on sunset, as the group shared a barbecue supper. Most of the couples sat in pairs, including Freya and her newly clean-shaven husband, Didy Aroha, who definitely looked a lot younger without his beard. Busily heaping a plate with food, ready to share it with David, Dulcy had been about to sit beside him on a cushion he'd placed in readiness for her comfort. Then Zelia sashayed in, swaying her hips and grinning. David had his back to the new arrival. Dulcy's intention stalled as the beauty zoomed in on her David. The romantic ambiance of the evening changed in a heartbeat.

"Uh oh." Boone uttered quietly, nudging Curly.

"Shit." Curly swore under his breath.

"Look who's here Davo." he urgently warned his mate.

David spun around, startled. His long time girlfriend was the last person on earth he wished to see.

"Zelia!" David exclaimed, standing up to face her.

"Surprise lover boy. Did you miss me?"

Zelia threw her arms around David and claimed his lips in a long and passionate kiss. David's hands held her waist as she humped suggestively into his automatic erection. He never could control that thing. Caught out, speechless, he didn't dare look at Dulcy. Zelia laughed, sure she'd stunned David with her spontaneous sexy greeting.

Dulcy froze. Put on the spot, she did not know where to look, or what to do. Everyone, except Zelia, knew Dulcy and David were in a relationship. Clever enough to save the awkward moment, Thaddeus forestalled Dulcy's instinct to run away. He promptly took the plate of food from her hands.

"Thanks my lovely," the tall guy said aloud. In a quieter aside, he whispered, "come sit by me Dulcy".

Benumbed and humiliated, Dulcy managed to spare a grateful look to Thaddeus. She sat beside the thoughtful law student, and somehow endured the evening. When everyone went back to the flat for ice-cream afterwards, David and Zelia stayed behind at the campsite.

Dulcy went to the bathroom to cry in private and splash her face with cold water. Opal and Keziah took pity. They stayed with their devastated friend rather than accompany their own new boyfriends for beach walks. In the long run, the trio shared the *OK Territory* bedroom. Most of the night, they sat up crying in sympathy with Dulcy and lamenting the dangers of holiday romances. Dulcy appreciated her friends' support but could not be consoled.

"I'm an idiot." she sobbed. "A stupid pathetic fool."
"No you are not at all. David is a prize bastard." Opal hugged her friend and rocked her like a baby.
"I'm sorry girls. I just can't do this anymore."

Dulcy went home early the next day, before the holiday ended.

Caught red handed, David had seen no way out of the predicament when his possessive girlfriend turned up unannounced. Neither could he get out of sharing his sleeping bag with Zelia, since she had nowhere else to sleep. Zelia took her welcome for granted, actively making love to David, who rose to the occasion without too much effort. Yet, all the while he longed to be with his new love interest.

Dulcy disappeared from his life before David could see her again. The two-timer regretted hurting the young girl so badly. He'd fallen in love with her, and the agony of heartbreak caught him off guard.

David Dubois determined to ease off with Zelia Wild and track down the seventeen-year-old who had won his avid affections during the beach holiday. Unfortunately, he had no idea how to contact her and Dulcy's loyal group of girlfriends refused to help him out. All he gained on appeal had been a severe telling off.

Chapter 3

THE SOLDIER

& The Stalker

As a full time recruit, David Dubois went into Kapooka Boot Camp for three months intensive army training. Sapped by strict discipline, his self imposed personal problems fell by the wayside. David threw himself into the army career he'd always wanted. In his absence, Zelia Wild tested someone else, and caught the law student Thaddeus Maekris on the rebound.

Despite Freya proving to be married, Thaddeus badly needed a quick boost to his ego. The tall guy wanted nothing more than a discreet convenience. But Zelia clung like a leech in public. Her exhibitionism clearly revealed what they'd been up to and Thaddeus rued giving in to easy temptation.

Mama Maekris would never believe her angelic boy indulged in a premarital physical relationship. Thaddeus' father, however, held no misconceptions. When the man took his grown son aside to stress the importance of safe sex, Thaddeus felt suitably rebuked.

When Zelia visited the Maekris home uninvited, such a major transgression of polite etiquette caused great offence. Thaddeus' parents ranted that the girl dressed too suggestively, spoke too coarsely, and lacked respectable manners.

"Son, you must guard your reputation. Need I remind you, any hint of scandal reflects badly on the firm."
"Yes. I am sorry to have encouraged her and it went further than intended. Of course, I will end it."
"That is the wisest course, my boy."

Thaddeus had made no promises to Zelia. He gratefully distanced himself from her with less than one iota of guilt.

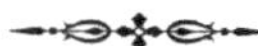

After the devastating holiday romance let-down, Dulcy Vestige tried to forget David Dubois by doggedly pursuing her chosen career path in the police force. Driven by her purpose, Dulcy advanced quickly.

Being teamed with a seasoned officer doubled Dulcy's chances of success. The grumpy senior detective, Dougall Grimslade, tasked with showing the novice recruit the ropes, only accepted the duty with a grain of salt.
The dour man doubted this fresh-faced sheila would last long. Surely the hardened criminals and seedier cases would soon have the young woman begging for a cosy desk job. He'd been wrong.
Dulcy Vestige proved a tough nut who won Grimslade's grudging respect. Shortly, the unlikely partnership achieved something akin to friendship and mutual admiration.

While Dulcy strove to get over David, he clung to hope they might meet again.

Zelia's temporary fling with Thaddeus did not alter her disposition. She still considered David Dubois as her prerogative. Attempting to ease away, David advised Zelia to see other people. He told her his army career would make him unavailable for a long time. Wily Zelia suspected David's ulterior motives and would not be put off.

"Will you be seeing other women yourself then?" Zelia pouted.
"I expect to be too busy for any of that." David hedged.
"But will you if you can?" Zelia persevered.
"I don't know. Play it by ear."
"You sound pretty casual about it." she accused.
"Just practical." he replied.

David and Zelia did not live together but a lot of her belongings ended up in his flat. To further ease her out, David decided to give up the rental and rely on army accommodation or temporary digs with mates. He hired storage space for his own use without telling Zelia in case she wanted to share it.

David recognised his short-comings in not facing Zelia's possessiveness more honestly. On the one hand he didn't like himself for it. On the other, he justified his decision as being kinder to Zelia by easing off gradually. He told himself he was setting her free.

Nonetheless, David Dubois' ulterior motive aimed at finding Dulcy Vestige again. He sought help from a good surfing buddy who had wed Dulcy's best friend.

Big brawny Angus married Opal and also thought it had been his own idea. Within a few years, Opal and Angus Bridcombe produced three beautiful brown-eyed daughters, including a set of identical twins.

As planned, Angus Bridcombe joined the police force. He and Opal often socialised together with Dulcy Vestige amongst their other mutual friends.

The poked club girls remained unforgiving for the heartache David caused Dulcy, having witnessed and shared her total desolation during the beach holiday.

Opal strictly forbade her husband revealing her best friend's location to David Dubois. The burly policeman held his tongue for his wife's sake, but he saw both sides to the story. In Angus's opinion, David's dazed and confused reaction when Zelia turned up at the beach bivouac had been understandable. He had felt sorry for him.

Angus wrestled with his conscience but his empathy for the man's dilemma eventually won out. Learning their group of friends would all be at a certain sports field for a cricket match, he gave a broad hint to David.

"I'll be there. I can never thank you enough Angus, mate."

"Just make it seem totally accidental and don't bloody dob me in it Davo, or Opal will have my guts for garters."

"Your little woman sure has you by the short and curlys."

"More by what rises in grandeur among the short and curlys. If you know what I mean." Angus replied.

Angus and David fell back on a common male ritual of sharing juvenile innuendos.

"You poor bastard. I guess being married has its ups and downs."

"Yep. It gets really hard at times."

Angus Bridcombe played on the local cricket team himself and knew David had leave from the army on that particular weekend. He also knew Dulcy Vestige had remained unattached. If she'd been turned off men, that would be another obstacle for his mate, but he could only do so much.

The day of the cricket match dawned mild and fair, bathing the sporting grounds in sunshine that brightened the emerald greenness of the grassy oval.

Dulcy and her best friend Opal spread a tartan picnic rug at ringside where they sat cross-legged enjoying the picturesque scene and the relaxing sounds of willow bats smacking leather. Eskies held substantial picnics to be shared with the men at lunch time.

David drove into the cricket ground public car park, anxious over how his presence would be received. He hung back, watching the friends for a while before braving a meeting.

As soon as he picked Dulcy out amongst the group, he couldn't take his eyes off her. She looked even more beautiful than he remembered. A few years maturity rearranged her weight in all the right places. Her hair was longer, lifting off her shoulders in a light breeze. David waited for the match to begin before making his way to her.

Dulcy had her face turned up to the warm sunshine, eyes closed, so Opal spotted David's approach first.

"Be buggered," Opal exclaimed, "look what's slithered in, and he's heading this way. It's bloody David, your slick two-timing surfer cheat."

Dulcy startled to instant attention. She'd just been daydreaming of sunny days on the beach. Jumping to her feet, she straightened her clothes and pushed a few stray hairs behind her ears. David heard Opal's put down which didn't help his nervousness.

"Dulcy. Opal." David greeted them briefly.
"Can you give me a moment please Opal." Dulcy asked.
"If you must...but..."
"Please Opal."
"Alright. Just yell out if you need me Dulcy."

Opal walked away out of earshot but kept a disapproving eye on proceedings.

Dulcy and David faced each other wordlessly for tense seconds. An inner quiver reminded Dulcy of her sensual attraction to the man, though she kept her cool. David swallowed hard, now that he stood in front of the girl he adored, after so long apart, he felt unsure what to say.

"What..." they both spoke at once. "Let me..."
"You go first." David allowed.
"What are you doing here?" Dulcy hoped to sound stringent. Failed.
"Please Dulcy. Let me explain about what happened at the beach."
She played it down.
"Nothing important happened did it?"
"You know what I mean Dulcy. Having Zelia turn up like that. Uninvited."
"Must have been an awkward surprise for you. Considering."

Dulcy couldn't help feeling snarky. As a naïve seventeen-year-old, she had rashly given her virginity to David and stupidly fallen in love. Puppy love, Pepper had called it, saying she'd soon forget him. But Dulcy never forgot. David continued with his plea:
"Okay. I deserve that. But look. Yes, I admit Zelia and I were seeing each other but I wasn't committed to her."
"Obviously." Dulcy retorted.

David regrouped, tumbling over random sentences he'd been rehearsing for hours: "Dulcy. I didn't plan how it happened. I just became so attracted to you. You enchanted me. I know I hurt you badly and I can't tell you how sorry I am. I'd like to start over and see you some more. If you will agree."

Dulcy's heart soared betraying her coldly aloof intention.

"What do you have in mind?"
"Can we please put it behind us and begin again?"

Morning tea break was called for the cricket. David didn't want Opal coming back to influence Dulcy.

"I'd like to take you to lunch." David added. "Just you and me. To talk."

"I could eat." Dulcy replied shortly, in a somewhat ungracious acceptance.

Opal had been watching and could see her friend seemed to be making up with David, however tentatively. Dulcy walked over to explain she wouldn't be sharing their picnic this time, but would see her later.

"I guess you are giving David another chance. I wouldn't. But it's your life Dulcy. Please be tougher this time. Don't wear your heart on your sleeve. "

"I'm a lot older and wiser now Opal." Dulcy replied quietly.

"I know. But remember he's shown himself to be untrustworthy before."

"Opal. I am really happy it worked out so well for you and Angus, but life doesn't fall so neatly into place for everyone."

"Dulcy, that is down to Angus being trustworthy."

"Opal, must you see everything in black and white?"

"That sounds racist."

Opal knew she'd replied stupidly due to concerns for her friend and received the expected barrage from Dulcy.

"Get the bloody chip off your shoulder Opal. My comment has nothing to do with racism. You know it, so just get off your flaming bandwagon about that."

Opal and Dulcy faced off. Neither ever liked to back down. Miffed, Dulcy walked back to David and allowed herself be ushered towards his car.

Zelia Wild had also gone to the cricket grounds that morning, hoping to re-connect with Thaddeus, who also played on the cricket team. She hadn't expected to see David, yet there he was in the flesh – *the sneaky bastard.* Incensed that 'her David' ushered an attractive woman into his car, Zelia stayed parked in the shadow of the clubhouse.

Angus, Thaddeus and some of the other cricket players came to sit on the tartan rug with Opal.

"Where's Dulcy?"

"You'll never guess. That two-timing David showed up and she went off with him. Will she never learn? Says she'll see us later. God I hope she has more sense about him this time." Opal ranted.

Opal's husband Angus tried to change the subject in a hurry, not wanting to admit his part in telling David where to find Dulcy. At the same time, Thaddeus noticed Zelia in the distance, which supplied a useful distraction.

"Hey. Isn't that Zelia Wild? Hell, I hope she isn't coming after me again. I thought we were through." Thaddeus groaned.

"Aha! I knew it!" Opal exclaimed, "I bet Zelia's back with David and she's keeping tabs on him because she knows he can't be trusted. Maybe I'll go have a nice little chat with her."

"No. Please don't do that Opal." Angus pleaded.

"Dulcy is my best friend, Angus."

"Dulcy knows her own mind my darling. Let her work it out." Angus replied.

Angus and Thaddeus both breathed sighs of relief for different reasons when Zelia drove off. Her departure took the decision to chat out of Opal's hands.

Zelia kept a couple of cars behind David's. When he turned in at a local pizza restaurant, she parked down the back, out of sight, prepared to wait for his return.

Chapter 4

DULCY & DAVID

I Could Eat

David escorted Dulcy into the pizza restaurant, placing a hand lightly on her back. Opal's advice not to wear her heart on her sleeve proved easier said than done. Trying to ignore how much his touch thrilled her required a great deal of self-control. The couple were seated at a table for two in a private corner. Dulcy placed her hands in her lap so David could not make an attempt to hold them.

"So. Dulcy. Thanks for agreeing to this." he began.
"As I said. I could eat." Dulcy replied stiffly.

The fact was, Dulcy wasn't entirely sure she could eat, considering her stomach was all aflutter on being near David again. She hoped not to betray her true feelings. It had been a desolate few years while she threw herself into work, trying to forget him.

In the interim, Opal and other girlfriends organised blind dates, embarrassing Dulcy. Their well-intended interference only made the young policewoman more determined than ever to remain unattached.

"I've missed you terribly. I tried to find you, you know." David said earnestly.

"Did you? Well, I wasn't that hard to find. I'm sure you must have been aware that Opal and your mate Angus Bridcombe became an item."

"It was Angus who eventually told me where to find you. He went against Opal's wishes because she strictly forbade him to do it. That's why it took so long. Angus didn't want to go against his wife, but he knew how much I longed to find you Dulcy. He hopes Opal never finds out he let the cat out of the bag."

Dulcy loved her friend Opal, but for the second time that day, felt irritated by her meddling. Nonetheless, Dulcy defended Opal:

"Opal and my other friends protected me from you."

"They all hate me."

"Hate is a strong word David, but they thought I deserved better."

"You did. And do. Will your friends' opinions be a deal-breaker to us getting back together?"

"I can think for myself David."

Dulcy resented attempts by her well-meaning friends to set her up with men in barely concealed elaborations, like being half of the only single pair at their dinner parties. Most of those single men seemed nice enough, but those intrusions fed into an opposite effect. Thaddeus might have stood a chance with Dulcy if not for his inadvisable fling with Zelia, which everyone knew about. The pizzas arrived pausing the tricky conversation. David tried again:

"Dulcy, can we talk?"

"We are talking."

"Can we start over. Please. I don't have long on leave, but I would love to spend what time I have with you."

"So, you got your wish to join the army." Dulcy replied, without agreeing.

"And I know from Angus that you are doing well in the police force, Dulcy."

"Yes, Angus and I have worked on some big cases together."

David felt it was like pulling teeth to get that much conversation out of Dulcy. But she agreed to have this lunch, so he surmised she still felt attracted to him, at least physically.

In optimism he booked tickets for a river cruise the following day. He chose it as a date where Dulcy could not easily walk out on him, unless she fancied a swim.

"If you're free tomorrow, how about a ferry boat ride up the river to see the koalas at Lone Pine?"

Dulcy gave his suggestion serious consideration. It would be helpful to spend a day with David, if only to sort out her feelings, perhaps even put her long held heartbreak to rest. To refuse only avoided the issue and would leave her feeling empty, without closure, never knowing how it might have gone.

Also, Dulcy had heard a lot about that koala sanctuary and always meant to go. She talked herself into it.

"Alright David. Thanks. That would be a nice change of pace for me."

"Where can I pick you up?" David smiled, delighted.

"No need. I know where to go. I can meet you at Southbank Boardwalk."

"Alright. Meet you at the ferry tomorrow. What now, after lunch? Do you want to go back to the cricket?"

"Yes please, my car is parked there."

"Just that...we could go for coffee somewhere."

David hoped in vain for an invitation to go to back to Dulcy's place, but she was not ready to let him know her home address. She had a lot to think about and would not be rushed.

"No, thanks anyway David. My friends will be waiting for me."

Dulcy didn't relish seeing Opal and the others again that day, but her car was parked there, as she said. Back at the cricket grounds, David got out and opened the car door for her. Dulcy consented to a chaste peck on the cheek and exchanging phone numbers.

"Thanks for having lunch with me, Dulcy. I'm very looking forward to tomorrow. Spending the day with you is a dream come true for me. I can't wait to be with you again."

Dulcy's heart flipped. It was difficult to appear cool and composed. More handsome than ever, David's clean-cut appearance held great appeal. Army training had honed his athletic stance and developed his physique to near perfection. Seeing her expression soften, David smiled.

Feeling elated, David waved goodbye as he drove off. He had eyes only for Dulcy and did not notice Zelia on the prowl. His ex-girlfriend stalked him to discover where he currently stayed and been rewarded to find it was not far from her own new flat.

Dulcy rejoined her group of friends back at the cricket grounds, ready to field any intrusive questions about her private life. Keen on telling they'd seen Zelia watching David, Opal fired up:

"So, you're giving him a second chance?" Opal cut straight to the chase.
"Just don't say anything Opal." Dulcy snapped.
"But Dulcy, we all saw..."
"I said don't say anything Opal. I mean it. Let me breathe. Please."
"Okay. I won't say I told you so when it all goes pear-shaped."
"Thank heavens for small mercies. Is there any chocolate cake left?"
"I saved some for you."

Opal grumbled her reply. In her opinion David Dubois had to be the worst possible man for Dulcy.

"Thanks. You're a good friend when you're not interfering."
"I'm a good friend even when I am interfering, because..."
"Uh! I don't want to know Opal."
"Go your own reckless way then."
"I plan to."

Dulcy accepted the big slice of mud cake her friend had set aside for her.

"Love you Opal."
"You should."

Dulcy and Opal parted best friends as always, despite their differences.

FERRY RIDE

Red Blooded

As arranged, Dulcy met David at 8.30 the next morning at the Southbank boardwalk pontoon on the Brisbane River.

Dulcy was not the only young woman with an interest in seeing David that day. Having found where David stayed, Zelia continued her hunt early enough to see her former boyfriend drive out. She followed obsessively keeping a few cars behind. Again, David did not notice being tailed, his head in the clouds, beside himself with anticipation of a day out with Dulcy.

Zelia seethed seeing David met with the same bosomy sheila from the cricket grounds. Foiled when the couple embarked on the river cruise, Zelia returned home to spend her day plotting and scheming.

Dulcy chose her outfit carefully, hoping it didn't seem she'd tried too hard, but with a view to looking attractive. She wore good blue jeans teamed with a striped cotton blouse in shades of pink, her sneakers were practical footwear for on board the river craft, and for walking about the koala sanctuary. Her blush matched her blouse when David squeezed her hand and said:

"You look gorgeous as always, Dulcy. You are more beautiful than ever."

David also wore denim jeans. His cool green cotton shirt went well with his dark auburn hair, which Dulcy commented upon. In return, David felt buoyed by her compliment. To keep the conversation general, Dulcy asked:

"Does red hair run in your family?"
"The colour only randomly crops up now and then. Supposedly a legacy of a distant forebear named David. So, a family tradition has been to always name the red-headed boys David."

Secretly, David entertained the notion that someday there might be another little red-haired David, perhaps his and Dulcy's. If he had anything to do with it, he'd be making that a distinct possibility as soon as possible.
Weather was sunny without being too hot, so the pair enjoyed the breeze on the upper outside deck of the river ferry. Dulcy couldn't help smiling for being in David's company and out on the ferry, away from her prying friends.

"You look even lovelier with the wind in your hair." David told her.
"Still the sweet talker aren't you David."
"I mean it wholeheartedly Dulcy. I feel so proud to be with you."

Dulcy knew she was far from over her first attraction to him. Ever cautious, she warned herself to go slowly. They enjoyed a wonderful day together, on the river and at the nature park.

At the end of the cruise, they disembarked back at Southbank, and David walked Dulcy to her car. With her car keys at the ready, she turned to say goodbye. Unable to back off with the car door behind her, David pressed in for a proper kiss. Masterful at taking the best opportunity, David caught Dulcy off-guard. His forceful eagerness brought back romantic memories of making love on the beach. Helplessly smitten, remembering how good that had been, Dulcy returned his warm kiss with more enthusiasm than she ever wanted to show. David pushed his advantage:

"I'm staying with mates at the moment Dulcy...could we go back to your place?"

Dulcy knew what he meant and what he hoped to get. Canny enough to see he aimed to strike while the iron was hot, she kicked herself for showing her helpless need for him. Opal's sage advice arose, and her own natural self preservation warned her to be cautious.

"Thanks for today David. I really enjoyed it, but I'm on call tomorrow."

"Fair enough. Can we meet tomorrow night? I'm back on duty soon too."

"See what happens." Dulcy remained non-committal.

Disappointed, David understood her hesitation and knew it to be his own fault. He continued his quest to woo Dulcy during the following week when they met a few more times, with no deeper intimacy than separating with a warm goodnight kiss. They both wanted much more, but past memories of humiliation when David two-timed her against Zelia stood between that for Dulcy.

In a moment of pique, a result of his growing frustration, David imagined Dulcy working alongside a bunch of sex-mad policemen. He succumbed to insecurity with a sulky comment:

"I guess you might have other guys interested in you now."

"No one special. I've been devoted to my career." Dulcy replied, honestly.

He wanted to believe her, and downplayed his lapse with more coaxing:

"Me too. I've been alone. And lonely. For you Dulcy. I've been waiting and hoping to get back with you, and only you. I don't want anyone else if I can't have you."

Dulcy's strict reserve began to melt. She had shied off asking if he'd kept on with the beautiful and trendy Zelia, although the question loomed unsaid, in the forefront of her mind. On the verge of yielding, Dulcy had been called up on an urgent case that took her away for some weeks. David envied whoever got to work with Dulcy. Just his luck, it would surely be some macho lawman.

Opportunely, Zelia chose this time to attempt a coup. The conniving ex-girlfriend orchestrated a 'chance' meeting. She faked a sprained ankle, where she knew David would jog by on his habitual dawn run.

"David! Ow. Ow. Ouch. I've turned my ankle. It's useless. How lucky to see you turn up just when I most need you. Can you please help me get home? I've got a flat on the other side of the park now. It's not far."

David could not leave his ex-girlfriend stranded. He offered a strong supporting arm to help her hop across the springy lawn, yet Zelia managed to trip and bring him down on top of herself. Part of David sprang to instant attention due to the close proximity. He missed intimate physical contact with a woman, and that ever ready part of him forever demanded satisfaction.

"Sorry." he said.
"Don't be." she replied.

David began to get up, but Zelia drew him down and hooked a long tanned leg firmly over his body. He didn't wish to rekindle anything with Zelia but his immediate carnal needs surfaced with a vengeance. Sorely tempted, his hard breathing and obvious bodily reaction gave him away.

"I've missed this." she crooned.
"Nothing has changed Zelia," he panted with sudden desperate need, "I can't be committed."
"That's Okay. I do understand. For old times sake then. Just for fun."

Frustrated with Dulcy's stand off, David could really use some immediate fun. They went back to Zelia's flat together. She recovered remarkably quickly from her sprained ankle, and they spent the entire day in an orgy of lust. At the end of the day, David felt he'd done Zelia a great favour.

Escaping back to army duty, David justified taking Zelia casually. It had been sex just for the sake of it. He convinced himself it had been excusable. He firmly believed a red-blooded man has needs that shouldn't be denied for the sake of his health. Zelia clearly wanted him madly, and she said it was just a romp for fun. His pleasure in the act had heightened imagining he was with Dulcy. So, he could argue he'd been sort of true to her.

He loved and admired the fact Dulcy remained sensible and virtuous. Assured he could always trust her, she embodied everything he wished for in a wife.

Both young women, Dulcy Vestige and Zelia Wild kept in touch with David Dubois.

Chapter 6

VESTIGE - DUBOIS

Eek

Guilt for spending an indulgent day of wild sex with Zelia, meant David could not wipe his old flame off completely. He had to back pedal from her advances once again. His own stupid fault and he knew it, which didn't help matters at all. He replied only with bland emojis to Zelia's frequent text messages, if at all, hoping she would get the hint and stop bothering him.

On the other hand, David reacted warmly to Dulcy's messages. Aware his pursuit neared a payoff, he promised they would soon meet again when they were both available and off duty.

While away working on a case, absence made the heart grow ever fonder. David's patient wooing created a slow burn build up making Dulcy crave seeing him again. It seemed high time to widen her horizons and explore interesting variations Opal and Pepper recommended to her years ago. The next time Dulcy met with David, she welcomed his overtures.

"Dulcy, I've got a whole week off and I plan to hit the surf. It's been a while."

"Will you be camping with your mates?"

"No. I prefer to motel it these days. Alone. Unless you want to come too."

Dulcy knew he engineered having a week together in a motel. Just the two of them, thrown together. David waited humbly for her reply, hoping he hadn't pushed the ticket too soon.

"Alright. I'm due some leave. I could take a week off." Dulcy agreed.
"Is that a promise? Can we seal it with a kiss?"

They kissed, elated, as their pulses quickened in shared rhythm.
David took his surfboard to the beach but spent precious little time riding the waves. Once the spark re-ignited to flames between them, Dulcy and David made the most of their short week, reluctant for it to end.

"I do love you Dulcy." David declared love for the first time to any woman.
"I love you too." Dulcy also said those words to a man for the first time.

Over the moon when David proposed marriage, level-headed Dulcy nevertheless took a practical approach to juggling their separate careers.

Privately, David wanted Dulcy to resign from the police force immediately and become a housewife and stay-at-home mother. He knew better than to suggest the domestic role, certain she would not readily relinquish her lifelong ambitions. Yet, he voiced his hopes.

"We could start a family together, Dulcy, you'd be a wonderful mother."
"I might opt for a desk job in the future. There's plenty of time."

Dulcy replied cautiously. Potential for real danger in their occupations had to be acknowledged as not ideal for rearing children. Underlining that fact, Dulcy wished to keep her maiden name.

"You don't want to be Mrs. Dubois?"
"David, if I use that name in my professional capacity, it could attract grudges from past felons. I'd rather safeguard our future family life."
"You'd change from DS Vestige to Mrs. Dubois once we have children?"
"Yes of course, once that happens."

David made the compromise, sure love could conquer all, confident that within a few more years, he'd have Dulcy 'barefoot and pregnant' to coin a phrase that suited his ideal of domestic bliss.

Dubious when told David proposed marriage, Opal bit her tongue for fear of sounding churlish. Repeating grave doubts about the man would not change her stubborn friend's mind anyway.

Dulcy Vestige married David Dubois in a quiet wedding, witnessed by family members and closest friends. Proud of her handsome soldier, Dulcy loved that David wore his army uniform. Dulcy knew she didn't rock frills well, so chose a simple cream shift dress overlaid with lace. An elegant 1920s style veiled cloche hat, and tan t-bar shoes complemented the outfit. David had never imagined such a beautiful bride would be his.

Dulcy's parents insisted on providing a lavish wedding breakfast, catered for at a top hotel venue. As the happy couple took to the dance floor for the traditional wedding waltz, they only had eyes for each other. Everyone, even Opal Bridcombe wished them well.

Nevertheless, Opal couldn't completely quash her mistrust of David. She whispered her fears to her own husband.

"Angus, mark my words, if this goes wrong it won't be Dulcy's fault. I hope he doesn't break her heart again."

"Don't be such a doomsayer Opal. Look at David. He really loves her."

"Yes, he professed to really love her the first time around too."

"I don't think he was wholly to blame for what happened at the beach."

"Well Angus, if you had another lover on the side, you'd have told me."

"How can you be sure I didn't? Maybe I had one or two or three." Angus teased.

"Huh. You didn't even know where it went until I showed you." Opal laughed.

"I've always been a good actor."

"Don't think I'll forget you said that."

"Eek." he said.

The motel holiday at the beach had been the unofficial Dubois/Vestige honeymoon, albeit before they wed. As husband and wife, they enjoyed an entertaining week in the city, dining out and taking in the latest shows.

The glorious idle days flew by. All too soon the newlyweds had to return to their separate work duties.

Chapter 7

THE TRAP

Blackmail

To avoid any unpleasantness, David declined telling Zelia of his marriage. He still hoped she would eventually get a clue from his cold shoulder and just go away.

However, Zelia remained a nuisance and continued chasing David online. It would be disastrous if Dulcy saw any of Zelia's messages. Most of them lewdly referred to their day long orgy. He had to put a stop to it. When Zelia begged to meet for a talk, David decided to bite the bullet, and relieve the pressure of her constant bombardments. He just wanted her out of his life forever.

"David darling. Thanks for coming. It's so good to see you again." Zelia gushed.

David hastily forestalled her enthusiasm. He had rehearsed what to say and said it all at once.

"Zelia, I've agreed to meet only because I have something that should be said to your face. The fact is: I have married. I thank you for what we once had, but this will be our final meeting."

Zelia's shocked disappointment rapidly turned to mutiny. David expected some form of dramatics, and was not fazed by her first reaction.

"I don't think so David." she spat.

Prepared to walk away, he shrugged at the woman he considered no longer his problem. But Zelia had an ace up her sleeve:

"I'm pregnant David. And it's yours."
"NO!" he cried in horror.

Judging by the triumph on Zelia Wild's face, David feared she told the truth. He could not have imagined a worst catastrophe.

"So you will just have to un-marry whoever she is."
"Never! That will NOT happen."
"You might have no option when she finds out." Zelia smirked.

Aghast, David stared at his ex-girlfriend.

"No Zelia. Don't do that. Please."
"It will cost you." she replied slyly.

He'd always seen Zelia as empty headed and ditzy, but now recognised her wily scheming nature.

"That's blackmail." he said.
"I have our baby to think of." she countered.
"How much? What do you want?"
Zelia named an exorbitant sum.
"I don't have that much."
"You've heard of loans I take it?"
"Be sensible and fair if you can Zelia."

"It's your duty David. You should know all about duty, right? Or will you defend the country but abandon your own child? This little story would make interesting click bait on social media."

"If you ruin my marriage Zelia, you won't get a cent out of me."

"I will. Because I'll sue you. No skin off my nose. Make it easy on yourself lover boy and do as I say."

Zelia had David over a barrel and he knew it. In a quandary of dread and panic, he paced up and down.

"Okay. Look. If a paternity test proves it, I will agree to some manner of compensation."

"You'll agree to my terms David, not your own."

David vehemently hoped a test would disprove his liability. He also hoped Dulcy would never find out. Yet his new bride was a detective and by all accounts, very good at her job.

In due course, a healthy red-haired baby boy entered the world. Even without the positive paternity test, the baby looked to be very evidently sired by David Dubois. Zelia changed her name to Zelia Wild Dubois before the birth, although David did not know she'd taken that step.

As far as David knew, Zelia named the baby Davy Wild, as this is what she told him. However, to underline the truth of paternity, Zelia had the child's name officially recorded as David Wild Dubois. The baby's birth certificate showed father as David Dubois and mother as Zelia Wild Dubois.

Completely unaware, Dulcy trusted her husband completely. At that point, she honoured her marriage as sacred, and would never act on a secret attraction she held for another man.

To steer away from Zelia causing trouble in his marriage, David paid an over generous weekly amount ostensibly in support of his offspring. Yet the sizeable sums Zelia demanded amounted to blackmail. At least his debt to Zelia remained his private affair, since he and Dulcy kept separate bank accounts.

Zelia insisted on cash, so the income did not limit her government single parent benefit. David sent the packets of money through the mail, always asking for receipts, which were never forthcoming.

David Dubois racked his brain to come up with another way to keep his illegitimate issue concealed, whilst satisfying its mother's demands.

To physically distance himself from Zelia, David applied for a transfer to Robertson Army Barracks in The Northern Territory. Dulcy took for granted this inconvenient relocation had been instigated by the army, as it meant they could only be together when he or she had leave to travel.

Deployed to The Middle East to evacuate Australians from a conflict zone, David pleaded with Dulcy to move up to Darwin. He missed her desperately and wanted her there on his return to Australia. Yet that had not been his only reason. He could not completely relax unless Dulcy and Zelia were separated by a great distance. At least his wife would probably avoid Zelia if she happened to spot her anywhere, but a risk existed that other friends could interfere. And that possibility played to Murphy's Law.

Torn with reluctance for leaving her current job and friends, Dulcy nevertheless applied for a vacant position with The Northern Territory Police Force. If successful, it promoted her to greater responsibility.

By chance one fine day Opal took her three daughters to a playground, where she spied Zelia pushing a pram.

By then, Zelia had acquired several tattoos and piercings. Opal considered the adornments to be tacky. As ever, she reckoned Zelia better suited David than did Dulcy.

When Zelia's baby threw his knitted cap out of the pram, into a rubbish bin, Opal noted his head of red hair.

Zelia scolded the child in her strident voice: "Naughty boy Davy, now Mummy has to wash that again."

Davy! With red hair! I've been right all along about that two-timing bastard Dulcy saddled herself with.

Opal bustled to confront Zelia, setting her sights on a fact-finding mission, only to be thwarted by her own children. Opal's eldest daughter chose that moment to fall off a swing. Xanthe screamed in anger and her younger sisters, in their twin pram, joined in. Kinta cried and Lirah laughed. Zelia hurried away, shooting a dirty look towards Opal's vocal mob, she said:

"What despicable loud brats. Come on Davy lets go."

Opal overheard the rude remark and regretted missing the chance to engage with Zelia. Whatever else might have been said, Opal had definite ideas about that red-haired baby.

Chapter 8

WHAT THE HELL

Variety

Zelia Wild always envied tattoos and piercings on others. Extravagant spending to acquire some of her own, often left the young mother short of money. A penchant for gambling on sports events depleted her finances further. Despite squeezing extra money from David Dubois, Zelia sometimes struggled to meet her bills and put food on the table.

When Zelia's cash fell short at a supermarket check-out, a kind check-out girl, name tagged as Isla, offered to put in a few dollars to cover it. Embarrassed, Zelia declined, and gave back some tinned baby foods and cereals. Little Davy would just have to chew on pizza for a while. Zelia thought it wouldn't hurt the toddler to be fed more solids and some variety anyway.

Not long after that humiliation, Zelia came across a coloured note in her shopping bag that read: *Want to meet? Tipsy Turnip Cafe 7am Saturday? BTW I have tatts and piercings.*

"What kind of devo stalker did this? Some nerve!"

Zelia crumpled the note and threw it into the kitchen tidy bin. Later, feeling lonesome with Davy sound asleep, and having insufficient funds to gamble, she retrieved the note and smoothed it out.

"What the hell." she muttered to herself.

Zelia made an effort to get to the Tipsy Turnip Cafe by 7am, taking little Davy in his pram. It seemed plain who had left the note when a cocky bloke with tatts and eyebrow rings confronted her. He waved a pink piece of paper. Zelia produced her crumpled blue note. They compared messages and saw both said exactly the same thing.

"I didn't write that." Zelia declared.
"Well. I didn't write yours either." the man argued.
Mystified, they puzzled over how those identical notes came about.
"This is beyond creepy. Anyway I'm getting a coffee while I'm here." Zelia said at last.
"Let me get it." the man offered.
"That's alright thanks. I can get my own."

Zelia had an idea the man might be scamming her with his identical message on pink paper, and that he had really put the blue note in her shopping bag himself. He looked perhaps in his late thirties or early forties. Probably fancies his chances trying it on with someone younger, she thought. Nevertheless, they sat at the same table with their coffees. At first, the man introduced himself as Will.

"Don't let on but I reckon whoever tried this might be watching us right now. Otherwise, why else would anyone do it?" Will said.

They shared a nervous laugh. Zelia, because she suspected Will, and Will because he felt to be set up by someone else. The man's assumption had been correct. The matchmaker, Isla Tickle, who worked on the supermarket check-out counter, watched from her usual breakfast table in a corner of the popular cafe. Isla wore a disguise of heavy rimmed spectacles and had her hair fully covered by a scarf. The crowded eatery made it impossible to pinpoint anyone who could be responsible for those notes. The targeted pair gave some thought to how those notes got into their personal shopping bags.

"The shop is usually busy when I'm in there. Anyone could have done it."

"Well, I'll be keeping a closer eye on my bags in future." Zelia said.

They parted company. With the hope nothing else fishy happened, Zelia began walking home, pushing Davy's pram against the sea breeze. Despite the odd encounter, the social interaction raised her spirits. The bloke wasn't a bad looking guy and he appeared fit and able. Perhaps she should have strung him along. It had been a while since she'd had a man, or even had one take any interest. Halfway home, a ute pulled over and the man from the cafe meeting got out.

"Look. Sorry you were freaked out back there. So was I." he said.

"That's okay. No harm done."

"My name's William Kirby. Will for short." he offered.

"Zelia Dubois." she replied.

As they spoke, an ice-cream van pulled in further down the esplanade.

"Can I buy you an ice-cream? And one for the little kid too?"

"That'd be really nice. Thanks." Zelia smiled.

Davy would love an ice-cream, and she hadn't had one in ages either. The upshot of Zelia and William getting together began that night. Zelia claimed to be widowed due to the war in Afghanistan. William Kirby offered condolences and platitudes for dead heroes in defence forces. Zelia played into the role, enjoying his sympathy. She didn't think it mattered what she told him. William, she found out, worked as a motor mechanic.

William Kirby serviced more than automobiles where he worked. He often lubricated the middle-aged married woman who owned the mechanical workshop. To deflect suspicion from that liaison, William paid false interest to the office gofer, a quiet and conservative young woman: Poppy Papadopoulas.

Poppy baked sweet treats to bring into work for William. He particularly relished the traditional Greek baklava she made. She'd also begun knitting a man-sized woolen jumper, planning to gift it to him.

To William's taste, Zelia's many tattoos and piercings turned him on. She amounted to a far hotter prospect than either female at his workplace. After regularly nailing the alleged widow, he sometimes fell short of pleasing his matronly employer, who blamed his lack of energy on the innocent office girl, Poppy.

If the women William Kirby used foresaw what the future held, they'd have bolted.

On reflection, after spying that red-haired baby, and hearing Zelia call him Davy, Opal cautioned herself to tread softly. Tactfully, she must not immediately blab her suspicions to Dulcy. In light of her past verbal disapproval of David Dubois, Opal feared her best friend would view any new allegations as spite. Dulcy would shoot her down in flames for having no proof. Now that Dulcy and David had wed, the ramifications were far more serious.

Opal did, however, have a quiet word with Thaddeus Maekris, knowing he'd briefly taken up with Zelia at one time.

"Guess who I saw at the playground today Thad?"
"Who?"
"The lovely Zelia."
"Lucky you." Thaddeus tinged his reply with sarcasm.
"She's got a baby now." Opal said, watching his reaction closely.
"Not guilty."
"Just saying."

"I'd rather forget about Zelia. She was a huge mistake for me. Thanks Opal."

"Alright. Keep your hair on Thad."

"Just so you know."

Opal never imagined Thaddeus would be responsible for Zelia's baby. In her estimation, he'd be way too smart to get caught by such a floozie. David Dubois starred as Opal's culprit. If only she could think of a delicate way to bring it up with Dulcy, without it seeming malicious gossip.

With some effort, Opal held her tongue. Her group of girlfriends had vowed never to jump to unverified conclusions after the mortifying gaffe during schoolies week. That unforgettable shemozzle could have gone so very badly wrong, since Freya's husband, Didy Aroha, turned out to be a really good guy.

Nonetheless, Opal dropped broad hints about deceptions to Dulcy, who misconstrued the clues. Opal's conversation skirted around infidelity issues so often it made Dulcy suspect her friend's husband, Angus, of misconduct. What the hell!

"Are you trying to tell me something Opal?"

"Just saying. Sometimes... not all is as it seems. You know. Between people."

"Are you okay though?" Dulcy asked.

"*I'm* fine." Opal replied.

That chat had been interrupted when Angus Bridcombe and Dulcy Vestige were called to inspect a possibly serious incident.

Chapter 9

A FAIR CRACK

The Other Angus

An email passed on by a police desk clerk on graveyard shift caused concerns.

"The message claims illegal workers being enslaved."
"Could be a hoax."
"Be stupid to send a fraudulent message with sender ID, and looks like it was cut off before it ended."
"Unless someone stole the device?"
"Sure. But we can't ignore it."
"No it could be a big deal. I want two officers as back-up."

The deprivation of liberty complaint turned out to be a very big deal. As investigators, Dulcy Vestige and Angus Bridcombe spearheaded the raid on a suburban terrace row of duplexes. A pair of armed uniformed officers accompanied them as back-up. The four gained access using skeleton keys. Dulcy sensed an evil aura pervading the silent residence, causing her intuition to kick into overdrive. They all barged through the living room to the kitchen beyond. Two chairs were knocked over, and a gory pair of garden secateurs sat on a blood-stained granite bench top.

"That seems excessive for a gardening mishap."

Angus led a charge up a staircase to the second floor where two huge bodies blocked the landing. The dead were lumped together in a doorway. Knife handles protruded from the eye of one man and from the jugular vein of the other.

"Cripes. What the hell went on here?" Angus exclaimed.

Dulcy's keen instincts had not let her down. The style of knife handles looked familiar. She had the same expensive kitchen set herself.

"Death by Baccarat." she said.

Blood seeped onto the floor and dark red splats spattered the walls. Slight noises, a creak of bed springs, and heavy breathing, were heard coming from the room beyond. Angus shouted:

"POLICE!"
A shaky female voice answered:
"How do we know you're the real police? We've already been tricked once by those heaps on the floor."
"We have ID." Dulcy replied.

Hearing another female voice reassured the fearful person.

"We've been locked in for hours," the woman replied, "did you get our message about the people smugglers next door?"
"That's what brought us here..."

Stepping across the bodies, the officers perceived the speaker to be an attractive young woman armed with a golf club, and poised to wield it. Two others accompanied her, an adult Caucasian male, wavering unsteadily on his feet, and a dark-complexioned smaller male who had an obvious injury to one hand. The three held golf clubs in defensive attitudes.

Angus asked that they identify themselves, adding: "...and please lay down your weapons."

The trio appeared to deflate, overcome with relief as they lowered their irons.

"I'm Arlo Marlowe editor of *The Crack Back*." the wobbly man said.

"I'm Verity Tripper, writer for the same newspaper. This is my house." the pretty woman replied.

"Eshan Madushanka. Illegal boat person. I killed in self-defence."

"He did. Eshan saved us all," the woman was quick to say, "and those horrible goons cut his thumb off. He needs an ambulance as soon as possible. Also there are more poor starving prisoners living in squalor next door."

Told to expect thugs guarding several illegal Sri Lankan boat people in the next door terrace house, Angus asked:

"Are the guards known to be armed?"

"They use poly pipe to beat us. I am unsure if they have firearms." Eshan replied.

"We must assume they might be armed." Dulcy said.

"We're on it." Angus assured the three distressed people.

Dulcy instructed the uniformed officers to call for ambulances and authorised a request for more armed police as back up:

"Send as many as can be spared. Urgently please. This could be big."

The man, claiming to be Arlo Marlowe, the editor of a local newspaper, sat down heavily on the bed. His face had turned a ghastly shade, yet he made a request in a quavering voice:

"May I ask you to also identify yourselves properly?"

"Sergeant Angus Bridcombe and DC Dulcy Vestige."

They flashed their police badges. Although younger than Angus, Dulcy outranked him. The ensuing conversation took a surprising twist. As Arlo Marlowe's condition deteriorated, he drunkenly brandished an arm to encompass both Sergeant Angus Bridcombe and the attractive young press writer, Verity Tripper.

"At long last, your wonderful meat man is here like a knight on his phone-charger. A bit slow on the uptake. Slack as last years underpants elastic if you ask me. But better late than never. Hey Verity?" Arlo slurred.

Dulcy Vestige burred up. Aha. So this was behind Opal's innuendos about infidelity. It seemed apparent that Opal's husband, Angus, had somehow been romantically involved with the alluring young female reporter, Verity Tripper. Dulcy looked daggers at Angus Bridcombe, whose nonplussed expression could be taken two ways, either as completely innocent or caught out. Despite Arlo Marlowe's diminished condition, Dulcy questioned his strange tirade that compromised her best friend's husband:

"Mr. Marlowe, what do you mean by saying 'your wonderful meat man Angus'?"
"Verity's boyfriend. The pork sausage roll. About time he showed up."
"What?" Dulcy angrily kept glaring at Opal's spouse.
"I have never met this lady before now." Angus declared.

Aware he'd gained a little weight since his marriage, Angus made an effort to suck his guts in. The pork sausage roll description offended the innocent man. Verity Tripper attempted an explanation:

"It's okay. Arlo has his wires crossed. I...um...used to have a boyfriend named Angus. A different Angus. Not this man. I am sure we've never met before now. If we had met, I'm absolutely certain I'd remember someone like him."

The wrongly accused wasn't sure how to take Verity's absolute certainty. It could be either a good or bad thing. The sergeant preferred to think he'd be unforgettable for being such a strapping big handsome fellow. Arlo Marlowe ignored Verity's account and added more to his rant:

"Or was it Haggis? Tell the truth, the whole truth and nothing but the truth. So help you dog. Or police dog. Whatever. Fix the grammar Verity. It's your job."

"Oh no. Arlo has lost the plot," Verity exclaimed, "he needs an ambulance too. He was knocked unconscious, his speech and his reason are obviously severely affected. Believe me, he is usually extremely articulate, and pedantic about absolute accuracy. Normally, he can split hairs three ways. I know for sure, he hasn't drunk any alcohol. I don't even have alcoholic based mouthwash in the bathroom."

Verity Tripper tried to apply a cool washcloth to Arlo Marlowe's perspiring forehead, but he batted her hand away. His annoyed reaction was so unlike her adored Arlo, Verity worried he could be suffering a slow brain bleed.

"Are the ambulances far away? Arlo is in dire need of medical attention."

Relieved to hear the strident sounds of sirens approaching, Verity finally addressed her own desperate need to re-hydrate. Her throat remained raw from an ordeal of being gagged unable to swallow properly, and her mouth had gone bone dry from talking too much. Ambulance personnel entered the house just as the troubled homeowner braved her sullied kitchen to get a cool soothing drink from her 'fridge. Sadly, Verity never got to enjoy that juice. There, within a bowl of blood-streaked lemon jelly, the severed digit gave a jaunty thumbs up. It did not take a master sleuth to deduce the crude surgery had been performed using Verity's garden secateurs. Verity's startled scream brought the medicos running. One of them commented mildly:

"Well that's a new one on me. We don't see that every day."

Verity acknowledged the bland observation from someone who probably encountered all manner of terrible injuries on a regular basis. The lack of panic had the effect of having her own professional side surface, and she pulled herself together. The horror photo opportunity was too good to ignore.

"Give me a tick, I just need to snap photos." Verity said.
"Better be quick." came the reply.

The ambulance man said a slim chance the member might be restored crucially depended on a time frame of less than twelve hours since its separation. Already time marched on. Verity managed a few snapshots seconds before medical staff wrapped and secured the severed part in a special container. Eshan, the Sri Lankan amputee and his thumb were taken to hospital without delay. Sirens blaring, lights flashing, police escorted the ambulance. As an illegal entry who'd also thrown the killing knives, Eshan Madushanka must remain under police custody. Arlo Marlowe also left by ambulance. Both the terrace houses involved were made crime exclusion zones. Verity Tripper could not stay in her own home, not that she wanted to after the terror and revulsion of what happened.

"Do you have somewhere to stay?" Dulcy asked.
"The newspaper office has a day bed and basic bathroom facilities. Plus, it's imperative I go there as soon as possible."

Verity stressed she must get the story written up for publication first thing, before anyone stole her thunder. This drama represented a huge chance for herself and the local newspaper, and her exclusive jellied thumb photo could drive it to great heights. Warning of a macabre image inside the pages provided an irresistible draw-card.

"I'll wrap it up as quickly as possible, should take no longer than an hour." Dulcy promised.

The main police focus shifted to next door. A specialised police squad ram-raided the front door, and prevented anyone leaving via the back exit. Angus Bridcombe supervised the arrests, assisted by several armed and capable officers. Dulcy Vestige stayed behind with Verity Tripper to address her personal concerns.

"Can you reaffirm to never having met my colleague Angus Bridcombe before?"
"Absolutely." Verity vowed.
"Why did your friend Mr. Marlowe think so? He seemed quite certain."

On further questioning, Verity Tripper admitted she had never had a real boyfriend named Angus. She invented 'her Angus' as a means of holding off Arlo Marlowe's amorous advances, fearing an affair with her boss would jeopardise her career.

"I take it you're together with Mr. Marlowe now," Dulcy said, "so will you be telling him your boyfriend called Angus is fake?"
"Tentatively together. Maybe I will tell Arlo. Guess he might have to be told eventually."
"Good luck with that." Dulcy sounded dubious.
"I admit to creating this ridiculous situation myself. So, I was thinking of having my Angus dump me. Or I could kill him off somehow. Well I don't mean I would personally kill him off, but he could get shot in a line of brave duty. Something like that. What would you do? Would you tell him?"
"Nope. I might want to use it again." Dulcy winked.

Dulcy liked to connect with people in a friendly way if possible, going on the premise *more flies are caught with honey than with vinegar.* Verity noticed the lady detective wore a shiny gold wedding band.

"It must be difficult at times, working with your husband." Verity commented.

"Angus Bridcombe? Oh, he isn't mine, but his wife is a good friend. You see."

"Well then. Lucky his missus has a detective on his case."

Despite the situation, Verity and Dulcy shared a small giggly moment, lessening tensions.

"It is a balancing act working with the nearest and dearest." Verity admitted.

"I'll never know," Dulcy replied, "my partner David is in the army. However, absence makes the heart grow fonder. As they say."

"That must be tough, especially for newly-weds."

"Yep. David is based in NT at Robertson Barracks. At the moment, we divide our free time between Queensland and The Territory, but it's not ideal. He wants me to transfer to Darwin permanently."

"That's a big step."

"It is rather out of my comfort zone but there is a vacancy in the NT police force, if I'm accepted for it."

If Dulcy's application went through, main regrets would be leaving her admired senior mentor Dougall Grimslade and her lifelong best friend Opal.

Dulcy let Verity leave, then hurried to assist Angus with their part in the sting next door. Arrests of the guardian householders were made, and several emaciated Sri Lankans were escorted to hospital for assessment. Eventually the illegal boat people would go to refugee camps on Nauru or Manus Islands of Papua New Guinea. The multiple arrests had been forceful, although achieved without resort to gunfire. The people guarding the slave workers surrendered in the face of so much opposition. The Sri Lankan victims had fallen to their knees and cried in relief. The whole day provided much to talk about and even more food for thought.

Dulcy Vestige and Angus Bridcombe were over tired and work-weary after the eventful day yet winding down proved difficult. The sight of the dead men stuck in their minds, as surely as the carving knives protruding from the face and neck of those bloodied bodies.

Wrongly suspected of being Verity Tripper's side dish, Angus invited Dulcy to share a late supper with himself and Opal that night. He didn't want his wife hearing of the awkward situation at the crime scene, second hand. Unaware Opal often primed her friend on matters of infidelity, Dulcy's pointed glare at the crime scene, seemed totally uncalled for and unnecessary to Angus. As he predicted, Opal picked up on it.

"Oh my goodness Angus, you mean you were accused of having an affair with the victim?"

"Yep. By her boss, Arlo Marlowe, ridiculous as that is. I never set eyes on the woman before today."

"Mr. Marlowe suffered a head injury and became confused." Dulcy explained.

"Yet you burred up right off, Dulcy." Angus sulked.

"I sincerely apologise Angus. My only excuse is being so het up. I was definitely on overdrive. Anyway, Opal, the female victim said you're lucky to have a detective on your case."

Opal knew the misunderstanding had been her own doing, and her prods about infidelity prompted Dulcy's distrust in Angus. At that time, and despite being a canny detective, it did not occur to Dulcy that Opal's hints were aimed at David. In truth, Dulcy doubted Angus would cheat on Opal, and she fully accepted Verity's explanation of inventing a fake boyfriend.

"But...how could that man Arlo become so confused?" Opal wanted to know.

"Verity invented a lover she named Angus, and made him out to be in the police force. Arlo Marlowe had never seen him, obviously, since the fake Angus didn't exist. Anyway, so when we turned up...well, the rest you know." Dulcy explained.

"Geez. Why would she make up such a silly thing?"

"Well, according to Verity, she tried to ward off her boss's advances."

"But weren't they living together?"

"Yes, but he only moved in with her after his apartment block burnt down."

"So the whole fake boyfriend called Angus thing was a waste of time?"

"Seems like it. She asked me what would I do. I said I'd keep the imaginary Angus up my sleeve, in case I wanted to use him again."

Opal and Dulcy shared a laugh. Less amused, Angus explored another aspect.

"That apartment block fire could be linked to the slave labour and cannabis farm fiasco."

"Why Angus? I don't think Arlo Marlowe is involved, given he exposed it."

"No not Marlowe. But that fire started at a unit owned by proprietors of a Chinese restaurant. There's evidence of a territory war going on with a similar takeaway food outlet. It's just the type of thing we've seen in the past... you know what I mean Dulcy."

"You're right Angus. Good thinking. The whole series of incidents could be somehow connected."

Appeased, Angus felt happily disposed towards Dulcy again.

"His bad luck to live in that building and lose his home unit. The whole place burnt to the ground."
"Lucky to escape though. Perhaps also lucky to be taken in by Verity Tripper considering he made unwanted advances towards her."
"Yes, and that's why she invented her fake Angus in the first place."
"She sounds scatter-brained." Opal concluded.

The three discussed the complexities of detective work late into the night, until Dulcy fell asleep on the Bridcombe's sofa. Opal gently covered her with a blanket and wondered where to go from there with her warnings about David. Opal felt certain Dulcy didn't know about Zelia's baby, and equally certain her best friend deserved to be enlightened of that distinct possibility.

Verity Tripper's pork pies led to relevant authorities cracking widespread drug related activities festering within Australia.

Vestige and Bridcombe received commendations for their work on the initial case.

THE JETTY

Catch

Dulcy Vestige and David Dubois were unable to enjoy much time in marital bliss while he served in the Northern Territory and she, in Queensland. The prospect of separations due to duties had been the subject of discussions before they wed. They'd accepted it would be a fact of life for themselves, during the early years of their marriage. Reunions at least made the times spent together special and kept their desires fresh.

Before her Northern Territory transfer was approved, Dulcy worked on another complex case, with her much-admired mentor, Dougall Grimslade. An old fisherman had netted partial human remains from under a jetty. Dulcy and Dougall strove to identify the body. They only knew it to be female, white, with a tattoo. It was not much to go on. The old fisherman said:

"Amazed there's this much left of the poor soul, given these are shark infested waters."

At the same time, an anonymous informant reported crimes to have occurred at a suburban mansion. Two slain men, their throats slashed from ear-to-ear mimicking macabre grins, had been found in the hallway of the impressive house. Shortly following that discovery, a dog walker let her spaniel off leash in bush land. The pooch promptly scented a shallow grave and dug into it. The naked occupant, a tall dark skinned woman presented few clues to her identity. Her scarlet painted fingernails provided little to go on.

"We've got bodies coming out of our ears." Dulcy remarked.

"We sure have. That's four counting the jetty remains." Dougall replied.

"The woman who complained of being obscenely videoed without her consent hasn't gotten back to us either." Dulcy mused.

"No, she has not. What was her name again?"

"She called herself Molly Malone. Probably not her real name. She admitted to being a sex-worker on that party yacht anchored offshore."

"I have dire suspicions about that. What do you think Dulcy?"

"Molly Malone is a likely contender for the jetty body."

"Good. Good. Very good Dulcy. We're on the same page with that then."

"Could all the deaths be connected?"

"I'd not be surprised."

Dulcy watched as Dougall doodled arrows and numbers trying to come up with a pattern. She knew he was deep in thought, so did not interrupt his process.

"All we've got to go on for the jetty body, is the tattoo design. We need some replicas to show tattoo parlour artists. They would know their own work."

"That's a start. We'll be busy. Could run into a lot of legwork."

"Good news is, we're getting a new recruit to help out with that. Goes by the name of Tim Fun." Grimslade said.

"Asian?"

"Chinese on his mother's side. I've got his file stashed away somewhere. Ah yes, here it is, I filed it under FAT."

"Is he?"

"Don't know. Never met him. But his employment file is headed F-A.T. as Funicular, Anwei Timothy, though he prefers to go by the name Tim Fun. He's said to be well-mannered and clever."

"Just like us then." Dulcy smiled.

Tim Fun proved to be a slim, unassuming young man. He was very keen to suss out the origins of the inking clue, and he did a sterling job on it. His diligent research connected that tattoo pattern to one used by a group of prostitutes known to work as escorts on the yacht Molly Malone had frequented. A high-flying playboy, Troy Van Baas, owned the royally appointed yacht where he held extravagant parties for various politicians and celebrities.

On the double murder case, the mansion proved to be a discreet brothel theatre, featuring live porn show acts. The murdered pair, who had been heavyweight muscle-bound men, were deemed to have been employed as thug bouncers. Researchers met with immediate difficulties trying to find who owned or leased the brothel lodge. Several title holders held shares in the impressive piece of real estate. It involved a complex maze of business ventures held across Asia and America.

"So a tentative connection links sex workers. Could it be a territory war between the mansion brothel and that yacht with the prostitutes?"

"Could be. If only we can marry it all up." Dougall replied.

Full details were kept from media as the case was ongoing. The investigators shied off warning the party-yacht owner that his vessel attracted intense scrutiny. If a raid could be organised, the element of surprise would be crucial. Ideally they'd catch the yacht owner off guard preventing disposal of any incriminating evidence.

"We need a spy on that boat." Dulcy said.

"Are you putting your hand up for it?"

"Sure. I'll go as a hooker."

"Do you own a pair of fishnet stockings Dulcy?" Dougall joked.

Dulcy played along.

"You bet. I've got a wardrobe full or fishnet stockings, leather mini skirts, and black lace suspenders. But I'm not getting a tattoo."

"We could fake the tattoo. Okay. So wear your hooker disguise in tomorrow."

"That'd be almost worth it to see your shocked face." she laughed.

Bothered by inappropriate mental images of his younger colleague in lace suspenders, Grimslade suffered a guilt trip. On his way home, he bought a bunch of flowers from the servo. The last time he'd given his wife flowers had been after a serenading mishap. He'd had a whiskey or two and been cavorting around the kitchen using a large spice mill as pretend microphone. The thing came apart and showered Bella with pepper that stung her eyes.

"Flowers! How sweet. Thanks Doogie. Or is there some catch?" Bella knew her husband well.

"No catch. Just being a lovable man. Maybe I still have it."

"You never lost it." she replied.

Vestige and Grimslade arrived at an impasse on the mystifying crimes, until out of the blue, a godsend break-through to the whole shebang walked in. Aiden Birdwhistle, owner and manager of a local private eye firm operating as Birdwhistle Solutions, volunteered vital information. The mild mannered PI who fronted up, looked to be a clean cut and respectable young man. Yet Grimslade took a dim view of private eye sleuths, he thought of them as wannabe proper detectives, and could barely disguise his contempt.

"So...Mr...er...Birdwhistle you're a private investigator yourself."

"Yes. Birdwhistle Solutions. I know it's BS. Thanks."

Aiden Birdwhistle forestalled the common interpretation of his business name initials, suspecting this grouchy lawman would discredit his business. Grimslade was indeed cross. He didn't like time wasters, didn't like private eyes, and had been about to tuck into his favourite salami and pickle sandwiches.

"You want to make a statement Mr. Birdwhistle?"

"That's why I'm here. I know the double murder house is a porn show brothel. I was there checking out an errant husband for a client. She is the man's wife of course."

"Hard work but someone has to do it, right?" Grimslade scowled.

Aiden Birdwhistle defended himself with a prudish sounding comment:

"There is a steady market for this type of surveillance. The industry might stink but so do the cheaters and criminals we get hired to expose. I'm sure you are aware that those we catch are just the tip of the iceberg. Sir."

Aiden Birdwhistle tacked on 'sir' as an afterthought, but it cut no slack with Grimslade. Irked by what seemed a mild rebuke, the senior police detective couldn't wait to give this upstart PI the bums rush. Grimslade huffed a barely tolerant reply:

"What can you possibly tell *us* that we don't already know."

The informant noted the officer's glance to a window where no doubt an equally dubious police colleague observed proceedings. Nevertheless, Aiden Birdwhistle soldiered on, telling what he knew in a rush of words he'd been thinking of all night.

"In a nutshell. I think that black woman found dead in the bush was in the porn show the night the murders took place. Everyone in the audience witnessed three tall Negroid men rush into the bedroom scene. They grabbed a woman matching her description and took her away. One of the men had a knife that dripped blood."

Grimslade startled to attention, suddenly all ears. Dulcy Vestige, who had been bored observing, entered the statement room. Triumph for stirring the instant reaction proved to be a short-lived coup for Aiden Birdwhistle.

"So you were in the audience yourself."
"Yes. On my surveillance task. Before those men barged in, a disturbance happened outside in the hallway. Thumping against the walls, things like that. Everyone scarpered and saw the two dead men. They couldn't miss them. One of the bodies had to be jumped over to get out of the viewing room."
"Did anyone touch the bodies?"
"One did. He robbed a wad of cash from the dead doorman."
"You say the body was the doorman?"
"Yes. He took the entry fees."
"Did the thief move the body?"
"He just slipped his hand into the guy's coat pocket. That's all I saw him do and he was quick about it. The big wad of notes had been pretty obvious."

Grimslade and Vestige asked how the private eye had gained access to the place, knowing the type of venue would employ strict security. He said passwords changed daily and were advertised within newspaper ads for dirt bikes. To his credit, Aiden Birdwhistle worked out that the various colours of the motor bikes were the entry codes. The officers grudgingly supposed he must be good at his job, although they did not award him any accolade. Questioning continued:

"Did you know any of the other men in the room?"
"I recognised the youngest one from somewhere, but I don't know him. Only that his name is Troy Van Baas."

Grimslade and Vestige already had that name, Troy Van Baas, on their radar as the party yacht owner, not that they would let on to Birdwhistle.

"You didn't know any of the others?"

"No. They were all older. Van Baas is about my age. He sports a bleached hip hairstyle that covers one eye, and he has an affected habit of flicking it back like a girl would. That's why I remembered him."

Grimslade jumped in quickly: "Sounds like you don't like him."

"No reason to like him." Aiden retorted.

In a quest to cover every possibility Dulcy joined in:

"Did you know anyone else you saw on the premises? Or that you knew to be on the premises? Either then or at any other time?"

Aiden Birdwhistle paused without answering as the clock on the wall ticked over several seconds. To the surprise of his interrogators, the PI's face crumpled. He broke down into gasped sobs, dropping his head into his hands. Dulcy poured a glass of water and Grimslade shoved a box of tissues across the table. They exchanged raised eyebrow looks and waited silently for the stressed man to recover his composure.

"I'm sorry," Aiden Birdwhistle said at last, "this has been a nightmare...is still a nightmare. I do know one of the porn show actors. My ex-wife Jenni. We divorced six months ago."

Grimslade gave Dulcy an imperceptible 'aha'. She got it.

"Was your ex-wife the real reason you were there?"

"NO!" he cried. "I gave you the real reason. I was following an ongoing case. It's all documented in my records at the office."

"We will check."

"You can."

"So your ex-wife was there?"

"Yes. And that was the first I knew of her being there. It was a terrible shock seeing Jenni playing the sexpot to a roomful of strange men. Her mask and wig fell off during the invasion."

"You're saying she was also present during the murders."

"Yes. She partnered the black woman in a lesbian capacity."

"And her name is Jenni Birdwhistle?"

"No. She goes by McKinstock. Jenni McKinstock. Her maiden name. I wanted to get her out of that place but I couldn't find her."

Birdwhistle blew his nose and sipped some water. Grimslade and Vestige exchanged another silent idea between themselves.

"Where is your ex-wife now?"

"I don't know for sure, but she might have gone back to our marital home. I moved out months before the divorce, but she kept on staying there. She recently auditioned for some talent scouts and supposedly landed a plum movie part and moved out."

That disclosure sunk in, with the unidentified body parts from under the jetty uppermost in the detectives' minds. Grimslade built on it.

"Does your ex-wife contribute to the mortgage?"

"No. She didn't work while we were married. I have always paid for everything."

"So you have every reason to want her out of your life."

"That is correct." Birdwhistle answered honestly.

Dulcy knew the troubled young man could hardly deny wanting to be rid of his slutty ex. She posed the question:

"Did it anger you seeing her in that pornographic role?"

Bitterness loaded Aiden Birdwhistle's reply:

"Not at all. I'm glad Jenni finally found a paying occupation. I'm sure she enjoys the part to be honest. It suits her. She's finally found her forte."

"It sounds like you have lost respect for your ex-wife." Dulcy prodded.

"Of course I have. Do you find that unreasonable?"

Grimslade for one did not find it unreasonable, but he applauded Dulcy's line of questioning. As usual, they were on the same page with their deductions.

"Why do you suppose your ex-wife went back to the marital home?"
"I don't know for sure if she did. Only that the cleaners said someone had been there after they thoroughly detailed the house for real estate inspections. Jenni had left the place in a terrible state and the house stunk."

It seemed shady that Aiden Birdwhistle employed a team of contract cleaners to blitz and disinfect the home. Listing the place for sale, in order to finalise his divorce, was given as his reason.

"Have you been back to the house yourself since?"
"No. I didn't want to see Jenni."
"But you assumed she was there."
"I don't know for sure. I just thought she might return there if she had nowhere else to go."
Dulcy summarised: "So. Mr. Birdwhistle. Aiden. Your ex has been a financial burden. She kept on in your marital home after the divorce. Her presence possibly prevented it being sold. Then you discover her in a compromising situation in a sex show."
"Yes. That is all true." Aiden replied.

Grimslade fixed him with a steely glare. Birdwhistle did not crack.

"Yet you tell us you tried to get her out of the porn show house."
"I did try. But the house seemed empty. I was sure she had already fled the place. Or course she didn't know I was there, or she would have appealed for my help."
"You believe your ex-wife would appeal for your help?" Dulcy asked skeptically.
"Yes. I am absolutely sure Jenni would use me."

"Did you search the entire brothel house?" Grimslade wanted to know.

"I only called out and knocked on the wall in the hallway. The two dead men were on the floor. Blood oozing. I could smell it. It really freaked me out. So I left."

Birdwhistle had waited a couple of days before volunteering information. The detectives suspected a possible delay to formulate his story.

"Why didn't you immediately contact the police?"

"I know I should have. I don't know. I was in shock."

"Is there more to this you're not saying?" Dulcy asked.

"Like what? I don't know what you want from me. I came in to help with what I know." he exclaimed, upset at their pointed insinuations.

"Let's go back to the men who invaded. You said earlier they looked African."

"I said Negroid."

"Okay. But couldn't they have been, for example, Indigenous Australians?"

"They didn't look Australian to me. They seemed be the same ethnicity as the woman they abducted, and I heard on the news she was described as Sudanese."

"But you didn't know that until you heard the news did you?"

Aiden Birdwhistle sighed in frustration. Clearly, he became fed up with the finicky probing.

"The first impression I got was that the woman must have been of some very tall African race. Even though I described it as Negroid. Alright? The men who took her all had the same appearance. Why is this an issue?"

"Just clarifying facts."

Dulcy placated while Grimslade smiled like a crocodile. Birdwhistle attempted to end the session.

"I need to get back to work." he said.
"Before you go. Has your ex-wife any distinguishing marks?"

Birdwhistle did not immediately pick up on that implication.

"There are plenty of photos of her if you need identification."
"Has she any distinguishing marks?" Grimslade repeated.

The ex-husband paused. His face paled.

"Has something happened to Jenni?"
"What distinguishing marks has she? Scars, tattoos, birthmarks?"
The question hung in the air.
"Jenni has a vaccination scar on her upper left arm. And a mole on the back of her neck. And another mole down below covered by her pubic hair. Her opinion of tattoos is they are a sign of lower class and even lower I.Q. There's irony for you hey? Anyway, I doubt if she'd get a tattoo. I didn't notice any when I saw her stark naked in the porn show."

The detectives did not respond but spent several moments staring at the man. He met their gaze. Dulcy thought Aiden was either a very good actor or was being completely honest with them. Grimslade privately agreed but would reserve judgement.

"Thanks for your co-operation Mr. Birdwhistle," Grimslade said, "we'd also like to inspect your house. Today."

The man appeared slightly annoyed at that demand, yet he complied without argument, asking that the house keys be returned to his office when they were done. Grimslade tasked their new recruit, Tim Fun, to change into street clothes and spend the rest of the day following Aiden Birdwhistle.

"What now Dougall? Do we search his house?"

"That would just be a waste of time Dulcy, he's had it professionally cleaned for one thing."

"So why did you say we would?"

"To get his reaction."

"He seemed truthful to me," Dulcy said, "I mean why would he admit to so much otherwise? Or even come in here to volunteer information at all?"

"Reverse psychology? Double bluff?" Dougall suggested.

"Anyway, if his ex-wife definitely has no tattoos that eliminates her from the jetty body." Dulcy said.

"If he isn't lying and she definitely hasn't, it would."

"Right." Dulcy replied shortly.

Dougall's cynicism was born of experience. Dulcy cringed. She'd erred by accepting Birdwhistle's claim as gospel, simply because the good-looking guy seemed genuine. She remembered stark embarrassment at wrongly judging the Freya case, years ago. Grimslade saw by Dulcy's face, her mistake hit home. So, he said no more about it.

"Remind me to get young Tim to drop these house keys back to Birdwhistle's office later." Grimslade said.

"I will. But I think it's high time for a nice cup of tea. I'm putting the kettle on."

"Good idea Dulcy. We're on the same page with that."

Dougall began unwrapping his sandwiches.

"Guess you've got salami and pickled gherkin again hey Dougall?"

"Yep. Bella knows it's my favourite. What have you got today?"

"Cheese and tomato sauce."

"Good grief. Is that actually a thing?"

"It's all I had. I need to shop. With Dave away I don't go to a lot of trouble."

"You want one of mine?"

"I could swap you one." Dulcy replied.

Dougall bit into the cheese and ketchup sanger.

"Actually, it's not that bad."

"I know."

They shared a smile. Dulcy loved when Dougall smiled. He was a very handsome man when he wasn't wearing his customary scowl. An improper attraction Dulcy felt for Dougall had to be quashed, telling herself it was only because she missed David.

Chapter 11

FUN ON THE BEACH

Gone In A Flash

Meanwhile, as Dulcy and Dougall shared their sandwiches, her husband made plans.

David Dubois thought of a shrewd way to stop cash payments to Zelia but still keep his illegitimate son a secret.

He planned to buy a small house in the sleepy coastal town of Zelia's old stomping grounds. The popular location should greatly appeal to her. In lieu of hefty cash instalments, he'd allow the house rent-free until the child came of age.

Parking Zelia and the boy in the quiet town, made it less likely anyone he knew would run into them. Aware none of his friends liked Zelia, and would cross the street to avoid her, David felt his plan to be a good one.

David doubly justified the expense as an investment in his future with the fond idea a beach house would be nice for eventual holidays with Dulcy. Perhaps the place could become their own retirement cottage, down the track.

Aiden Birdwhistle agonised over how volunteering information to police degenerated so badly into implicating himself in wrongdoing. He cursed himself for not staying out of it and wished he hadn't gotten involved. In his mind, he dubbed Grimslade as *that bloody prick of a detective.*

Hot to tail the informer, Tim Fun quickly changed into beachwear kept in his car, and parked in sight of Birdwhistle Solutions car park. Before long, the quarry drove out again, taking no notice of an old jalopy driven by a teenager following some distance behind.

The new recruit revelled in being given the surveillance task of following a suspect. It represented an exciting variation, different to his usual more mundane research work.

Aiden Birdwhistle drove to an old jetty where he walked to the end and sat a while. Since relevant case details were withheld from the public, the man did not know partial human remains had recently been fished out from beneath that pier. By the same token, he was unaware his ex-wife, Jenni McKinstock, joined Molly Malone as an alternative contender.

Privy to police information and sworn to secrecy, Tim Fun couldn't wait to get back and report to his superiors:

"He drove to the old jetty where those body parts were netted."

"That's interesting. What did he do there?"

"Walked to the end and just sat for a while, looking out to sea, then he got up and drove back to his office."

"Maybe he was thinking about his interview." Dulcy supposed.

"How long did he sit there Tim?"

"Less than ten minutes."

"Hmm." Grimslade frowned.

Again, it wasn't much to go on. Tim Fun missed seeing Aiden adroitly drop a small flash drive through a crack in the jetty boards. The item had momentarily bobbed on the choppy surface, before sinking from view.

The storage device contained sexually explicit footage of Jenni McKinstock committing adultery with a number of different men. Suspicion led the PI to install hidden cameras in the marital bedroom he used to share with his wife. The betrayed husband now lived alone in a flat above his office, and kept the steamy bedroom scenes for his own shameful titillation.

After the implied accusations of that morning, Aiden Birdwhistle feared the material to be a damning factor against himself if a police search found it. As soon as returning from his police interview, he removed his secret stimulant from his sock drawer, soaked the device in boiling water and driven to the jetty. He'd been half relieved and half regretful for its disposal.

Back at police headquarters, Tim Fun added an incident he'd observed two days ago on the esplanade:

"I don't know if this is relevant, but I recognised the man Birdwhistle as a bloke who almost started a fight at the beach recently." Tim said.

"Are you sure it was Aiden Birdwhistle? He doesn't seem the type."

"Yes. I am quite certain." Tim replied, "also the girl he was with works at his agency."

Dougall Grimslade took more of an interest.

"What happened with this almost fight?"

"This other guy walks up and says something while the girl and Birdwhistle were engaged in a pash. Everyone was watching them. I mean, it seemed a bit...um...overdone for the time and place."

"A pash?" Dougall asked.

"Kissing." Dulcy explained patiently.

"Is that all? Go on."

"Whatever he said hit a nerve with Birdwhistle. He pushed the other guy backwards into a tree. The other guy recovered and posed himself into an attack stance. Karate or something like that."

"Did this other guy look like a martial art fighter?"

"To me, he looked comical, but I'm not qualified to judge." Tim admitted.

"So did Birdwhistle back down?"

"No. But some lifeguards stood up. They seemed ready to break it up."

"I guess there'd be kids and families around." Dulcy remarked.

"Anyway, so the karate guy hurdled the fence into the car park. He took off in a sports car, tooting the horn, giving the finger."

"Would you recognise the karate guy again Tim?"

"Sure. He's often at the beach. Hangs out with the glamour set."

"How would you describe him."

"He'd look macho except for his trendy blond hairstyle. Short one side and longer on the other, with a floppy girly bit in front. Only my personal opinion of course." Tim replied.

"Troy Van Baas." Dulcy declared.

"Has to be." Grimslade agreed.

"So the plot thickens. Good work Tim."

Tim Fun was sent to ask Aiden Birdwhistle to come in for further questioning, the next day.

"Why? Am I under arrest."

"No. Just a courtesy request Mr. Birdwhistle. If you have no objection that is."

During the second interview, Aiden Birdwhistle thanked the officers for promptly returning his house keys.

"I hope you didn't make a mess of the place. The real estate agents are due to inspect the property and take photos for their ads."

"I think you'll find it is in order." Dulcy replied.

If the place was not in order, it wasn't down to police inspections, as they hadn't gone to the house at all. Aiden Birdwhistle's questioning continued, most of it recapping what he'd said last time. The PI knew the reason would be to catch any changes to his original statement.

"Can you remind us of why you believe your ex-wife went back to your house?"

"The cleaners said the bathroom had been used. The towels were damp. You can check with the lady manager. She told me this in case I thought they'd been neglectful in their duty."

"We will check. She must be a highly diligent cleaning lady."

Aiden Birdwhistle caught the dubious slant to Grimslade's reply. In return, he explained the deal, very clearly and slowly, as if speaking down to a halfwit.

"I will attempt to explain so you can properly understand the cleaners' duty to fulfil their contract: The firm specialises in preparing homes for real estate inspections. They detail everything down to the last wrinkle and speck of dust. They will even come in and replace fresh flowers in vases and fresh fruit in bowls if necessary. For a price. I hope that clarifies it for you."

Grimslade and Vestige did not visibly react to Aiden's reciprocal sarcasm, though Dulcy chalked one up for his exacting rejoinder. She imagined a guilty man wouldn't be so bold with a smart-arse reply and thinly veiled insult. Yet, Grimslade's warning about double bluffing and not jumping to conclusions rang in her ear.

Confident he'd won that round, Birdwhistle claimed the high ground:

"Has something happened to my ex-wife? Otherwise, I can't see why her whereabouts is so important."

"You seemed sure your ex went back to your house after the incident at her place of work."

"No. As I have said more than once, I was not sure. I only thought she might have. I don't know where else she has to go to. We've been divorced six months. I don't keep tabs on her."

"Except you were present at the peep show."

"That was coincidental. I was on a case of my own."

The detectives did not reply. They'd attempted to trip him up, but he hadn't change his original account at all. Staring him down, Aiden Birdwhistle's face reddened. Dulcy put it down to irritation at their needling. Grimslade kept an open mind.

"Is that all? I have a business to run. And since you won't or can't tell me anything about Jenni, we are just wasting each other's time."

In a huff, Birdwhistle stood up to leave.

"Just one more item we'd like you to clarify for us concerning Troy Van Baas."

The man sighed, clearly fed up with the inquisition. He sat down again.

"I will if I can." he conceded.

"Your previous claim not to know Troy Van Baas is at odds with the fact you engaged in an altercation with him two days ago."

"What has he been saying?"

"We want your version."

Grimslade spoke sternly. He did not let on the information came from their own Tim Fun, and not from Troy Van Baas.

"I pushed him. That's all. He backed down and took off in his car."

"What was your reason to push him."

"He made crude and disparaging comments."

"You allege to not know the man. So why do you think he did that?"

"I was accompanying a young woman named Isla Tickle who works at my agency. Van Baas used to be her boyfriend. The slurs were directed at Isla."

"So Van Baas backed down after you pushed him?"

Grimslade made it sound absurdly unlikely, even amusing. Aiden blushed. He knew himself to be more of a lover than a fighter.

"At first, Van Baas did some martial art posturing, shaping up to fight. But I have friends at the surf club who were watching. When a bunch of them stood up ready to help me, Van Baas leapt over into the car park."

Aiden's younger brother, Ethan, had been among the lifeguards who had his back. But Aiden did not want to bring Ethan into it. Naming Isla Tickle had been bad enough yet he saw no way out of that. He thought the detectives probably had her name from Van Baas anyway. Furthermore, Isla had not done anything wrong. The detectives referred to some notes and drew conclusions.

"You named Troy Van Baas as being at the brothel saying you only knew him by name. Then you become embroiled in an altercation over his ex-girlfriend, an Isla Tickle, who happens to work for you. You, Troy Van Baas and your ex-wife Jenni McKinstock were all present when the Sudanese abduction and double murders all took place at the mansion brothel. A lot of coincidences here."

"Nevertheless, that's how it is."

Aiden Birdwhistle began to sweat, due to the nature of their summary. The detectives knew his nervous reaction could indicate guilt.

"Have you reason to believe your ex-wife and Van Baas are known to each other?"

"I have no idea."

"You made sure to tell us Van Baas was at the brothel."

"You asked me if I knew any of the other men. I told you I knew Van Baas by name. Why do you keep going over this? I volunteered to tell you what I know."

Birdwhistle's agitation made Grimslade feel he might be getting somewhere.

"You wanted to implicate Van Baas, didn't you?"

"I had no reason not to tell his name. And since he seems a complete and utter arse hole, yes, I hope you do investigate him. Please do."

Failing to crack Aiden Birdwhistle under pressure, Grimslade and Dulcy could only meet his gaze blandly. Grimslade gave him his official calling card after writing his own personal phone number on the back.

"Call me anytime if you think of more to add." he said.

Aiden made a show of slotting Grimslade's card into his wallet, all the while hoping the irritating man would hold his breath, turn purple, and pass out waiting. He had absolutely no intention of contacting that *bloody prick of a detective* ever again.

The detectives combed over everything again after the peeved man left.

"We have to interview the girl, Isla Tickle." Dulcy said.

"Yep. First thing tomorrow." Grimslade agreed.

Chapter 12

ISLA TICKLE INTERVIEWED

Grimslade Speechless

Tim Fun was sent to Birdwhistle Solutions office to request Isla Tickle come with him to assist with inquiries. Isla imagined he wanted Aiden again.

"Hello," she said, "I'm afraid the manager is out at the moment."

"I've been sent to accompany a Miss Isla Tickle downtown." Tim replied.

"That's me," she said, "but I can't leave now. I'm here alone and in charge of the office."

Tim Fun did not expect a refusal. Noticing the junior officer's momentary confusion, Isla Tickle compromised, albeit rather reluctantly:

"...but if the interview can be done here, I am happy to assist."

Isla hoped they'd postpone the interview, but Vestige and Grimslade soon arrived at Birdwhistle Solutions. The detectives formally introduced themselves. Dulcy aimed for a friendly approach.

"Call me Dulcy." she smiled.

Grimslade did not say to call him Dougall. In fact, he said nothing at all, just rudely stared at Isla Tickle.

By her mutinous expression, the girl took personal offence at Grimslade's intense ogling. Known for her quick outspoken retorts, Isla Tickle longed to tell him off. Yet she disciplined herself against brash back-chat in case it prolonged their visit. The night before had been extremely energetic and she needed a siesta.

"Miss Tickle. Can you confirm you were in a relationship with Troy Van Baas?" Dulcy began.

"Yes. I was. He broke it off with me because he needed someone more suitable."

"More suitable for what?"

"To further his career or his image as a high flyer. I don't even know why he picked me for his girlfriend to begin with."

Dulcy tried for a sympathetic face. Her mute senior colleague still only gaped at the girl, saying nothing. Dougall's silence began to disconcert Dulcy. It seemed so unusual for the man who so enjoyed grilling people. Raising an eyebrow, she cast a questioning glance at her senior colleague, but Grimslade kept his unblinking gaze and full attention riveted on Isla Tickle. Dulcy soldiered on alone:

"How did you meet Troy Van Baas?"

"To put it bluntly, he picked me up on the beach. I was charmed by his handsome face and smooth talking. Pretty soon I began dating him seriously. I didn't know his true nature at the time. If I had known what he was really like, I wouldn't have touched him with a barge pole." Isla declared.

"Had you seen Troy Van Baas on the beach before?"

"Sure. I noticed him. Hard not to. He was always the centre of attention, hanging out with a bunch of bikini girls. That's why I was flattered when he asked me out because I am the opposite of a glamorous bikini girl. I don't even wear bikinis. I only go to the beach for swimming or surfing and not to parade about. I always wear plain ordinary one-piece bathers with baggy board shorts as well. I haven't tried to impress anyone, that's for sure."

Dulcy waited in vain for Dougall to offer any input but his mute state forced her to go it alone. She'd certainly be having words with him later.

"Were you with other people when Troy Van Baas spoke to you?"
"No. Not really. But there are always others I know around on the beach whenever I go. Usually there would be some people I recognise who shop at the supermarket and a few of the regular lifeguards and other locals."

Aiming a sharp eye at her senior colleague, wishing she could kick start him into action, Dulcy decided not to say another word until he roused himself out of his coma. As the silence stretched out, Grimslade took the hint. He cleared his throat and found his voice at last:

"Miss Tickle, did you ever go out on the yacht with Troy Van Baas?"
"Yes. A few times. But usually he took me to his big house. I have to admit, his wealth impressed me at the time. Now I know he isn't worth it."

Dulcy questioned an inconsistency.

"You say he broke it off with you. But the altercation with your employer, Aiden Birdwhistle suggests jealousy."

Already in a bad mood from Grimslade's rude staring, Isla snapped a reply:

"Troy neither wants or needs me. If he did, he wouldn't have dumped me. Right? He just can't hack that I wasn't thrilled to accept his terms."
"What terms?" Grimslade frowned.

"He wanted a loose arrangement where he did whatever he liked with his fancy women but still had me as a sideline. And he thought I would go for that! Well, sorry for the language, but to put it crudely, I told him to go fuck himself."

Both Dulcy and Dougall hid instant inclinations to grin. Isla Tickle went on:

"…so he's been really peeved because he thought it was a reasonable arrangement. I guess he couldn't stand seeing me with someone else. And while I'm on that subject, someone threw a brick through the plate glass window here. It's just been fixed. But there was a nasty note tied to the brick. I believe it was probably Troy who did it. We kept the note. I'll show it to you."

Isla retrieved the note from the desk drawer where she knew Aiden had it locked away. The scrawled black block letters read as WHAT A SLUT. BONKING THE BOSS IN THE LUNCH HOUR.

"Can we keep this?"
"Sure. We only kept it in case any clue ever came up over who did it. No luck for us. But it's the type of thing Troy said about me and why Aiden pushed him that day."

Grimslade managed a further query, carefully worded.

"Apart from work, are you in a close relationship with Aiden Birdwhistle?"
"Yes," Isla admitted, "I am now. Just beginning. But I wasn't at the time the brick was thrown. In fact, that happened on my first day of working at Birdwhistles. I was still on trial. And I only met Aiden the day before."

The detectives digested that information leading their questions down a different path.

"Did you know Jenni McKinstock before meeting Aiden?"
"Who? Oh, is that his former wife Jenni? We sort of met once."
"When was this?"

Isla took a deep breath and gathered her thoughts regarding Jenni McKinstock.

"She accosted Aiden at a hotel restaurant when I was with him in a work-related meeting over dinner. I had only just met Aiden that same day and agreed to trial the job. I hadn't even started work at Birdwhistles yet..."

Grimslade surmised Aiden Birdwhistle would have been attracted to Isla Tickle and possibly used the job meeting excuse for the dinner date. The dour detective could see the attraction, but he did not mention this to Dulcy. Isla continued with her account:

"...anyway, she must have imagined we were on a proper date, and I guess she was jealous. The woman was really offensive and quite drunk at the time. I only saw her that once. The place wasn't well lit and she was ranting and wild looking."
"What became of that?"
"Hotel security escorted her out. She had a little dog that peed on the floor, and they used a rule of no dogs allowed. Otherwise, I think she might have kicked up more of a stink. Aiden apologised and said that was his crazy ex who loved to make a scene."
"Did you or Aiden say anything to her at the time?"
"No. Nothing. We just sat there stunned. It was so unexpected and embarrassing."

Hotel CCTV had already been checked. Isla's version did not differ. Dulcy Vestige opened a briefcase. Two professional studio photos of Jenni McKinstock as a fashion model were shown.

"Is this the same woman you know as Aiden Birdwhistle's former wife? And are you sure you hadn't seen her on other occasions?"

Isla Tickle inspected the photos but felt unsure.

"Yes and no," she answered, "I think it's the same person but she looks a lot better in these photos than when she made that drunken scene. I don't remember seeing her before but she might have been amongst the models who partied on Troy's yacht. They were all like clones of glittering film stars. Flash jewellery. Heavy make-up. False eyelashes. Probably wigs as well. I can't be certain if she was one of them, after all this time. Obviously I was really outclassed amongst the glitterati."

"There's more to class than paint and bling." Dulcy remarked, somewhat primly.

Isla ran a hand over her eyes. She felt weary and rather worn out. The detectives' visit delayed Isla's need to catch up on sleep. Her fatigue resulted from an energetic night of passion with Aiden Birdwhistle, in their first ever physical intimacy. Aiden suggested she close the office for an afternoon nap in his upstairs flat. He wanted his new lover fresh and rested for a second wild night together. It had been what they both looked forward to. Little did they know, their wishes were not to be granted that night, nor for many nights ahead.

"Is that all?" Isla hoped the police people would just shut up and go away.

"Not quite."

Grimslade gave a slight nod to Dulcy, who went ahead with a pre-determined ploy, though asked gently.

"Isla, were you aware of being video taped while you were privately occupied with Troy Van Baas?"

The implications of that question sunk in. Isla Tickle looked aghast. She visibly paled then reddened. Her hands flew to cover her opened mouth, and her eyes widened in shock. The detectives paid close attention to her reaction. They predicted she wasn't faking. Isla gasped:

"What? NO! I hope you don't mean... is that what you mean?"

Grimslade and Dulcy fished that line to expand on the Molly Malone complaint. They did not yet know Isla Tickle had also been filmed without her consent while indulging sexually with Troy Van Baas. The detectives neither confirmed nor denied the suggestion.

"Thanks Miss Tickle. We might want to talk another time but that is all for now."

Isla Tickle had to be left fuming and upset. Murder investigations favoured no one. Grimslade and Vestige returned to their office.

"If she was filmed by Van Baas, I'd say she certainly didn't know." Dulcy said.
"Agreed. And I doubt if she would agree to it. That young woman doesn't seem the type to do so. She's been badly treated by Van Baas and a pity she was taken in by him. Without seeming too judgemental, in the interests of maintaining a fair and unbiased perspective, I nonetheless gather Van Baas is something of a despicable creep." Grimslade expounded with a lengthy reply.

Dulcy couldn't resist the reprimand she'd been holding in:

"So Dougall, now you can talk it up. You didn't have much to say at the interview. I felt totally stranded while you just gaped like a stunned mullet at the poor girl."
"Sorry." he replied.

"That behaviour is so unlike you. Normally you enjoy the verbal duels."

"It's just that...the girl reminded me of someone. Don't ask."

Dulcy swallowed her curiosity but vowed to get to the bottom of Dougall's odd reaction to Isla Tickle before too long.

Deep in thought, Dougall Grimslade went home to his wife and dinner. Bella was too busy cooking to notice her husband's unsettled mood, or that he spent some time peering closely at their framed wedding photo on the mantle.

Chapter 13

ABDUCTED

Showdown at the Hacienda

No sooner had Dougall sat down at the table to eat dinner with Bella, than a frantic call arrived on his private phone number.

Aiden Birdwhistle, who had no intention of ever contacting the irritating *prick of a detective* had cause to do so. He spoke quickly in a somewhat garbled account.

"Slow down. Say it again."

"It looks like Isla has been taken. She isn't here. I found her car keys on the ground and all her things are still in her car... we had arranged to meet for dinner... so I am sure something is terribly wrong."

Bella Grimslade frowned knowing another meal would be put on hold. Dougall felt famished, but he only stuffed some bread in his mouth while pulling his shoes back on.

"Can't it wait long enough for you to eat?" Bella asked.

"Not this time." Dougall could not expand on the dire urgency he felt to rush.

Within minutes, another call came in from a different Birdwhistle: Ethan.

"I'm Aiden's brother. We are driving to that big white Spanish place on the cliff. Well Aiden is driving. He believes Isla could be there. But she might also be taken out on Troy Van Baas' yacht. Aiden says to alert the Coast Guard. Please."

Grimslade phoned Dulcy saying to meet him at the marina. Dulcy understood the urgency. This was another link tying a missing woman to that damn yacht. Dulcy abandoned her husband Dave, who had a short leave before beginning a mission overseas.

"I'm sorry Dave my darling. I must go. This could be a life-or-death thing."

Dave Dubois felt very let down. Dulcy seemed to be forever going off with that blasted Grimslade bloke. Acute disappointment reminded David of his lapse in succumbing to a convenient day of sex with Zelia that final time. That led to worrying over his ensuing predicament. At times David had been on the verge of confessing all to Dulcy... his rash encounter with Zelia, the unplanned pregnancy, the child being definitely his own... perhaps it could be a problem shared. But he wasn't brave enough to face the consequences. Fearing Dulcy would leave him stifled David's intention to reveal all. David booted up his laptop and continued searching affordable seaside cottages. He hoped to convince Zelia to agree to his new plan, and by moving her out of town his guilty secret might be safe. While David Dubois browsed real estate ads, his detective wife addressed more pressing problems in the line of duty.

The Birdwhistle brothers made it to the clifftop hacienda before Grimslade and Vestige got there. The detectives found a traffic cop already in attendance, since he had chased Aiden for speeding. That officer had already called for additional police back-up and ambulances by the time the detective team arrived. The entourage met a gruesome scene. Troy Van Baas and Jenni McKinstock, had been grotesquely mutilated. Aiden's ex-wife suffered excruciating pain, but despite dreadful facial injuries, her wounds were not life-threatening. A man known as Fergus Rudin, a local supermarket manager, had died of stab wounds. Van Baas had also expired as a result of trauma.

Dougall Grimslade's greatest concern had been for Isla Tickle. Aiden Birdwhistle stood protectively over Isla as she lay prone, wrapped in white towels, on a narrow bed. Ethan Birdwhistle hovered in a supportive role, but left the room when more police drove in. He followed Jenni McKinstock's small poodle outside.

"I better see where the little dog is going in case he gets hit by a car." Ethan said, as he quickly exited the crime scene.

The dog hid himself underneath Rudin's vehicle. While coaxing the poodle to come out, Ethan took the opportunity to remove a tracking device he'd placed under Rudin's car. The device had been used to track the man for his wife, Sylvia Rudin, who wanted to know where he went at nights. Ethan slipped the surveillance device into his jeans pocket and pulled his shirt down over it. A policeman on guard duty questioned Ethan about the dog.

"Is that your dog?"
"No, he's a family pet. My brother bought him." which was the truth.

Aiden had given the pup to Jenni during their marriage. It had been the only gift she never had any complaint about. Jenni loved that spunky animal.

"What's its name?" the officer asked.

Ethan always thought Jenni gave him a ridiculous name. He mumbled Pitbull but the policeman thought he'd said Pebbles.

"Come on Pebbles. Good boy."

The officer got down on his knees, looked under Rudin's car, and smooched to the small dog. The name Pebbles sounded enough like Pitbull to the dog, so he came out and promptly bit the policeman's proffered hand.

"Ow. He's a right little carnivore isn't he?"
"Dogs will be dogs." Ethan replied.

At that stage, neither Ethan nor the policeman knew what delicacy Pitbull/Pebbles had recently eaten. It had been a substantial snack that culminated in Troy Van Baas' demise. With no one left capable of looking after the poodle, Ethan took him home.

Aiden Birdwhistle accompanied Isla Tickle in the ambulance and sat by her bedside for most of the long night. Nursing staff advised Aiden to go home and get some sleep himself, as the patient had been heavily sedated. While Aiden went on a bathroom break, Dougall Grimslade looked in on Isla Tickle. Unconscious, she knew nothing of his visit, and did not feel anything when he pulled a few hairs out of her head by the roots. Bleary eyed, the dour detective approached Aiden in the hospital canteen, very early in the morning. Grimslade tried for a friendly opener:

"How do they make this coffee taste so bad?"
"Morning Grimslade. How did it end up?"
"Van Baas dead. Rudin dead. Jenni McKinstock scheduled for surgery today sometime. Probably early this morning."
"So now you know I didn't do away with my ex." Aiden said.
"Why would I think you did?"
"Your line of questioning about her distinguishing marks. Also the comments about me wanting to be rid of her, and losing respect for her."
"Those were mainly run-of-the-mill prodding. But the distinguishing marks question was to eliminate your ex from another case."
"Give me a lift home Grimslade, and I'll let you tell me about it."

Since Jenni McKinstock turned up alive, if not well, Molly Malone regained prominence as most likely to own those bits found under the jetty.

Before police arrived at the hacienda, Ethan Birdwhistle detected hidden spy cameras, while Aiden attended to Isla. Instead of being used for future blackmail, the spy camera footage could now provide a record of what really happened during the deadly hour at the clifftop house. Without that proof, events would have been difficult to fathom.

Footage proved old Fergus Rudin, in a fit of rage, lopped off Troy Van Baas' impressive penis as the younger man flaunted it at him, as a taunt. Van Baas fell to the floor unable to fully comprehend the horror. Then, Jenni McKinstock entered the games room followed by her poodle. Troy Van Baas screamed in horror as the little dog ran outside with his most cherished part in its mouth. Subsequently the ruined man suffered a catastrophic failure and died.

Too late, Jenni became aware of Troy's injury only when she knelt to take his hand. A bloodied stump replaced where his proud manhood had recently reigned supreme. Knowing it had to be Fergus Rudin who maimed her lover, Jenni McKinstock knifed the supermarket manager in the guts as retribution. Nonetheless, jealousy consumed Jenni seeing Isla tied to a bed ready for Troy's pleasure. She selected a long corkscrew with the intention of hurting the helpless girl.

Fortunately, at that point, Sylvia Rudin entered the room scolding caustic comments to her errant husband, who remained standing upright in a state of delayed shock. Sylvia had no idea Fergus had been stabbed. Jenni McKinstock lunged at Sylvia with the corkscrew, but Fergus collapsed between them at the same time. Aiden's ex-wife tripped over Rudin and the corkscrew pierced her own face. Sylvia hit Jenni over the head with a champagne magnum while delivering sage advice:

"Don't mess with the big girls honey."

Unaware her husband Fergus had been fatally wounded, Sylvia Rudin left the scene. Her husband's prior lecherous interest in the check-out chick had never escaped Sylvia's notice. For some time, she'd held Isla Tickle as much to blame. Disgusted by the hacienda scenario, seeing Isla tied down naked, Sylvia realised her mistake in thinking Isla consented to anything with Fergus.

Rudin's distraught wife felt sorry for throwing a brick through Birdwhistle's plate glass window, in misplaced fury against Isla. The contrite woman had been unable to release Isla's bonds, but at least covered her up with big towels she found in the bathroom.

Dulcy Vestige tasked herself with finding what Mrs. Sylvia Rudin muttered as she covered Isla's nudity. Those words remained a loose end as the only unclear part of video evidence. Grateful for having her humiliating exposure covered, Isla never told anyone that Sylvia Rudin quietly confessed and apologised for throwing that brick with the rude message.

Dulcy found Isla Tickle had been brought up in institutions and bore the brunt of that childhood. The girl's tough attitude came of a constant need to stick up for herself, and put offenders in their place. Isla impressed Dulcy as a kindred spirit, and the two feisty women forged a friendship during those hospital visits.

Another friendship grew out of that event: Dougall Grimslade discovered he liked Aiden Birdwhistle, and felt deeply sympathetic towards the younger man's ordeal. Happily married to Bella for twenty-one years, Dougall could only imagine what revulsion Aiden suffered over Jenni McKinstock's lewd antics.

Grimslade approved of Aiden being with Isla, and had an exceptionally good reason to care about that.

Pursuant to the jetty body case, regular attendees on the Van Baas yacht were brought in for questioning. Only one, the woman known as Molly Malone, could not be found.

Grimslade ordered that the yacht be classed as a crime scene. As such, it remained anchored off-shore, divested of all crew and personnel. The detective checked that no cats or other pets were on board. None were found, because Troy Van Baas abhorred animals. He often described people who kept pets as suckers and losers. One of his workers commented:

"Troy would laugh that the sharks around his yacht were his only little pets."

Therefore, no life had been aboard when, one dark night, the party yacht disintegrated in a massive explosion. The blast lit the sky and the surrounding ocean with a bright and fiery mushroom of smoke. Apart from what wreckage sunk to the seabed, only shards of blackened flotsam remained afloat, to be washed away by strong ocean currents.

Tim Fun worked diligently on an unresolved aspect of the yacht case.

"I've accounted for all the yacht regulars except the one calling herself Molly Malone." he said.

"While I caution everyone never to jumped to unverified assumptions, I'm willing to bet the missing Molly Malone is not alive, alive, oh." Grimslade replied.

Puzzled, Tim Fun looked askance. The turn of phrase 'alive, alive oh' seemed to him strangely quirky coming from the gruff detective.

"Unlike her cockles and mussels." Dulcy added.

Tim Fun was perplexed by the apparent code-speak from his superiors. Not wishing to display ignorance, he sussed it out. Googling Molly Malone, Tim linked the name to an old Irish song he'd not heard of before. Apparently the tune known as the unofficial anthem of Dublin, also sometimes went by the titles *Cockles and Mussels* or *In Dublin's Fair City.*

Before long, Tim Fun's sterling efforts came up with a useful finding.

"Perhaps the assumption regarding Molly Malone can be verified. One of her close friends supplied hairbrushes and personal effects that might be DNA matched with the jetty remains."

"Well done Tim." Grimslade nodded.

"We're giving the QFSS plenty of work." Dulcy added.

Queensland Health Forensic and Scientific Services (QFSS) also had samples taken from the slain brothel men and the female Sudanese body. The investigation worked on the assumption the woman's killers would be kin. Further testing proved decisive. Arrests eventuated for the murders of the Sudanese woman and the two mansion brothel bouncers.

Shortly, Dulcy Vestige picked up another phone call from the QFSS.

"Dougall, did you authorise DNA testing on Isla Tickle?"

Dougall Grimslade took the handset from Dulcy. He had not expected a phone call despite that he'd flagged the test as urgent. His colleague only heard his side of the conversation:

"Uh huh. Okay. Yes, it is very helpful. Thanks." Grimslade said.
After ending the call, Grimslade muttered:
"I knew it. I just bloody knew it."
Dulcy said nothing, but wondered what he just bloody knew.
Forced to own up, Dougall replied:

"Yes Dulcy. I did authorise it. It was a private concern. I put it through official channels hoping for speedier results than might be had from other laboratories."

Again, Dulcy offered no reply. Dougall appeared discomforted, truly a rarity. It belied his usual practice to deadpan. She waited for some enlightenment.

"Dulcy. I admit using QFSS for myself is highly irregular. Please hear me out."

"I know you wouldn't do so if it wasn't important, Dougall. I thought you had some private issue with Isla Tickle that first time we interviewed her. The way you stared her down, I wondered if you suspected her of some prior thing. But you don't owe me."

"I feel I do owe you an explanation."

Dougall Grimslade walked around the desk and closed the door. Clearly, he did not want anyone else hearing.

"Turns out I am Isla Tickle's father."
"What?"

Dulcy imagined herself inured to hearing shockers, yet Dougall's disclosure astounded her.

"You are Isla's father?"
"Yes. It's true. Actually, Bella and I are her blood parents. She is the image of Bella at the same age. Long story. No one else knows. Not even Bella. Certainly not Isla."

Dulcy took a minute to digest the surprise, she sat open mouthed for moments before asking:
"Are you sure?"
"I am now. Confirmed by DNA. Absolutely."
Dulcy addressed logistics: "When did you get material for testing?"

"I pulled hairs from Isla's head while she was unconscious in hospital."

"There's no doubt then."

"I felt certain of it even before the DNA result, to be honest." Dougall replied.

Dulcy thought about Isla's sorrow for having no family. Dougall went on to tell Dulcy how it came about. In his youth, he sung in a rock band. His ardent fan, Bella, looked a few years older than her fourteen years. He assumed she was of age and did not know he made her pregnant. They lost touch when he joined the police force and gave up the band. Bella ran away from home and gave birth alone. With no options, she left the newborn in a cardboard carton inside a church vestibule. Later as a young policeman, Dougall met Bella again when he arrested her on drug charges. He visited her in re-hab often, and they fell in love properly. They had no luck trying to find what happened to their baby. They didn't even know her name.

"In any case, we believed she'd certainly have been adopted into a good family and we had no right to disrupt her life."

Dulcy felt for Isla's sad childhood which prompted her to say:

"Unfortunately Isla was raised in institutions and has regrets."

"I know that now, Dulcy. I blame myself for what she's suffered with Troy Van Baas and Fergus Rudin. Thank God it was not a lot worse."

"You can't blame yourself Dougall but I can see why you might."

Dulcy wrapped her arms around Dougall in a long comforting hug. It seemed the only right response at the time, though they lingered over it for rather too long.

"I'm glad she is with Aiden Birdwhistle though. He seems a decent type of young man."

"I agree. But Dougall, you must tell Bella and Isla. Surely?"

"I will. Of course. Just marking time to allow Isla to recover from the abduction ordeal. Claiming Isla as our daughter consumes my thoughts. Not sure how to go about it. I am well aware that Isla doesn't like me very much."

Dulcy could not disavow him of that notion.

"Aiden might be a good go-between?"

"That's true. Good thinking Dulcy."

"I'm not just a pretty face." she replied with a smile.

Dougall had always been well aware of that fact but would never let on. He loved Bella dearly, yet he was a man with eyes in his head and was not blind to Dulcy's undeniable charms.

Chapter 14

FAMILY TIES

Some Things Best Unsaid

Dougall Grimslade had not told Bella or Isla his findings, before a surprise wedding invitation arrived. Isla Tickle was to wed Aiden Birdwhistle.

Dulcy and Dougall were delighted to learn the young people they liked so much were to marry. A double wedding planned with Aiden's brother Ethan and his youthful partner Tiffany, would have wedding breakfasts at Ethan's surf club. Marriage ceremonies beforehand were to be held on the beach.

"By the sea too. I am so looking forward to it. David will be on leave then as well, so we can go together." Dulcy enthused.
"Did you notice the celebrant's name? Francis Funicular."
"Betting she is related to our Tim."
"Has to be."

Anwei Timothy Funicular, known as Tim Fun, did not know the betrothed couples, but he assured them his Aunt Francis Funicular would provide fitting rituals.

"My Aunt Francis is lovely," Tim said, "and she also breeds toy poodles."

The senior detectives knew of one such little poodle. That small silver-grey dog known by three names, Frou-Frou, Pitbull and Pebbles, had quite innocently triggered the carnage at the hilltop hacienda.

Sadly, the double weddings of the Birdwhistle brothers with Isla and Tiffany, did not go smoothly. A couple of prison escapees tried to run down the wedding party on the beach. The deranged pair in an SUV had axes to grind with three of the group. If not for the silver poodle, they might have succeeded. *[cite The Peckish by Jo Milanne]*

In the midst of that near tragedy, Bella Grimslade reeled over a discovery that shocked her to the core. Bella almost fell and had to be escorted to a chair. Just as her husband had experienced, she recognised herself in the bride, Isla. Only Dougall and Dulcy knew Bella's swooning spell must be in shock reaction to seeing Isla for the first time. Dougall covered for Bella's near collapse, by saying they'd been running late so had skipped breakfast.

Within the surf club wedding breakfast venue, Isla arranged sustenance for the older couple, without any inkling she was caring for her very own birth parents. Dulcy observed the interactions and shared a look with Dougall, who nodded imperceptibly. They were on the same page with their thoughts.

In a quiet aside, Dougall promised he would reveal the family connection after the honeymoon trips. He dearly hoped Isla would not be traumatised on learning they, the Grimslades, were her birth parents.

"Yes, they should have time to relax before facing more dramas," Dulcy agreed, "otherwise another upset could ruin their honeymoons as well."

Having lost his own parents, Aiden identified a father figure in Dougall for himself, so he requested the Grimslades be at his wedding. At the time, Isla disliked Dougall, but she agreed Aiden should invite whomever he wanted. Since the Grimslades were coming, Isla wanted her friend Dulcy there as well.

Isla also invited her prior landlords to the wedding, as she'd rented a flat from them for three years, and acquired their old car at a good price, with driving lessons thrown in. The friendly old couple were glad of the chance to bid Isla good luck, and to say goodbye. Due to advancing age, they were moving back with family in New Zealand, and their Australian beach house must be sold.

Seated at the same table at the wedding reception, Dulcy's husband pricked up his ears and asked about that house sale. Available homes near to the beach were few, and he hadn't yet found a cottage for Zelia and his secret offspring. David Dubois made his interest seem merely polite comments within general conversation. Distracted at the time by Dougall's family dilemma, Dulcy did not hear the exchange between David and Isla's old landlords.

David Dubois noted his wife's gaze often meshed with *Dougall bloody Grimslade's* and the degree of their shared interest seemed loaded with private messages. He jealously imagined the detective partners might be too closely involved with each other.

Earlier, at the surf club venue, an attractive girl, Chantel Chiron, had been blatantly coming on to David Dubois. The man knew he could be 'in like Flynn' with that one. Among a few kids at the venue, one ran up to them.

"This is my boy Dominic." Chantel said proudly.

The young mother wore no wedding ring, and her forward approach suggested she would be easy. David regretted missing out due to his loyalty to Dulcy and considered he could be a prize mug for being faithful during their marriage. He had a healthy libido and his wife's frequent absences, forever going off on some exciting adventure with her manly colleague, irked him.

Unashamedly easy, Chantel Chiron didn't know who had fathered her child and didn't particularly care. A visiting Yank contestant in an iron man event was her best guess...unless it had been the visiting Kiwi. Dominic didn't look like either, he took after herself with Continental good looks.

Chantel could only be certain her son's father wasn't Ethan Birdwhistle because he, among very few, rejected her advances. The knock backs proved just as well, since Ethan married Chantel's best friend, Tiffany, this day.

It struck David that Chantel's boy Dominic would be about the same age as his own illegitimate son. It reminded him he must do something about a house for Zelia. He decided to follow up on the place he'd heard of from Isla's old landlords, as soon as possible, before it got snapped up by another buyer.

Numerous and various undercurrents swirled about on that memorable wedding day, and everyone gleaned a different take on events.

After seeing Isla for the first time since newborn, Bella Grimslade later confronted her husband in the privacy of their own home. It was not a conversation to be had in front of others. All day, Bella tried to think of a way to voice what she suspected. In the end, she did not mince words:

"She's ours isn't she Doogie?"

Dougall's wretched expression, left no doubt. He confirmed, their daughter had been found and positively identified as Isla Tickle, now married as Isla Birdwhistle.

"I've been dying to tell you Bella, but I had to be completely sure. Now I can say with certainty, yes Isla is our baby girl. DNA proves it. Of course she doesn't know yet."
"Oh my God! And she is so beautiful." Bella cried.
"Yes she is. Just like you Bella, my love."
"But what will she think of us? How can we ever explain? What if she doesn't want to know us?"
"Well, Aiden knows Isla best. I plan to enlist his help in breaking the news to her."
"Does Aiden know?"
"Not yet."
"At the very least we attended her wedding." Bella choked out.
"Yes. How blessed is that?" Dougall replied, taking his wife into his arms.

Bella broke down and cried non-stop. She felt happy, sad and afraid all at the same time. Dougall knew he must soon fulfill his pending obligations. Once the honeymoon trip was over, and the newlyweds returned home, Dougall called upon Aiden to meet him privately. The rest is history, the Grimslades and their abandoned daughter found each other at last and were united. Dulcy congratulated Dougall on achieving the difficult meeting and a long overdue reconciliation with the past.

"Happy families?" she asked.

"It was tricky at first." he admitted.

"Must be hard for Isla. I mean in view of the abduction tapes and whatever else was on that yacht. She knows you witnessed her humiliation and the rest of it. The knowledge must be so much worse for her, finding out you are her father."

"I assured her Van Baas' tapes from the hacienda had her identity blurred out. I made sure of that myself."

"And of course, the yacht blew up." Dulcy added, eyeing her colleague closely.

"Yes." Dougall replied shortly, unable to meet her gaze.

Dulcy would never ask how such total destruction of such a large yacht came about. Some things were best left unsaid.

Chapter 15

THE BEACH COTTAGE

Free Rent

Deployed on army rescue in Gaza, David Dubois had wishful dreams of Dulcy intermingled with unsettling thoughts of Chantel and Zelia. Three women and only one of him...an absorbing burden that also vividly coloured his many waking hours.

Before leaving Australia, David Dubois at least secured vacant possession of the house he heard about from Isla's old landlords. The beach cottage needed some repairs and cosmetic updating, so was just within his means.

To Dubois' great relief Zelia accepted the offer after seeing the homely place in the pleasant location. He hoped it resolved one of his woman problems. She had not brought little Davy to the house viewing and David did not ask to see him. At that stage, the reluctant father had viewed his offspring only once, curious to see if the child took after himself. He couldn't really tell, so many babies looked fat, pink and bald. No way could he pick his own out of a nursery of similar newborns. His interest had been clinical, with no desire to touch the baby.

David had to resist emotional attachment to his son. Any on-going relationship with his wild oat would be impossible in order to avoid Zelia. At least she liked the free rent arrangement.

"It will do us okay. Little Davy can have his own bedroom instead of sharing mine. Now I can really look forward to you being with me when you're on leave from the army, David."

The man recoiled. Zelia seemed delusional. Did she imagine he wanted that? He'd offered the house only to get her off his back. At the time, he managed to fob her off.

Well aware she'd rattled him, Zelia laughed to herself. She couldn't resist taunting to see him squirm. Quite happy with a new man in her life, Zelia no longer needed David Dubois to warm her bed.

Well before Zelia moved into the seaside cottage, she had a new man in her life.

Zelia Wild and William Kirby began a convenient relationship after meeting at *The Tipsy Turnip Cafe*. The blind date had been orchestrated by someone they did not know. The couple never discovered it had been Grimslade's daughter who set them up on that blind date.

Working in the boring supermarket job, Isla Tickle's fun hobby involved placing secret notes in customer's shopping bags. Zelia and William counted among her successful pairings although she did not learn their names until much later.

Following a complaint about spam dating notes in customer's bags, the supermarket manager Fergus Rudin hired the local PI firm Birdwhistle Solutions to expose the culprit. Rudin suspected Isla Tickle, an outspoken employee who gave him cheek. Her behaviour made her most likely to be doing the notes.

Isla scorned his sport of touching up his young female shop assistants, calling it sexual harassment. When Rudin's wife Sylvia shopped one day, Isla pretended a fancy condom order had arrived for Fergus. The old lech had reasons to want Isla embarrassed, insisting she be confronted on the job at her check-out station in front of everyone.

The Birdwhistle brothers, Aiden and Ethan, considered the case trivial but it paid so well they couldn't afford to turn it down. They regretted it led to the young check-out operator getting fired. It seemed fair to offer her alternative employment, and they had already been thinking of getting a third. Primarily, the extra help would manage the office but also assist on surveillance cases if necessary.

The brothers spied on Isla Tickle, noting her potential for disguise and covert observation at *The Tipsy Turnip Cafe*. She chose that busy venue for her blind date couples to meet, so she could watch how it went. A major part of surveillance work involved waiting and watching too.

Isla had her eye on Aiden when he shopped at the supermarket, with an idea to set herself up with the handsome guy. The admiration had been mutual. Aiden's attraction to Isla began from day one, when she'd run from the supermarket, embarrassed by being exposed as a sneaky matchmaker.

Aiden caught up with Isla in the car park and convinced her to consider working at his PI business. Learning Isla had excelled in business studies at school had been a bonus. Isla proved to be an admirable choice from the outset. Broken hearted by her flamboyant ex-lover, Troy Van Baas, Isla found Aiden's shy conservatism tempting by contrast. Eventually Aiden set up a romantic date in his flat, but it had been Isla who initiated a seduction.

Zelia jumped at David Dubois' offer of several years free rent in the homely beach cottage. Knowing the child to be taken care of, Davy's absent father resolved to stay away.

Believing Zelia's story, William Kirby assumed she came into ownership of the cottage through some army widow settlement. Kirby moved in taking advantage of the no-rent deal. They were well off as a couple. She had her single parent benefit, and he earned a reasonable wage from his grease-monkey job.

The couple wanted to live together but did not want to limit Zelia's social security payments by having the man's income taken into account. William suggested a way Zelia could keep her government stipend: Ostensibly, he'd pretend to be a tenant in the flat under the house. The plan benefited them both in more ways than one.

Looking to his own future, William undertook to renovate the house and garden. His efforts enhanced the property value and made it an even more desirable piece of real estate.

The very much alive army soldier, David Dubois, knew nothing of the handy arrangement Zelia made with the cottage he provided rent-free. In any case, he would not have cared, as long as she kept off his back.

Relieved Zelia stopped contacting him, David did not visit his beach house until deceptions caught up with them all.

Chapter 16

THE BRUISER

The Chase

Regrets for parting company with her several girlfriends and her colleague in Queensland, Dulcy half hoped to be knocked back for the NT job. In the long run, her outstanding record worked against her, and she was awarded the duty.

Thankful his wife and Zelia became distanced far apart, David found suitable married quarters and happily set up house in Darwin with Dulcy.

Soon after Dulcy Vestige gained her Northern Territory promotion, a missing person report became her first important duty. That case evolved into a homicide and a lengthy chase across much of Australia.

Dulcy sought Dougall's advice. He had been inordinately happy to hear from Dulcy and have her ask for his input. He had missed the playful banter they enjoyed together, and the way their minds so often meshed on the same wavelength. When evidence led the chase from

The Northern Territory across to the east coast, DI Grimslade became officially involved.

Kirkwood Bonn, the missing person, had been incinerated in his Landcruiser, found upside down in a dried creek bed. The vehicle gear stick had been in neutral, rather than in-gear as it should have been if it had been driven into the ravine by accident. Further forensic testing ascertained the driver died from a blow to the lower back of his head. A head injury resulting from the crash would logically impact the front or top of the head. It did not look like death by misadventure. Everyone on the case agreed on a murder verdict.

Initially, the only clue had been a text from Kirkwood Bonn to his partner, Damien Cresswick, to say a hitchhiker named Richie had been picked up. Kirkwood messaged Damien saying the hitchhiker would help out with fuel cost and provide companionship on the long and lonely road ahead. Richie the hitchhiker became the prime suspect for killing Kirkwood Bonn, and with nothing else to go on, he'd been the only one.

Dulcy's efforts pounding the beat to question people living in outlying areas, found a landowner gave a foot traveller safe lodging overnight. Hikers on foot were rare and at great risk in the vast arid countryside. Notably, this one had given his name as Kirk.

Dougall concurred with Dulcy, hypothetically, that drifter could have murdered Kirkwood Bonn and destroyed the Landcruiser. It gave reason for him to be on foot.

"If he's stolen Kirkwood Bonn's ID he'd be calling himself Kirk." Dulcy said.
"Yes he would. And it isn't a common name. It's possible the hitchhiker Richie is misusing the victim's ID."
"It could be someone else though. Not Richie."
"Of course. But he is our best bet."

As such, they agreed the murder and stolen ID must be kept strictly confidential until the killer thief could be nabbed. The only chance of catching the felon might be if he misused the stolen credentials. Damien Cresswick, the victim's partner cooperated, telling friends and acquaintances Kirkwood died in an off-road accident.

"Damien Cresswick says Kirkwood habitually carried a lot of cash. His killer would be right for ready money."

"So, the murderer would be cashed up, but it wouldn't last forever. He might try looking for casual work. If he were stupid enough he might even use Kirkwood Bonn's ID as we hope." Dougall replied.

"Let's dote on him being stupid enough."

"He probably thinks himself smart. They often do."

The murderer, Bruce Luck, did not suspect detectives were already sniffing him out. He had called himself Richie after an admired mate in prison.

Another adventure caused him to flee a teen beach party stark naked. A scheme to distract the man with group sex and rob his backpack, backfired on the youths. Fighting back had been easy for the hardened criminal. He inflicted serious injuries on the kids and stole a new car belonging to one of them. Clothes the criminal had worn, complete with Kirkwood Bonn's laundry tags, were found in the sand dunes.

The teenagers concocted a tale saying an older man attacked them. In the wake of individual questions, Grimslade pulled their story to pieces. Having a bigger fish to fry, he tasked a local policeman to deal with it. Grimslade surveyed the beach party crime scene and contacted Dulcy to bring her up to speed:

"Seems our most wanted is on a one man crime spree. Now he's targeted a bunch of schoolies having a picnic. I'm not sure the kids are as innocent as they make out. But their injuries are real that's for sure...and by the way, Richie is now calling himself Ricky."

"Richie, Kirk, Ricky, he gets around if it's one and the same man."

Grimslade and Vestige decided it had to be the same man. The trail ran cold until Grimslade caught a breaking news report on TV about a heist on a prayer meeting. Footage showed signage naming a guest speaker as 'Brother Richie'.

Acting on a slim hunch connected to the name Richie, the detective sped to the scene. The guest speaker, Brother Richie, had by all accounts, absconded via a second story window. The description given of the man sounded very like their prime suspect wanted for the Kirkwood Bonn murder. Dougall called Dulcy again.

"What are your thoughts?

"Could it be him?"

"I don't know. They say a girl was taken hostage and it involved at least two others. Our suspect acted alone in the past." Dulcy mused.

"I agree," Dougall replied, "though much of what I've heard sounds like him."

Dougall told Dulcy the speaker had given a speech on finding Jesus.

"It could feasibly have been him doing the speech. Maybe not the heist. I think he is more likely to act on his own."

"Yes. The theft could be completely separate."

"He'd want to get out of there before police arrived."

"That's it. He would. And it seems he did. Going out of an upstairs window. It's quite a drop too."

"That adds up." Dulcy replied.

"Were the organisers co-operative?"

"They tried but they followed an agenda of their own."

"How's that?"

"They asked if I'd found Jesus."

"And?"

"I said, so far HE wasn't on my suspect list."

"Bet you scarpered after that." Dulcy laughed.

"Scarpered? Well, I did have to get back."

"To work on the urgent case of course."

"Anyway, jokes aside, I'm betting our prime suspect did it." Dougall said.

"Found Jesus?"

"Get real Dulcy."

The heist incident became unofficially titled *The Bible Thumper* - a description shared only between Grimslade and Vestige for their own amusement.

After doing away with the poor loser in the Landcruiser, Bruce Luck went by the name Kirk only one more time after staying at Alba Jenkins' place.

Chapter 17

THREE GIRLS ON A FARM

A Nod to Sport

Prior to Severe Tropical Cyclone Larry impacting the region, police searches discovered Kirkwood Bonn's credentials misused to obtain casual farm work.

The person seeking employment had been sent to an outlying farm known as Calenda Market Gardens. In the interim, the whole area had been flooded and roads cut off.

"Eureka Dulcy. We found Kirkwood Bonn's ID in use. Or to be exact, in misuse."

"So the killer is stupid enough to use it. Well done Dougall. What now?"

"As soon as roads are passable, I'll pay a visit to Calenda Market Gardens and see if the management can shed any light on the subject."

"Here's hoping you catch up with the impostor. But of course, if you can get in, he can get out." Dulcy replied.

"I doubt if he is still on the farm. He won't want to stay in one place for too long."

"But you tracked him down and are hot on his tail. You're a bloody legend Dougall."

"Shucks. Thanks for the accolade but I'd rather you just threw money."

"Noted. But don't hold your breath." Dulcy laughed.

Despite roads being potholed and boggy from flooding, Dougall managed to get through to the market garden farm in his capable 4WD vehicle. He drove right up to the farmhouse where he met three young lookalike women, wearing gumboots and making their way further down the farm.

Alighting from the 4x4, he introduced himself as DI Dougall Grimslade of The Queensland Police. He flashed his badge as well.

"Oh great!" the youngest looking girl exclaimed.

Grimslade pretended to miss an elbow nudged into her side by another one.

"Pardon?" he asked.

"Just saying. Oh great. The roads must be open now."

Grimslade deduced the three had to be sisters. They gave their names as Marcha, July and Nova. He surmised their names probably linked to their birthday months. Marcha seemed the eldest and Nova the youngest. Ignoring the younger girls' reactions, Marcha stepped up.

"Good morning Inspector, what can we do for you?"

"I'm asking after a man who was scheduled to work here. A Kirkwood Bonn."

Marcha answered without pause, as if she expected the question.

"He was working here. But I'm afraid he is no longer with us."

Grimslade caught a stifled snicker from the girl named July. Unless it had been a sneeze, nevertheless, he kept it in mind.

"When did he leave?"

"All the workers left because of the cyclone."

"But when did Kirkwood Bonn leave? How long ago?"

"Um. He was the last. I believe it was less than a week ago."

"Don't you keep pay records? I mean, that would pinpoint his departure time more accurately."

"No. the backpackers work only for food and lodging. I don't count every bean."

It did not seem a tightly run ship, but Grimslade kept a poker face. July added to her sister's comment:

"They don't only get beans you know. Marcha is a great cook, and they are really well fed. A lot of them say this is the best place they've ever worked at."

The canny detective regarded the identical fair-haired blue-eyed sisters while the trio gazed back, pictures of pure innocence. Only the youngest blinked and she had a sticking plaster over one eye. Grimslade voiced an idea:

"Did you have any problems with Kirkwood Bonn?"
"He was a good worker. Fit and strong." Marcha replied.

The detective knew all about prevarications and this sounded like one. Not to be put off, he repeated:

"Did you have any problems with that man? At all?"
A hasty three-way chorus answered his question:
"We were glad he was gone before having to invite him to sleep in our house."
"Because the workers' place took on floodwater."
"We like to keep our place private."
"Uh huh. Hmm. I see. Of course you would." Grimslade replied.

The three seemed rather quick with those explanations. Dougall couldn't pinpoint why but felt they were railroading him for some reason. He noticed what looked like dwelling further down the slope and below that, a big barn sitting in a couple of feet of brown floodwater.

"I guess the man left before the flood rose too high. Do you know where he went?"
"Couldn't say." Marcha replied shortly.

Grimslade pointed towards the dwelling below. It looked like an old schoolhouse.

"Is that the workers accommodation?"
"Yes. We were just going down to clean it up. The floor will be covered in mud."
"Could I take a look at where Kirkwood Bonn slept?"
"Sure. If you like," Marcha handed him a torch she held, "could be snakes under the beds and lockers."
"Have to be tough handling all this."

He almost added *for girls,* biting his tongue in time, aware the comment would not be well received by any of the womenfolk close to himself. At first, the girls let him make his way down to the workers cottage on his own.
Entering via a covered barbecue and kitchen area, the first thing Grimslade faced was a menu blackboard chalked with JULY U ONLY PITY FUCK HA HA.

"Hmm. I wonder what this implies?" he muttered to himself.

As he re-read the blackboard, the three girls followed him into the eatery. Grimslade noted their triple dismay. Apparently, they had not known that intriguing message existed.

"It's about me." July blushed.
"She turned him down." Marcha added in swift support.

"Apparently you did have problems with him." the canny detective said.

"Yes. Well, it was just too unpleasant. That's why we didn't say."

"I'm not here to judge you. I only want to determine when and where Kirkwood Bonn went."

"Can't say." Marcha repeated her earlier stubborn response.

Dougall Grimslade searched the workers' quarters and found nothing more of interest. He surmised the girl, July, probably had a fling with the man misusing Kirkwood Bonn's ID. Par for the course, he supposed. Perhaps the worker had overstepped his welcome and been run off the place. Faced with the triple cold blue-eyed stares of the three sisters, Dougall imagined they could be formidable adversaries when angered.

"How do your workers leave here? I understand they are usually backpackers. Do you drive them into town?"

"No. Most of them just hike out or get a lift with a delivery driver."

"Did Kirkwood Bonn hike out?"

"I can't say he did," Marcha answered, "we just woke up one morning and he had apparently gone."

The fair-haired trio faced the detective blandly, but their wide-eyed gazes seemed deliberately guileless. Again, Grimslade strongly suspected they had their guard up and were stonewalling for some reason. His instincts were accurate.

Grimslade did not know that particular worker, calling himself Kirk, had been caged in the barn after attacking the youngest girl, Nova, almost a week ago. Overnight, floodwater rose to inundate the building, so the girls believed the man they had locked in a metal crate, must have drowned. They'd been on their way to get rid of his body when Grimslade drove in. Nova and July almost gave it away until Marcha stepped in to cover up.

Fearing blame for killing Kirk, the sisters decided discretion to be their wisest choice. They had planned to drag the body with his knapsack in place, into the raging creek. It would look as if Kirk had been swept away trying to leave the farm. The plan seemed foolproof until the nosy police detective drove in.

Grimslade felt sure the girls had not been as helpful as they might have been. Yet he thanked them. Perhaps they'd decide to be more forthcoming at some future time.

"Thanks for your help. I may want to speak to you again. Please take my card and let me know if anything else comes to mind. Anything at all. Anytime."

"Will do." Marcha nodded, with no intention of that ever happening, if she had anything to do with it.

Grimslade surveyed the surrounding countryside. If evicted during the flood event, the criminal had only one obvious option. He would have to hike over the wooded hills.

Shortly after Grimslade left Calenda Market Gardens, the sisters discovered Kirk had escaped the cage. They hadn't known he had a pocketknife, which he used to saw through nylon ropes securing the crate. The rope lay in tattered pieces around the barn floor.

"We were going to use that rope to drag him." July moaned.
"July, honey, we don't need to drag him now."
"I know. But that was a damn good roll of rope, was that."
"It was always going to be wasted on him." Marcha said.

"That must be when he wrote that rude message on the blackboard."

"What does pity fuck mean anyway?" Nova asked.

"Charity." Marcha replied.

"Wow. He was really up himself, hey."

"Almost inside out." July agreed.

Checking GPS, the nearest settlement looked to be a small township on the other side of the low range.

That village became the detective's next port of call. Signage on a church hall informed Grimslade it had been an evacuation centre. Looking inside the empty building he saw it had been cleaned up. Trestles and folding bunks were stacked neatly against a wall. The place smelt of pine disinfectant. Dougall walked outside and came across an elderly gardener pruning roses in the small church cemetery.

"Good morning sir. I am looking for someone who might have stayed in the evacuation centre during the flood. Can you tell me who might know anything about it?"

The old gardener liked being addressed as 'sir' and been happy to help. Directed to the CWA tea rooms, Dougall found the mature ladies far more amenable than the young Calenda sisters.

"I'm chasing a missing person who might have stayed in the evacuation place recently. Chap going by the name of Kirk. Or Kirkwood. Surname Bonn."

One sturdy matron with a voice like a town crier, yelled:

"Anyone remember a man named Kirk or Kirkwood being in the evacuation centre?"

Two other women appeared from the kitchen area.

"You know what? We found some good clothes binned that had that name on the laundry tags. Kirkwood something. Sounds a bit posh."

Grimslade thrilled to that information. He'd enjoy phoning Dulcy later with that news.

"Well done," he replied to the ladies, "but you remember no man going by that name? No one who seemed new to the area?"

"There was one we didn't know. Named Richie. He was really helpful too. Helped to serve out breakfast."

Richie! Another eureka moment. With some effort, Grimslade managed to keep an inscrutable face.

"Does anyone know where this fellow Richie went after here?"

"He was hiking. Poor thing. He said his car was a write-off. Tree feel on it. His face was all scratched up too. We dabbed iodine on it for him. Must have stung like hell."

In light of the outlaw's scratched face, the deal with the blue-eyed farm girls began to make sense. Dougall considered going back for another talk with those feisty young women. Obviously in cahoots, the stubborn sisters were unlikely to break ranks without thumb-screws. Maybe not even then. They probably wouldn't know or care where the man went anyway.

DI Grimslade pushed ahead. It helped that only one road led out of town. Further down the highway, he was held up with roadworks. Speaking to a stop-go lollipop man, the detective learnt that only one hitchhiker had been through. That foot traveller cadged a lift in a delivery van, and the road worker had been vaguely familiar with that van driver.

"So, you know the van driver who gave the hiker a lift?"

"Just to look at. Old bloke. Big sort of van probably refrigerated."

"If you see him again, it would be really helpful to let me know. Or ask him to call me." Dougall said.

He gave the man his card.

"You're with the police?"

"I am. And I want you to know that van driver is not under any suspicion, but his hitchhiker might be."

"Always glad to help the men in blue."

Grimslade gave that claim a fifty-fifty chance of being true. The road worker turned his sign to GO and Dougall Grimslade went. Back at the office, he phoned Dulcy:

"Goodness Dougall. You've done well."

"But that's where it runs cold. A slim chance a traffic controller might put me onto a driver who gave a man a lift."

"We can be certain our murderer likes calling himself Richie, Ricky or Kirk."

"It seems so. And using Bonn's ID is his first major mistake. We have to keep the case under wraps, so he isn't warned against using it again."

"We must. It's really our only chance of nabbing him. Do you think we can assume he resembles Kirkwood Bonn's ID photo?"

"Maybe. Or, you know, perhaps it wasn't scrutinised all that well by the recruitment mob."

"True," Dulcy replied, "there can be a sameness with even featured faces. Crooked, scarred or disfigured ones are more memorable."

"Sure. No one forgets my ugly dial as far as I know." Dougall laughed.

"Now you're fishing for compliments."

"Don't knock it Dulcy. That's my only nod to sport."

Chapter 18

THE GAME CHANGER

Fantasies

Despite Kirkwood Bonn's killer moving over to Queensland, Dulcy Vestige in The Northern Territory, cracked the game-changing breakthrough. Dougall Grimslade put it down to his younger colleague's diligence, although Dulcy humbly counted it as a fortunate fluke. Truth be told, it had been a bit of both.

Early on, when the missing person investigation led to the outback doorstep of the lone homesteader, Alba Jenkins, Dulcy had her work cut out to extract information from her. The woman was not elderly, perhaps only in her thirties but she came across as being mentally challenged. After the homesteader admitted to giving a hiker called Kirk a bed overnight, Dulcy's intuition kicked in. She felt Alba Jenkins possibly entertained the man intimately. The notion somewhat accounted for the householder's reluctance to speak up.

The name, Kirk, triggered alarm bells. Connecting the names Kirkwood and Kirk already suggested the likelihood that the hiker stole the murdered man's ID. Grimslade and Vestige discussed this at length and doted on the ID being misused. Eventually that did happen, hitting partial pay dirt when it led the chase to The Calenda Market

Gardens, where those three blue-eyed sisters put one over on the senior detective.

Another opportunity to quiz Alba Jenkins occurred at Kirkwood Bonn's funeral. In an informal chat, Dulcy learned Alba kept a rum bottle handled by her unexpected house guest. The slow witted homesteader had made sure to keep that particular bottle, as it had a Merry Christmas label. Dulcy jumped on the possibility of lifting the suspect's fingerprints.

History confirmed Dulcy's original theory to be true. Kirkwood's killer did call himself Kirk as the overnight house guest. Also, the backward homesteader had taken the drifter to her bed, proven by her ensuing pregnancy.

The hiker also left another reminder of his visit, a nice sample of fingerprints on Alba's Christmas rum bottle. Dulcy ran the prints through the system and identified Alba's one-night-stand as a known criminal, Bruce Luck, recently released from prison in South Australia. Dulcy excitedly conveyed the news to Dougall Grimslade.

"I spoke with South Australian authorities to find out more of Bruce Luck's background. He escaped justice on technicalities several times, eventually going down for two years for abetting a robbery. That had been in his late twenties, so he'd be perhaps be aged about thirty by now. Records showed a long list of violations beginning in his youth, theft, vandalism and sexual misconduct."

"Sounds like a real charmer." Dougall replied.

"Well that may be so, but he only made one friend in prison, a convicted rapist named Donald Rich. This Rich guy dubbed Bruce

Luck as 'Bruiser'. I'm told the pair were known inside as Richie and The Bruiser."

"Sounds like a musical pop duo." Dougall quipped.

"But with no fans. They were feared and avoided by other inmates."

"Aha. So that's why he favoured using the name Richie."

"Role playing?"

"Some sort of idolatry would be my guess."

Dulcy went on to say local officers had been sent to Bruce Luck's Adelaide address, finding only his aged and demented father in residence. The old man told them Bruce probably took off with someone called Greta. He'd said you couldn't trust either of them.

"Wonder who this Greta is?"

"That isn't clear. The old man waffled off on a rant. No one could get any sense out of him."

"Hmmm. Could Greta be Bruce Luck's girlfriend?"

"Whoever Greta is, he was definitely alone when he got to Alba Jenkins' place."

"He's acted alone every time that we know of. Including attacking the kids on the beach, and when he took that farm job too."

Grimslade and Vestige mused over what little they had to go on. Dulcy summed up her take on it:

"I still don't want to make the crimes public. This Bruce Luck suspect might use Kirkwood Bonn's ID again. As you say, if he's stupid enough. Also, I should let Kirkwood's partner know of any developments before he sees anything on the news."

Dougall agreed with Dulcy's stance and gave her his usual endorsement:

"Good. Good. Very good Dulcy. We're on the same page then."

Disturbed by another murder report, Grimslade was unable to give the current Kirkwood Bonn case his undivided attention.

Grimslade attended the newest crime scene at an impressive rural residence in the outer suburbs. The incident came to attention when neighbours reported a broken front fence. They worried a big savage guard dog would be on the loose. Afraid of the dog, none braved entering the property themselves. The lone female householder kept to herself. She had never befriended anyone in the street, and the woman's privacy had been respected.

An RSPCA officer, Pamela Burn, sent to inspect the dog situation, found the kitchen door ajar and a bag with jewellery spilling from its ripped seams on the concrete floor of an empty carport. It looked like a robbery gone wrong. It seemed plausible that a thief had been chased off by the missing guard dog.

Pamela made a cursory inspection around the house and been shocked to come across a huge dog standing over a bloodied body. The RSPCA officer backed off slowly and called police. Her first impression suggested the dog killed the person. Pamela soon revised that idea. The woman's body was naked, so she reasoned the death had to involve human intervention.

By the time police arrived, the RSPCA officer had tranquillised the enormous canine with a dart gun. She'd called for colleagues to help lift and secure the heavy animal into the back of her van. Pamela Burn rightly decided the dog had been guarding his owner's body, and feared police might shoot the loyal hound dead, out of hand.

Police established the homeowner, Amelia Boole, as the victim. Her obese and bloodied body, lay in an odd warped position, twisted over her broken neck. Estimated time of death had been assessed as no more than fifteen hours since discovery. Apparently Miss Boole had fallen or been pushed from a balcony above. Strewn across the yard, a number of knives surrounded the body.

"Sexual assault?" Grimslade asked the coroner.
"Definitely. I'm afraid this is a particularly nasty one."
"What do you make of all the knives on the ground around her."
"Could be ritualistic."
"Are you thinking satanic?"
"Can't rule it out. Something definitely unholy sent on here, that's for sure."

The extent of unholiness escalated when a farm shed search turned up sickening results. The outbuilding housed a crude butcher shop. Fridges and freezers contained dismembered human body parts. Aghast at the find, police responders wished they could erase the memory from their minds. Yet the grisly sight became the source of numerous nightmares for years to come.

Adhering to duty, Grimslade pulled himself together to inspected the contents of the ripped bag in the carport. Astounded, he found Kirkwood Bonn's ID within. It seemed all roads led to the wanted man, Bruce Luck.

"Aha." Grimslade exclaimed in triumph.
"You've had a find?" an officer asked.
"I certainly have. This is gold. And I don't mean the bling jewels."

That night, Dougall couldn't wait to phone Dulcy:

"You're never going to believe this..."
"You're kidding! How likely is it that our charmer has joined the others in the freezers?"
"Remains to be seen. No pun intended."
"That sounded intended Dougall."

Dulcy almost stifled an inappropriate impulse to laugh, but Dougall's dry humour got the better of her. At times, the colleagues resorted to dark humour as coping mechanisms in horrible cases.

⸺⸱❖⸱⸺

Busy cooking the evening meal, Dulcy had her phone on speaker when Dougall called about the freezer bodies. David Dubois monitored their conversation and was far from amused.

"You and old Grimslade get off on some weird stuff."
"Old? Dougall isn't that old."
"Reckon you've got a thing for him Dulcy." David sulked.
"Yep. I sure have. I greatly admire Dougall Grimslade. I'm incredibly lucky to be mentored by him. He's an amazing detective."

David's mood did not improve.

"Sometimes I think you've got bloody Grimslade on your mind while I'm making love to you. I feel like he's in our bed with us."
"Only sometimes? Like when?" Dulcy teased.
"Like after one of your giggly phone calls. Which is most of the time Dulcy."
"Really. Do you ever imagine anyone else? Like Zelia for instance? When you get into some of your rough stuff?"

David back peddled with a mental curse: *Zelia! Shit why did I ever start this.* He did not want his old flame brought up, yet he did use Zelia's more inventive moves to spice it up with Dulcy. His detective wife inadvertently identified his secret fantasy spot on.

"Never." he lied.
"I bet you do David. Therefore, in your imaginary world of whodunit that puts Grimslade and Zelia in bed together." Dulcy laughed scornfully.

Dulcy's ridicule needled David, as intended. She refused to cater to his fits of jealousy. Yet, she knew his suspicions were not entirely unwarranted. An unspoken attraction to Dougall enhanced Dulcy's own dreams. When her earth moved with David, she often thanked her imagination. To be fair, it seemed a good idea to appease her husband's doubts.

"I'm thinking of you now David."
"You'll burn the steak." he grumped.
"Not in two minutes."
"Alright. Come on. You might get lucky."
"So might you."

The Bruiser case came to an inglorious end. An unidentified body of a man who had fallen ill on a train journey, turned up a fingerprint match with Bruce Luck. Detectives Grimslade and Vestige were duly informed.

"So not eaten by the dog."
"But the dog killed him in the long run."
"Karma?"
"Tetanus."

The Kirkwood Bonn/Bruce Luck case evolved as the freakiest of many incidents jointly investigated by Grimslade and Vestige. The victim and his killer turned out to be blood brothers, though neither knew the other existed.

Chapter 19

YOUTH CRIME

Grief & Deception

Bizarre circumstances and people they dealt with, united the detectives beyond officialdom. They often spoke on the phone in the evenings, recapping findings, or just as a means of winding down. Sometimes their conversations endured late into the night, when they would switch to sms chats.

The chat line also represented relaxed down time... until one brief shocking text, struck dread in Dulcy's heart. *NO! OH NO!* Horrified, she reread the message repeatedly to fully grasp the terrible meaning, hoping there must be some mistake.

Despite the late hour, Dulcy immediately phoned her friend and colleague. Dougall Grimslade picked up immediately.

"Are they sure? Can there be no mistake?" Dulcy cried.

"Yes. I'm afraid it is true. Bella is not expected to survive." Dougall gasped.

Dougall's beloved wife, Bella, mother of Isla, had been hit by a speedster running a red light. Stolen by youths for joy riding, the car then crashed into a pylon head-on and split apart, killing its five occupants.

Bella went to hospital, in a coma, life support sustained her life for five hours before she passed quietly. Dougall, Isla and Aiden Birdwhistle, were by her bedside. Dougall held one of Bella's hands, and Isla the other. Isla had only been granted one Christmas with her mother before losing her to senseless youth crime.

Stark grief assailed Dulcy for Dougall and Isla. They had not so long ago united as a family unit. Dulcy had met Bella and liked the down-to-earth woman, but did not get to know her well. Dulcy knew she must attend Bella Grimslade's funeral, to show her respect, and to support the family. She took the soonest flight back to Queensland.

Such a sad and tragic loss left Dulcy depleted, yet she strove to stand in for Dougall in his absence, to allow him time to cope with his sorrow. Due to the dire circumstances her temporary engagement back in Queensland had been sanctioned by police hierarchy.

Dulcy Vestige stood in for Dougall Grimslade with the newest recruit, Tim Fun, as her aide. Being back on the East Coast, Dulcy met with other friends, particularly taking comfort from seeing Opal and Angus Bridcombe again. Opal insisted Dulcy stay with them. She enveloped her friend in a firm hug, making Dulcy cry.

"It beggars belief Opal, poor Isla only just discovered her mother, to have her ripped away so cruelly."

"And they only got to spend one Christmas together as a family? I didn't know Isla or Bella, but I feel heartbroken too. It is just so tragic." Opal commiserated.

"This will hit Dougall hardest. He'd been with Bella for over twenty years."

"It will. There will be hundreds of reminders. Big ones and small ones." Opal agreed.

"He's taken time off. I will be filling in. I don't know for how long."

"Yes, so Angus says. He went to Bella's funeral...of course you would have seen him there Dulcy. I'm not thinking straight. Angus was a first responder at that accident. He saw some horrific carnage. It keeps him awake at night, so we've both lost sleep over it." Opal replied.

Dulcy could only imagine the shambles Angus must have witnessed.

"The funeral was heartbreaking. And now Isla has invited me to a lunch at her house. I'm such a coward for feeling reluctant to go and cope with the family's grief. But I must accept the invitation of course." Dulcy said.
"You of all people, have never been a coward, Dulcy." Opal smiled.
"You're a good friend, Opal."
"I try to be."

Dulcy fronted up to the luncheon at Isla and Aiden Birdwhistle's home. Dougall came as well. Everyone struggled to put brave faces on their despair. Arrival of Aiden's brother Ethan, and his young wife Tiffany, helped fill any silences in the conversation. Ethan brought wine and beer. No one turned down a bracing aperitif. Aiden acted as chef, serving a light but tasty seafood stir fry.

"This is lovely, you've gone to so much trouble." Dulcy complimented her hosts.
"This dish is Aiden's speciality," Isla said, "he makes it on very special occasions, like the night he proposed to me."

Aiden winked at his wife and their guests managed to relax somewhat and segue into general conversation. Everyone pretended not to notice the family dogs, Pebbles and Noodle, creeping in under the table. No one ordered them outside.
Aiden cleared the table, made coffee and, without asking who wanted any, served a tangy lemon meringue pie on individual plates, with cake forks. No one could easily refuse dessert since it was placed in front of them. In fact everyone needed a sugar hit at the time and the sweet treat went down well.

"Oh. I nearly forgot," Isla mentioned, "my old landlords sent a Christmas card from New Zealand with a letter. They said their beach house sold to your husband, Dulcy. Does that mean you and David might be moving back here permanently? I hope you do by the way."

"Oh. Did they say that?"

Perplexed, Dulcy thought the information could not possibly be true. She did not like to contradict Isla, and felt to be put on the spot. Dougall had been very quiet, but joined in following Isla's comment. He imagined Dulcy would have mentioned any plan to move back into the area.

"Is that right Dulcy? David bought the place?"

"Um. No. Perhaps those old folks got David mixed up with someone else."

Isla and her father exchanged puzzled glances, aware that Dulcy's husband might have acted without her knowledge.

Isla glossed over her remark: "Maybe I misread it."

Dulcy's bent for getting to the crux of a mystery came to the fore.

"Did you keep the letter?" she asked, smiling, hoping not to seem picky.

"I have it somewhere." Isla replied vaguely.

"It's in the sideboard drawer." Aiden said.

Ever helpful, Aiden got up from the table, rummaged around in the drawer and found the card and letter. The letter confirmed it. Isla's prior landlords wrote that the nice young man named David eventually bought their beach house. They even remarked he and his wife Dulcy sat at their table at the wedding reception.

"There must have been another David there. Maybe one of the life-savers."

"Yes. That must be it."

Dougall Grimslade's detective mind-set kicked in. He had an inkling all was not right. At least it gave him something else to think about apart from the enormous loss of Bella.

As a life-saver at the surf club wedding reception venue, Ethan Birdwhistle knew of no other David. Suspecting a looming marital glitch, he felt it prudent to say nothing, but Aiden, head of their private eye agency, put his ever helpful foot in it again.

"Is there another David among the lifeguards Ethan?"

"No, not amongst the lifeguards. Maybe Chantel Chiron or someone had a David as their other half."

Ethan cast an enquiring eye towards his wife Tiffany. He recalled Tiff chattering on about a David her friend Chantel had gone for. Chantel was always falling in and out of love so it went in one ear and out the other for Ethan.

As close friends who went through school together, Tiffany and Chantel told each other everything. Tiffany replied:

"Chantel went on and on about some great hunk she met at the wedding reception. I can't remember his name. It could have been David. She said he turned out to be married anyway. So that was a bummer for her."

Dulcy remembered something:

"Isla, that name Chantel rings a bell. Wasn't she the one keeping David amused after your wedding got trashed?"

"That's right Dulcy. I remember that now. I said *not the dreaded Chantel, she's the worst*. And you said *I'll see about that*."

"Oh well," Tiffany said, "that David must have been your husband, Dulcy. Geez, lucky Chantel didn't get her hooks into him. She used to go after Ethan too. But he managed to stave her off. So he says. And I believe you honey. Thousands wouldn't. But I know Chantel would have shouted it from the rooftops if she'd nailed Ethan."

"Tiffany darling. Not so much of the in depth reporting. Okay?" Ethan smiled.

"He's just afraid I'll say something inappropriate." Tiffany laughed. "Like that time you asked Isla if..." Ethan abruptly buttoned his lip.

This was neither the time nor place to bring up the first time Tiffany and Isla met. Aiden helpfully summed up:

"Anyway, apparently there was no other David."

Isla regretted bringing the subject up. Clearly, Dulcy knew nothing about her husband buying the beach house. Dulcy let it pass, sure there must be a mix up, some crossing of wires. Dougall later discussed the possible house sale with Isla in private, both glad of the distraction.

"How likely are your old landlords to be right in thinking Dulcy's husband bought their house?"
"They're fairly old people, but nimble minded. Apparently both of them believe David Vestige bought their property."
"Actually, his name is David Dubois. Not Vestige. Dulcy kept her maiden name."
"Oh did she? How very modern."

Isla applauded that choice, it suited the fond image she held of her feisty friend.

"Dulcy is always on the ball, she's a capable detective, but I could see she didn't know about that house purchase." Dougall mused.
"Could her husband have bought it as a surprise for her?"
"Hmmm. Not impossible. I suppose. Though it seems unconventional."
"Well, they must have an unconventional marriage. Dulcy keeping her maiden name for one thing." Isla said.

In her own case, Isla loved taking Aiden's name of Birdwhistle in place of her prior surname, Tickle. Abandoned at birth, left in a cat's box with a sad note saying *can't keep it* she'd been dubbed her name from the cardboard carton printed with Tickles Thousand Island Dressing. With initials I.T. Isla Tickle became the 'it' girl. She saw her new initials I.B. as a new beginning: 'I be'.

Dougall's daughter liked and admired Dulcy, counting her almost as an older sister. But Isla did not know Dulcy's husband, David Dubois, having only met him briefly at her own wedding reception. During the upset after their wedding party narrowly escaped tragedy, socialising with guests took a back seat.

The double wedding event with Isla, Tiffany and their Birdwhistle grooms made news headlines. *[cite The Peckish by Jo Milanne]*

During her stand in position back in Queensland, Dulcy stayed in the home of her good friends, Opal and Angus Bridcombe, for several weeks. The night following lunch at Birdwhistles, Opal and Dulcy shared supper and a bottle or wine together, as Angus had work duties that night.

"So how did the awkward luncheon go?"

"It wasn't too bad. No tears or beating of chests or anything. Actually, Aiden is a good cook. His seafood stir-fry was awesome. So was his lemon meringue tart." Dulcy replied.

"That's good then. I know you dreaded going."

"Just one thing struck me as being a bit off kilter..."

Dulcy paused, not sure if she should share her confusion with Opal, who had always been mistrustful of David Dubois.

"Oh? What was that?"

"...well, Isla had a letter from her old landlords. They'd moved back to New Zealand and sold their house where Isla used to rent a granny flat before she met Aiden. Anyway they claimed to have sold the place to David."

"Your David?"

"That's what they reckon."

"Could they be mistaken?"

"They described the David who sat at their table at the wedding reception. And we did sit at their table. Also no one knew of any other David."

Opal's radar kicked in. Her mistrust of David Dubois began when they'd all first met, during schoolies week holidays, when the girls shared a holiday cottage. Camping nearby with mates at the beach, David managed to win Dulcy's heart. He'd been her first lover. In Opal's opinion, the handsome surfer took unfair advantage of her gullible friend.

That holiday romance went pear-shaped when Zelia, David's current and long-time girlfriend, turned up unexpectedly. He'd failed to mention having another love interest at home. At the time, Dulcy suffered total humiliation. Her friends circled the wagons to protect her, refusing to tell David where she could be found. Dulcy tried to forget him by concentrating on her career.

Within a few years, David met Dulcy again and they eventually married, much to Opal's disgust. Now sipping wine in Opal's living room, Dulcy could see her best friend bit back on something she was dying to say.

"Spit it out and get it over with Opal. I know you've never trusted David."

"Alright. I know you won't thank me for this, but I saw Zelia that time at the cricket."

"When?"

"When David re-appeared after so long, and you went off with him. It looked like Zelia was keeping tabs on him. Once a two-timer...."

"Zelia had been going with Thaddeus by then." Dulcy retorted, cutting her off.

Opal took a deep breath and soldiered on:

"Thaddeus broke up with her pretty quickly. He even said he hoped bloody Zelia wasn't stalking him again. We all saw her watch you and David get in his car and drive off."

"Opal, my dear, David did break my heart when I was young and silly but I still had strong feelings for him. Couldn't help it."

"Obviously you forgave his two-timing since you married him."

As a guest in Opal's home, Dulcy avoided further argument.

"Is that all Opal? I know you have my best interests at heart, but yes, I married David and that's that."

Opal topped up their wine glasses, draining the bottle. She decided to have it out to the bitter end:

"I wish it was all Dulcy. But there is more."

"Okay. Do we need to open another bottle to get this over with?"

"That's not a bad idea."

Opal fetched another from the fridge. Dulcy felt a prickle of anxiety.

"Don't keep me in suspense."

"It's just that... a while after you married David, I saw Zelia at the playground. She had a baby. A red-haired baby."

"So?"

"I told Thaddeus and he said 'not guilty'. He said Zelia was a big mistake for him, plus, he never wanted to hear anything about her again."

"So Thaddeus more or less told you to mind your own business?"

Opal avoided answering and sipped her wine, because Thaddeus had done exactly that. Never a wilting violet, Opal regrouped quickly:

"You are my business Dulcy. Who'll tell you if I don't?"

"So you deduced because Zelia had a red-haired baby and my David also has red hair, he must be it's father?"

"But that dark auburn red. It's not a common natural colour. Also I heard Zelia call the kid Davy."

"It's a popular name. She might have called him Davy after David simply for having the red hair and that reminded her of him."

"Come On Dulcy...you must suspect..."

"Give it a rest please Opal. I don't need this."

Opal held up her hands in surrender.

"Alright. Okay. Have it your own way. But now I've said it, I'm not sorry Dulcy. I've kept my mouth shut for ages for the sake of our friendship, because I knew you wouldn't thank me for warning you. Just that I care about you, you damn ungrateful white girl."

"Maybe you should be the detective. And don't call me white girl."

Opal waved her hands theatrically and hiccupped drunkenly.

"A rose by any other name...hic".

"What's Shakespeare got to do with anything?" Dulcy slurred a bit.

Opal expounded: "Shakespeare? Well I reckon your Davo's been shaking his spear around where angels fear to tread."

"Where angels fear to tread?" Dulcy laughed at Opal's flowery turn of phrase.

"Yeah. You know. Fools rush in and all that."

"You're rattling sabres here my friend." Dulcy advised.

"Well I'm not the only one. I'm afraid it's David who's been rattling his sabre, that's my point Dulcy."

"You stick to Angus's pointed sabre and we'll...get...or do...something or other...now I've lost my train of thought. I blame you for that Opal."

"You would. Anyway, we might as well finish the bottle."

"That's the best idea you've had so far Opal."

The best friends finished the second bottle of wine. Angus returned home after his night shift to find them both snoring in the lounge room, with not two, but three empty wine bottles on the coffee table. He'd never let them live it down, and would bring up their state of inebriation time after time. It wasn't often he could get one back on that pair of outspoken females.

The morning after Opal's boozy heart to heart talk, Dougall drove Dulcy to the airport for her return flight to Darwin. He decided to return to his duty rather than mope around at home.

He noticed Dulcy looked rather seedy.

"You alright?" he asked.
"Splitting headache." Dulcy groaned.
"Self-inflicted?"
"Opal inflicted more like."

Dougall shared a sympathetic grimace and gave Dulcy a careful hug.

"Take care." they said both as one.
"Great minds think alike." Dougall added with a watery smile.

His eyes gleamed with unshed tears. Dulcy's heart broke for Dougall's recent loss. She could only nod and quickly turn away to board the plane.

During her return flight, Dulcy went over Opal's suggestive disclosures, adding her friend's distrust of David to the knowledge that he supposedly purchased that beach house. If true, Dulcy could not fathom why her husband would buy a house without telling her. She'd have to use tact and find the right time to broach the topic with David.

Chapter 20

TWO TIMING

This Stinks

David Dubois looked forward to his wife's return. Dulcy seemed subdued but he thought he knew a sure-fire way to jolly her up. He eagerly reached for her in bed on their first night back together prepared to administer some good cheer.

Dulcy's less than enthusiastic response, David put down to the unhappy reason for her trip back to Queensland. He guessed she would get over it, once into her normal work-a-day routine. In the meantime, he'd try to be understanding.

His good intentions lasted until the stand-off strung out beyond his endurance. Losing patience, David spent more and more time drinking with mates at the end of the day.

Fearing an unpleasant outcome, Dulcy agonised over how to bring the subject up without igniting a major blow up. After a further fortnight rehearsing tactful intros on why or whether David bought that beach house, she decided on a roundabout ploy.

Sundays, the couple shared breakfast over the weekend newspapers, when their separate duties allowed that luxury. Dulcy spread out real estate pages and made a show of circling various ads in red biro. She knew David's curiosity would nudge him to ask:

"What are you doing?"

"I think of this Northern Territory stint as only temporary," she replied, going for a casual tone of voice, "although it could be a few years, I hope to get back to the East Coast eventually. I miss my friends down there."

"I thought you liked it up here. I mean, your promotion and all."

"I'd never have transferred way up here except for your army relocation, David. I thought you knew that."

The conversation paused while David got up to refill his cup. He asked a question while turned away at the coffee pot, so his face would not betray anxiety.

"So... are you thinking of buying a property for later?"

"Yep. I could rent it out in the interim. Don't you agree that's a good idea?"

"Maybe." he muttered.

Dulcy noted his ears redden as he spent an overly long time stirring his coffee. She had given him an ideal opportunity to admit to buying that beach house, if he had indeed done so. David's blush and mumbled reply were very telling to Dulcy. Alarm bells jangled in her head. Hoping he might come up with some viable explanation, she decided not to push it at this stage.

During the following week, Dulcy phoned Dougall. His return to full duty assisted him in facing life without Bella. Brooding alone at home did him no good, and there remained young Tim Fun's ongoing induction to be considered.

"Is Tim Fun learning the ropes?"

"He shows potential."

"Well, Dougall, you got me through, so clever Tim should be a piece of cake."

"Despite my initial qualms, you were easy Dulcy. Tim seems blessed with some instinctive insight too."

"What! You had initial qualms about me? Why?"

"Just that... um... nevermind." Dougall hedged.

"Because of my sex I bet." Dulcy exclaimed.

"You have sex?" Dougall tried for a cheap joke, to restore their usual banter.

Dulcy laughed half-heartedly but decided not to go there. She'd felt cold towards her husband since suspecting his deception, so had avoided intimacy. It now felt too much like sleeping with the enemy.

"Anyway, perhaps my fabled instinctive insight is working overtime. But Dougall, that thing Isla brought up about my David buying the beach house..."

"Has that caused a rift in your marital bliss?"

"Not yet. I'm skating around it so far, but I'd like it resolved."

"You mean, find out for sure?"

"Yes. Either way. Can you help me out here Dougall?"

"I can do that. It sounds like a nice little detecting exercise for our Tim Fun."

Dulcy knew she could count on Dougall, and felt a weight lift from her shoulders. She acknowledged his help:

"You're a legend Dougall."

"I know. Sorry about the stupid sex joke."

"Oh! Way to dig yourself deeper Dougall. So you think I'm of the stupid sex?"

"No! That isn't... you're pulling my leg now aren't you?" Dougall realised.

"You're so easy." Dulcy laughed.

"You are not the first person ever to say that."

Dulcy knew what he meant: She had the run-down of when the Grimslades confronted Isla as her biological parents. Mother and daughter, Bella and Isla, laughed that both their men had been easy. At the time, the frivolous moment helped break the ice in an awkward first meeting.

Reminded of Bella, who was never far from their thoughts, Dulcy and Dougall ended the call on a sober note.

Dulcy salved her guilty conscience for checking up on David, telling herself she must never disregard her intuition. It held her in good stead in the past and been instrumental in solving cases.

Tim Fun relished the chance to do some under cover spying. As a keen surfer, he had joined the local surf club. His new friends amongst the lifeguards included Ethan Birdwhistle.

Ethan told Tim of a possible cheap flat for rent at the very same address Grimslade tasked him to suss out. Tim already knew the place in question, he'd driven past it a number of times on the way to the beach. As a long-term tenant of the humble accommodation, Ethan's sister-in-law, Isla, allowed him use of that flat after she began spending her nights at Aiden's apartment.

Tim knew through surf club gossip of Ethan's legendary list of conquests before he married Tiffany. Intrigued, Tim eyed the bikini girls who hung around the surf club, hoping some of Ethan's charisma might be catching. In the meantime he had a job to do.

Set the sleuthing task, Tim took pains to play the part. On arrival at the address in question, the young recruit came across a heavily tattooed man busily painting the front fence. William Kirby smiled at Tim who had dressed down, looking like any other teenaged beach bum surfer. William greeted the young man amicably:

"Gidday mate. What can I do for you?"

"Hi. I need somewhere to lob, and someone said there could be a cheap flat to rent here." Tim replied.

"Oh?"

"Yeah. Friend of a friend used to live here but she moved out, I'm told." Tim explained.

The flat was vacant. Currently William Kirby pretended to be its tenant while sharing the main house with his partner, Zelia. The subterfuge let Zelia keep her single parent benefit, while they lived as a couple.

William's mind whirled. With his pay and Zelia's social security benefit they raked in a good income. The man realised that actually renting out the flat served a far better long-term purpose. He supposed it wouldn't hurt to show this young bloke around.

Zelia had taken her small boy to a playschool group and would be out for most of the morning. William would discuss his ideas for renting the flat with her later.

"What's your name son?" William asked.

"Tim Fun."

Tim replied truthfully, he hadn't been in the area long enough to be known or recognised as a member of the local constabulary.

"That's a fun name." William replied.

Tim chortled as if never hearing that old one before. William credited himself for making such a good joke. Off the cuff too. It put him in a generous mood.

"I'm William Kirby. Come in and I'll show you around. The flat is a bit plain by the way."

"I don't expect a palace."

Tim made a good show of inspecting the flat. The bathroom, semi-outside, accessible via a patio, allowed a backyard view. Tim noted a full clothesline pegged with clothing to suit men, women and children. There were also some outdoor toys strewn about on the lawn.

"You got kids?" Tim asked.
"Just the one. Don't worry, our youngster is quiet and well behaved."

Tim sought to confirm William Kirby as the homeowner, knowing a renter might also sublet spare space if they could.

"You were lucky to get this place, so close to the beach and all."
"Yep. I know. It was pretty run-down but I've done a lot of work on it. Mostly painting but I've installed a new kitchen as well." William replied, proudly.

In Tim's assessment, only a homeowner would undertake such extensive renovations. Tim congratulated himself for sussing William Kirby as owner of the beach house.

"It looks great... so would the flat be available to me if I could afford it?" Tim asked.
"To be honest. We hadn't thought of renting it out. Can you give me until the weekend to think on it? I have to discuss it with my partner Zelia." Will replied.
"Yeah. Of course you have to clear it with your wife." Tim replied.

William Kirby did not disavow the notion that Zelia was his wife. Tim Fun memorised the number plate of Kirby's vehicle, and parted on friendly terms.

Tim Fun seriously considered renting the sparse flat. Currently, he lodged with his Aunty Francis Funicular and her family of poodles. He loved everything about that accommodation apart from the commute. The flat under the beach house offered great incentives to move in there, being in close proximity to work and the surf beach.

Back at the office, the budding detective checked the number plate of the vehicle parked at the beach house, finding it was registered to William Kirby, as he fully expected.

Pleased with his half-hours work, Tim wrongly assumed the home owners to be a married couple, William and Zelia Kirby, who had one child. He didn't get the kid's name, not that it mattered.

Tim Fun reported his findings to his senior, Dougall Grimslade, who proceeded to pick apart the young detective's assumptions.

"You took a lot for granted here, Tim."

"But he said... and he was painting the fence..."

"Here's the thing, lad, nothing is gospel unless proven. Nevermind. You did well to check the bloke's number plate. Of course, he might have only been a contractor working there. Pulling your leg."

"Why would he?"

"Who knows? Some people like to take the mickey out of the police."

"I wasn't in uniform."

"But he still might have recognised you. It's a small community if you don't count tourists."

Later, it occurred to William Kirby that Tim Fun's visit could be a covert government investigation into their rort of social security benefits. He mentioned it to Zelia.

"Would they do that?" she asked.

"Sure. I've heard private eye firms actually expose a lot of fraud."

"So what will we say if he comes back?"

"I'll say I've been renting the flat myself but I want to move in with you."

"That might work," Zelia replied cautiously, thinking quickly, "but I'll have to declare a change in circumstances and have my benefits reduced."

"But Zelia, this could be a good thing. The rent should nearly cover your lost benefits. And we'd be legal."

Legal? Zelia sincerely hoped William wasn't hinting at marriage. She hadn't looked too far ahead. Marriage would mean coming clean with her little white lies. As it stood, Zelia had William Kirby renovating the house at his own expense, because he believed, as a widow, she owned it. A fly in the ointment would be William learning her tenancy ran out when little Davy came of age, and why she had the beach house rent-free.

"No one is going to pay much rent for that hovel." Zelia said, to put him off.
"I'll do it up. Enclose the patio. Put in a kitchenette. It could be a nice little earner." William enthused.

Trickier and trickier. Zelia saw that William Kirby imagined himself eventually becoming co-owner of the desirable beach house property. She knew that boon to his prosperity was never going to happen, even if they did marry.

Tim Fun felt downcast. Adding to Grimslade's slight reprimand, renting the handy flat hung in the balance. He thought grumpy old Grimslade to be exceptionally picky, but had to knuckle under and suck it up. Subsequently, Dougall ordered Tim to conduct a proper search of the title deed on the beach house. Dougall phoned Dulcy:

"Found anything?" she asked.
"Nothing solid. Young Tim thinks he has it wrapped up though."
"What does he reckon?"
"Says the homeowners are a William and Zelia Kirby. No proof, only assumptions. I've sent him on a title search."
"Zelia!" Dulcy exclaimed.

Dulcy felt her heart ice over.

"What?"

"David's old girlfriend's name is Zelia...it isn't a common name."

"Don't jump to conclusions Dulcy."

"What else did Tim find?"

"Just that they have one child. He didn't get its name."

Dulcy thought about that one child, betting it had dark red hair like David's.

"Dougall, I hope I am wrong but my best friend Opal reckons she saw Zelia with a baby. Red-haired like my David... and then there's the thing Isla said about her landlords selling their house to my David."

"Now, now Dulcy. Don't do a 'Tim Fun Run'. There could be many explanations."

Although Dougall placated Dulcy, he also harboured grave doubts. He underwent his own search and found the beach house to be indeed in the name of a David Dubois. Tim Fun completed his training exercise and gleaned exactly the same result.

"I am so sorry. I should have been far more thorough." Tim apologised.

"A lesson learned my young friend. How about putting the kettle on now. I could use a brew."

Tim relaxed. Old Grimslade wasn't that bad, when all was said and done.

Among many things Dougall missed by the loss of his wife, having no ready fresh cut-lunch gave a daily reminder. He now made his own sandwiches, missing the notes Bella often included. Even if only shopping lists, she'd always added a heart and xxx.

That day, Dougall had been all out of pickled gherkins and salami so had to settle for cheese and tomato sauce, Dulcy's go-to combination, in a pinch. That reminded him of his unsavoury task: Dulcy was about to suffer a major disenchantment when he next phoned her. He bit the bullet and got on with it.

"Dulcy. I fear this is not what you wanted to hear."
"It's true then? David did buy that house?"
"The search showed it's in the name of a David Dubois."
"Of course that has to be him." Dulcy's heart sank.
"There could be an innocent reason, Dulcy. He might have invested for your futures."

Dougall felt Dulcy's immense hurt and tried to play it down.

"What about Zelia living there?"
"She might be a different Zelia. Tim said a couple apparently lived there, so..."
"No Dougall. You know this stinks to high heaven."

In Dougall's private opinion, Dulcy's nearest and dearest surely two-timed her. Outlaying on a house and installing an ex-lover certainly reeked of a major deception.

"Guess you have to sort it out with David. If you want my advice, wait until you cool down before bringing it up."
"Yeah. I really should do that. Thanks for your help Dougall."
"Good luck Dulcy."

Dulcy knew if she waited until she cooled down, it could take her beyond a few more Christmases.

Chapter 21

THE KILLING SHIFT

Fate Don't Tempt Me

Dulcy Vestige dragged her weary feet home, over-tired from a gruelling day at work. Her chore that day had been to inspect hate-graffiti spray painted all over the outside of a business: *The Brilliant Health Clinic and Wellness Centre,* an address she'd had cause to visit in the past.

The naturopathy clinic, once run by partners Damien Cresswick and Kirkwood Bonn, thrived, until the latter met his death at the hands of a murdering thief. Vestige and Grimslade worked the Kirkwood Bonn case together, tracking the murderer from The Northern Territory, across to Queensland and down to Adelaide in South Australia. Informing Damien of his partner's tragic demise, a result of murder, had been Dulcy's onerous responsibility. It left her torn by the man's abject grief. She and Damien formed a sympathetic friendship during the extended proceedings.

It had been a long day. Upset over David's deceit, then witnessing the disgusting slurs on the wellness clinic, culminated in abuse from the graffiti artist's parents. There had been no doubt of the culprit, caught with spray cans in his possession, and paint on his clothes that matched the graffiti. Unsettled by the days events, Dulcy knew it wasn't the best time to confront her errant husband. Yet, a reckless need to get it resolved overtook her patience. Taking the bull by the horns, she did it anyway.

Totally oblivious to impending disaster, David Dubois arrived home rather late, having enjoyed a few extra drinks with mates. Feeling amorous, he tried for a kiss and cuddle with his seething wife, waiting for him in the kitchen. Her face pale and furious, Dulcy pushed him away. Despite being tiddly, her husband twigged her lack of a friendly greeting did not bode particularly well for what he felt like doing. He couldn't recall if it was her time of the month but thought it likely.

"What's up with you Dulcy darling? It was only a few amber ales with the boys." he cajoled.

He attempted another squeeze and a tweak. She usually liked him doing that. But not this time.

"Seems you've been keeping some very big secrets from me, David."

A first inkling of impending doom filtered through his alcohol induced state. Ashen with her anger, Dulcy delivered her precise accusation in a low voice. Had she screamed and shouted, it would have sounded less forbidding to David. Struck with alarm, a sick churning in David's guts threatened to expel his recent beers with the boys. Realising the jig was up, and his savvy detective wife had discovered the worst, there seemed little point in denial.

"I can explain." he said, without any idea of how he could.

"When were you going to tell me."

"It's complicated." he replied.

"I'll bet it is. Give it your best shot David."

Dulcy walked around to the other side of the kitchen island to physically separate herself from David. Coincidentally, her move brought the kitchen knife rack within easy reach. She cast a glance at the arsenal of razor-sharp cutting utensils. *Fate - don't tempt me.* Dulcy imagined herself whipping a meat carver out and throwing with perfect aim to pierce David's cheating heart. As a realist, Dulcy knew she'd probably cut herself and miss or he'd nimbly jump away. Seeing a calculated purpose harden Dulcy's eyes, her husband backed off a step. Combat training identified a killing intent in adversaries. David feared the same shift possessed his wife, in that moment. His voice quivered:

"Zelia tricked me." he began.

"How?"

"She...well um...I thought she'd always been on the pill...but...that is..."

Dulcy helped him out: "So you've been hiding a child you spawned with Zelia."

"I didn't know how to tell you." David cried in anguish.

"And I take it, you have bought her a house as well."

"NO. I bought the house for OUR future, yours and mine Dulcy. It's in my name. Zelia can only live there until the boy comes of age. It's a way to provide my share for the child and make sure he has somewhere decent to live."

David made the appeal with pleading eyes and a hand on his heart. Once upon a time, the sincerity of the gesture would have seemed touching. Now it only represented more of his bull dung.

"What then? Once the boy comes of age?"

"Then...that's it. I guess."

"So you don't see any ongoing obligation to your own flesh and blood?"

"I'm providing rent-free accommodation. A roof over his head without actually giving money to Zelia that could be misspent."

Dulcy's head reeled. It stung hearing her husband acknowledge his guilt. Bile rose in her throat, like acid. No longer trusting David, she wanted to know if there were more to his story.

"So other than free rent, Zelia supports herself and your child."

"She gets a government entitlement, a single parent benefit."

David did not confess to the exorbitant amounts of cash he'd previously paid Zelia, before buying the cottage. He didn't want to appear more of an idiot to Dulcy, knowing those payments had been closer to blackmail than mere child support.

"When do you see this boy of yours?"

"I don't see him at all. I couldn't without having to see Zelia as well, and I've avoided her like the plague. I love you Dulcy. The child is just collateral damage."

"Oh is that all he is? Hopefully the poor kid never hears it said."

"I meant...it...that is he...was unplanned."

"When was he born?"

"In the New Year before I transferred up here."

Dulcy computed the information. David regretted his wife's lightning quick brain and acute skills of analysis.

"His conception had to be very close to when we got back together."

"Before we were married."

"How soon before?"

"What does it matter?" he riled up.

"It matters to me David."

David couldn't believe his life had taken such an abrupt downturn. Anger and a skin full of alcohol fuelled a frustrated reaction. He said too much that could never be unsaid:

"Why Dulcy? Are you jealous because I have child and you don't? You have never even shown any maternal inclinations. So that's rich coming from you."

Sorely affronted, Dulcy spun away from the tempting knives in the rack.

"How can you turn this on me David? That is an incredibly low blow."

"It's not as if you haven't had it off with old Grimslade. You think I'm deaf to your cosy fucking phone chats? Every fucking night?"

"I never hid that from you David. It's usually on speaker phone too. Your problem is that you judge me by your own low standards."

David knew he was in the wrong and had hit out with uncalled for retorts in rage. He strode towards the door. Dulcy got in a parting barb: "We're through David. I could never trust you again."

Desperate to escape the unhappy circumstances, David stomped out, slammed the door, got into his car and floored the accelerator. Dulcy didn't expect he'd be back that night. She retired to bed, tossing and turning, sick with the barrage of disappointments weighing her down. David's accusation of no maternal instincts, made her feel less of a woman. Barren. Aware he'd said it out of spite, cut her deeply.

In the small hours of next morning, called to investigate a car crash, where a vehicle had run through a fence and damaged a house. Dulcy rolled reluctantly out of her lonely bed.

David had wrecked his vehicle and been taken to hospital. Observing no allegiance to her husband, Dulcy Vestige recorded alcohol and excessive speed causal to the accident. She duly reported it as such, uncaring that David would be up for a heavy fine, possible suspension of his drivers licence and a large bill to cover repairs. Fortunately no one else had been injured.

Dulcy dutifully visited David in hospital. The airbag prevented serious harm. He emerged largely unscathed but bruised and sorry. If not for that self-inflicted mishap, Dulcy would never have chosen to speak to him again. Arriving at his hospital bedside, she said:

"Could you make anything worse David?"

"I know. I'm a stupid idiot. Dulcy I love you. Please don't leave me."

"I find your deceptions cowardly and hard to swallow David."

"I'll sell the beach house. We can buy a house together in both our names. You and me." he said.

"The house isn't the point David."

"Is it the boy? I will pay child maintenance through normal channels. I should have done it in the first place instead of the free-rent arrangement."

"Why didn't you then?"

"I don't know. I just wanted to get Zelia off my back and provide for the boy."

David feared Dulcy would call out the blackmail if she knew of the large sums he d given to keep Zelia quiet. It would only make himself look more cowardly for bowing to the extortion. Going over it carefully, he saw no way Dulcy could learn of the large instalments of cash Zelia gouged. No receipts at least worked in his favour for that.

"You've always had this thing with Zelia haven't you David? Obviously before our first involvement and even after I took you back."

"I'm only guilty of falling in love with you before I finished up with Zelia. Having her turn up without warning at the surfing holiday was truly awful. I know it really hurt you."

"At least you acknowledge that."

"And I am truly sorry for it. I wanted to break up with Zelia. I tried to find you, Dulcy, but you ran home and your friends all stonewalled me."

Dulcy knew what her girlfriends thought of David. Opal's regular warnings came to mind. David went on with his plea:

"I only found you because I knew you might be at the cricket match that day since Angus was playing, so Opal would be there."

"So, like a fool, I put my trust in you again, but you managed to make a baby with Zelia on the side. That reeks of you wanting your cake and eating it too."

They faced off. The deceptions tolled a death knell for their marriage, yet David held high hopes he could still win Dulcy over.

"Dulcy, you were rejecting all my advances at the time. I'm only human. Zelia has always been really hot for me and...er...anyway she tricked me into giving her one for old times sake."

"A quickie for old times sake hey? Well that really hit the magic spot didn't it."

David prayed Zelia never bragged to Dulcy of the indulgent whole day orgy.

"It just happened. Spur of the moment." he replied lamely.

Nausea almost overwhelmed Dulcy. Opal had been right all along, and she'd had her head in the clouds, sticking up for David like anyone would, who loved and trusted a partner.

"You got Zelia into a house you bought so you'd always know where she lived."

"No. As I said, it's to provide for the kid and to keep Zelia off my back."

Dulcy could not admire David anymore. Disappointment weighed heavily. Her erstwhile brave soldier showed a yellow belly, and to her, cowardice tainted him beyond redemption.

"I need a break away from you David. I have a lot to think about."

"I want to make it up to you." he pleaded earnestly.

"Then leave me alone. I need some space."

"I love you Dulcy."

David's pleas hung in the air. Dulcy walked away without a backward glance. An eavesdropping nurse bustled in to plump up pillows for the handsome patient. She rather fancied him for herself, and it seemed likely he would soon be available.

Immediately back at the office, Dulcy requested a transfer back to Queensland. She wanted no delay but it could take months. Packing a couple of suitcases with essential clothes and toiletries, Dulcy moved out of the army lodgings. David could keep everything else. She wanted no reminders of her disappointing marriage.

Tightly wound up with marital problems, in dire need of a relaxation treatment, Dulcy revisited Damien Cresswick at *The Brilliant Health Clinic and Wellness Centre.*

"I have such an awful headache Damien, and my neck is killing me."

"I can help with that."

Damien began a soothing therapeutic massage. Face down on the treatment stretcher, Dulcy's tears began to flow.

"Goodness Dulcy. You are really tense and knotted up. Not surprising I guess with your stressful work."

"I'm afraid it's caused more from a domestic issue, Damien. I've had the most awful let down."

"Do you want to talk about it?"

"I could use a coffee."

"Coffee is the last thing you need right now, my friend. I prescribe chamomile tea."

Dulcy's suitcases were in her car. She asked if Damien had a spare room she might rent, while awaiting transfer back to Queensland. He offered her Kirkwood's empty room for free, thinking there was no one he'd rather have in it. Dulcy's eyes brimmed with thankful tears. She had really needed that kindness.

"Are you okay?" Damien asked gently.

"I will be, Damien. Thanks."

Over evenings spent in Damien Cresswick's calm company, Dulcy related everything that had happened to cause disillusion with her marriage. He offered a sympathetic ear. It irked that loyal partners like his long-dead Kirkwood suffered, while cheats like Dulcy's husband endured. Life seemed so unfair.

Back at the beach house, Zelia couldn't think how to curb William Kirby's enthusiasm to renovate the dreary flat. The capable handyman went ahead and began work on it, spending his spare time and much of his wage on building materials. Tim Fun returned to the beach house to ask if they'd decided about renting the flat to him. Suspicious of his motives, in case he was indeed covertly working for the government, William Kirby put him off.

"Sorry mate," William said, "change of plans. We decided the flat needs upgrading so it won't be available for a while."

"That's a shame. Well, I might apply for it again later, if I can still afford it after the upgrades." Tim said.

Once again, Tim left on reasonably good terms. William felt the young surfer was on the up and up, he seemed genuine, but the wily man took no chances.

David Dubois came out of hospital to find Dulcy had moved out. He knew she would seek a transfer back to Queensland. He lamented her absence even more assuming her admired partner, Dougall bloody Grimslade, would be sympathetic towards her. *The bastard* David fumed. The dumped husband decided listing the beach house for sale to be his best course of action. Once he could show proof of his intention, he imagined Dulcy would relent.

As Dulcy did not answer his calls, he emailed a message to let her know.

Chapter 22

THIS IS MINE

Davy

David Dubois expected Zelia to be livid with anger learning he'd sell the beach house and pay future child support through a solicitor. He had no wish to face his old girlfriend again, but felt it only fair to tell her of his plans in person. While back in the area, he could suss out some local real estate agents as well.

Obtaining a short leave from the army, David travelled back to the east coast, arriving unannounced at his beach house on a Saturday morning.

Zelia had gone out shopping, leaving little Davy at home with William Kirby. The little boy played with several toy matchbox cars in the front yard, while William worked inside re-painting the drab under-house flat.

David Dubois set eyes on his son for the first time since the boy's birth and been unprepared for the effect. Looking over the front fence, David saw at once, the sturdy little chap indeed took after himself. Awestruck on seeing the handsome, solidly built red-haired lad, the man greatly admired his child.

David choked with pride to have sired such a beautiful boy. The long-absent father stood for a while, on the footpath, overwhelmed with regrets for the years missed seeing this son of his grow. The boy looked up from his game and acknowledged David's presence with a friendly greeting.

"Hello." little Davy smiled.

David's heart, already in meltdown, almost burst seeing the child's bright and ready smile.

"Hello yourself. That's a nice collection of cars you have there." David replied.
"Yes, and Mummy is getting me a new one from the shop in town."
"You're a lucky boy then. Which one is your favourite?"

Little Davy held up an army truck patterned in camouflage.

"This one. It's for soldiers. See it can hide in the garden so the *'emeny'* can't see it."
"That would be my favourite as well."

David felt in danger of tearing up when his son picked an army vehicle as his best.

"You can hold it for a bit if you like."
"May I? That would be super. Thanks."

David briefly brushed the boy's chubby little hand as he passed the toy over the fence. That first touch felt electrically charged to David. He had never even held his son as a baby. Now he yearned to get to know his beautiful child. David managed a suitable reply, as he handed the toy back.

"It is a nice one and you've taken very good care of it."
"Taa." Davy thanked him politely.
"Is your Mummy going to be home soon?" David asked.

"Before lunch. But Will is here."

In that instant. William Kirby sprang from under the house, ready for a fight. He'd caught the tail end of the conversation.

"What's your game then? Chatting up a little kid are you?" William yelled.
"Steady on mate." David retorted in anger at the implication.

Little Davy's face fell as he looked from one man to the other. William chided:

"Get in the house Davy. You've been told not to talk to strangers!"
"I was just..." the child began crying.
"Stop your sooky snivelling. I said get inside. NOW!" William yelled.
"No need to take it out on the kid." David burred up.

David noted Kirby's paint spattered overalls. He took the angry man for a hired tradesman, unless Zelia rented the flat out, which would come as no surprise.

"Who do you think you are giving orders. Now you've upset the boy."
"I'm taking care of him."
"By leaving him out in the front yard alone?"
"What business is it of yours?" William advanced, fists clenched, ready to fight.
"Not that it's any of yours. But I am Davy's father." David shot back.
"Bullshit. Davy's father died."
David twigged, the aggressive bloke must know Zelia quite well.
"Is that what Zelia told you?"

It had been exactly what Zelia told William Kirby, who felt a twinge of misgiving. He couldn't miss that Davy looked exactly like this 'stranger'. The two men faced off for several seconds.

"If that is true. Where have you been all this time?" William demanded.
"Overseas. I'm in the army."
"Zelia thinks she is a widow." William said.

Confused, the man wondered if Zelia's husband had been missing in action and believed dead. David Dubois relieved him of that misconception:

"No. Zelia knows she is not a widow. We never married."
"Then...shit...how?"

Davy wandered back outside. He eyed the men cautiously as he gathered his toys. William brought the child into the argument.

"Davy. Do you know this man?"
"Well...no, but he likes my army truck." Davy looked uncertain.
"I mean. Do you know this man's name?"
"No."
William's mouth fell open as the unwelcome visitor said:
"My name is David Dubois."
"Hey! Same like me!" little Davy exclaimed in awe.

The boy's statement surprised David. Zelia told him she named the child Davy Wild. The six-year-old imagined owning the same name made everything good. Both men tried to make sense of it.

"Sounds like you left Zelia in the lurch." William surmised.
"I did not. She knows the score. So who are you?" David asked.
"My name is William Kirby."
"What's your role here?"

"I'm with Zelia."
"That explains a lot." David nodded with a wry twist to his mouth.

David did not imagine Zelia would remain alone for long but hadn't given it much thought. For the first time, he noticed his investment house looked spic and span, newly painted. The garden beds bloomed with bright flowers and the lawn appeared lush and well-trimmed.

"We seem to have gotten off on the wrong foot, William. You are right. I'm only a stranger to the boy." David apologised.
"Well, he has been told never to talk to strangers. But you know...kids. So why are you here now?"
"I have business to discuss with Zelia."
"I see. Well she should be back soon." William replied.
"By the way, you have the old place looking really great." David mentioned.
"You've been here before then?" William asked.
David dropped the bombshell:
"Of course I have. I own this place. I let Zelia live here so the boy has decent housing. It was rather run-down when I bought it. I see a lot of work has been done since then. I suppose I have you to thank for that, William."

Kirby did not know what to say. His face reddened as the penny dropped. Zelia didn't own the place! He'd been knocking himself out working on another man's house.

Zelia, drove in at that fraught moment. William jumped into his ute and sped away without greeting his lover. Zelia took in David's presence and William's angry departure with foreboding. She did not like this unexpected development at all.

"So you've turned up like a bad smell." she said.
"That's a nice hello." David retorted.
"Why are you here?"

"I came to tell you I'll be putting this place up for sale. Maybe your handy pal William might like to buy it? Looks like he's been busy painting."

Zelia reacted in anger and disbelief. The unexpected turn of events put a spanner in the works.

"Why now! You owe me for Davy whether I'm with another man or not."

"I know. I'll make other arrangements to pay my share for the boy. It will be through a solicitor this time. No more cash in the mail and no more free rent."

David appreciated an upside to having Dulcy know. Subterfuge had become unnecessary.

"I've kept your secrets from your darling wife, yet you don't trust me." Zelia spat.

"Why would I trust you Zelia? Seems you've tricked your new bloke as well. Did you tell him you were widowed? Apparently, that is what he believed."

"What I do is none of your business David. I don't owe you my life story."

The conversation degenerated into laying blame and delivering insults, until they both noticed Davy watching and listening, seriously taking it all in.

"You said a bad word Mummy."

"Davy. It's okay. Mummy didn't mean it." David said gently.

"Yes Davy. All okay. Did you find the new toy car I got for you? It's in my bag."

Davy ran to look into his mother's shopping bag.

"I'd better go. I guess." David said. "Sure. Leave me to pick up the pieces. As always." Zelia scowled.

David departed with a heavy heart, feeling sorry for himself. He hoped Dulcy appreciated the sacrifices he'd made for her.

Selling the beach house and wrangling some other deal with Zelia, made no difference to Dulcy. Her husband had fallen off the pedestal, landing flat on his handsome lying face, leaving her crushed and disenchanted.

Dulcy did not reply to David's ongoing messages vowing his everlasting love to her.

Chapter 23

Boo Hoo Will

Domestic Violence

After David Dubois' visit to the beach house, William Kirby had no desire to speak to or even look at Zelia. He drove to an old timber jetty. At times, that barren wind-blown place had drawn others contemplating life changes.

Hands in pockets, William strolled to the end of the pier to crouch alone and upset, on the heavy timber planking. He lit a cigarette. It was the last one left in the packet. A new unopened pack of Marlboro sat on a bedside table at home. He enjoyed a smoke after a romp with Zelia. Now he wished he'd kept those cigarettes in his ute and his dick in his pants, at least with Zelia.

Looking out to sea, William smoked his last cigarette right down to the butt, tasting bitterness that matched his thoughts. He scorned how carefully Zelia embellished her tale, even going by the name Dubois. Her deceit struck him as calculated and cruel. William invested all his leisure time and spare funds on renovating that beach house, with the idea he would wed Zelia. The time had felt right, he'd been on the verge, with every expectation his proposal would be gratefully accepted. As a stand-in father figure for Davy, he liked exercising his authority over Zelia's kid too. Now, even that fond role curdled sourly.

Yet, Zelia simply never looked too far ahead. She hadn't expected the macho mechanic to stick around forever. Claiming widowhood seemed no big deal when they first met. The sham had been easy to keep up after the relationship jelled. Zelia knew David Dubois avoided her on purpose, so she did not foresee he might ever turn up unannounced.

Learning Zelia hoodwinked him dealt a rude awakening to William Kirby. The rough grey ocean reflected his stormy mood. He hoicked a golly into the choppy waves but couldn't get rid of the acrid taste in his mouth. William Kirby had loved being Zelia's man too. She knew how to really turn him on. *The lying fucking bitch!* Estimating his lost expenditure in time, money and emotional support, Kirby's anger burned white hot.

Young Davy had been overtired, yet his mother dosed him with a children's analgesic to ensure he would sleep deeply. Anticipating voices might be raise, she did not want her son waking up afraid. Zelia chose to sit on the front steps of the beach house, to keep the argument outside. She stressed out, knowing Will had to get the undeniable likeness between Davy and his very much alive father. *God knows what else David said to Will.*

Ahead of the awkward encounter looming with William, Zelia tore open a new packet of Marlboro she found in the bedroom. She rarely smoked except to share a puff with William when he lit one up after sex. Waiting made Zelia so nervous, she chain smoked. Three butts were flicked under the stairs before she heard William's ute approaching.

Zelia stood up as William drove in late, in the darkness of midnight. Kirby got out of his vehicle and clicked the car door shut quietly. Zelia hoped that meant he had cooled down. Unfortunately, his rage had not lessened but manifested silently. The force of his emotion palpable in a hissed accusation, imbued his tone with sinister purpose.

"You've lied to me all along."
"What about?"
"Don't play games Zelia. You said you were widowed."
"He was dead to me."
"Yet you live in HIS house? You go by HIS name?"
"The house is a business arrangement. His way of paying dues to Davy. I named Davy for his father and it seemed logical to use the same name."
"You led me on."
"How Will? You've done whatever you want without my say so."

William seethed over all the effort he'd put in on another man's house, mistakenly assuming he'd become its joint owner when the time was ripe to wed the widow. He felt well and truly gazumped on all sides.

"You let me do this place up. Shit Zelia. All the work and money I've put in!"
"You were on a good wicket. Why shouldn't you make some effort?"
"Some effort?!"

William became more riled as Zelia stood her ground. In her opinion, he only had himself to blame. Arguably she'd been good to William, shared her bed, done his washing and did more than half the cooking and household cleaning. As William's voice rose, Zelia was glad to be outside. She hoped Davy would not be woken by the argument.

"David wants to sell the place anyway, Will. He suggested you might like to buy it. I'm sure you'd get a housing loan easily enough."

Following Zelia's casual support of David's suggestion, William's mood worsened. His hands trembled as he raged:

"I come out as the fucking prize sucker. The great fixer of everyone's crap problems. Wouldn't that work out just dandy for you both?"

"No Will. Don't you see? We could make this place a good home together, and even rent out the flat."

"And the doting daddy will forever be in the picture. Turning up to smirk."

"What does David matter. He has never tried to see Davy at all"

"I'm betting that will change. He looked pretty taken with his kid this morning."

Zelia calculated that if Will bought the place, and they married, the cottage could really become hers in the long run. Plus, she'd have the last laugh on David, which would truly be golden. Annoyed that William's reaction obstructed possibilities, Zelia mocked and cajoled in equal measure.

"Boo hoo Will. Try to be mature for once in your life."

"You bloody bitch Zelia. Can't you see how this effects me?"

"Only if you let it, Will."

"I find your lies hard to swallow." Will growled.

"I told you David was dead to me. I was pregnant and vulnerable when he stooped to let me know he'd married someone else."

Will added it up but still couldn't get over Zelia's trickery. At a low ebb, he wasn't thinking straight, hadn't eaten since breakfast, and still wore the stiff paint spattered overalls. He noticed she'd been smoking his cigarettes too.

"So who was two-timing? You? Him? Both of you?"

"That's in the past and really none of your business, Will."

"Doesn't look good for you, does it Zelia? You've been shady all along. Lying. Scheming. Reeling me in. Using me. And that was my last pack of Marlboros you've helped yourself to."

Zelia became incensed. She spat out a scathing retort:

"Now you deny me a couple of cigarettes? And turn everything on me? Like you're the saint in this? Don't think I haven't seen through your money grabbing motives, Will. You saw yourself profiting by getting this place for free, complete with a live in housekeeper and a ready made kid to boss about like you're lord of the frigging manor."

That truth hit so close to the bone, the man couldn't take any more. William Kirby grasped his tormentor's throat and shook her with all the weight of his fury. Zelia's head thrashed from side to side and her hands flailed about uselessly trying to stave off the attack, before she slumped, unconscious.

The furious man continued violently shaking Zelia until an ominous crack brought him to his senses. It sounded no louder than snapping a fresh carrot in half, yet he instinctively knew what it meant. Kirby recoiled in horror as his lover's body buckled to the ground. The murderous act had been noiseless, and the dark of night hid the crime.

What have I done? No No No! Kirby's mind whirled in panic, trying to think how he might escape blame. He rejected his first impulse to run away since fleeing would make him look guilty as hell. Also, he had nowhere to go and very little money in his bank account after the recent renovations on the flat.

A perfectly obvious solution came to him after he'd smoked two cigarettes to calm his nerves. *Yes. It's karma. Payback.* William Kirby hit on a plan to implicate David Dubois.

With luck, some nosy neighbour might have seen Dubois there during the day, and even better if any arguments were overheard. Plus, the pair shared a troubled history: Dubois left Zelia in the lurch, pregnant with his child. That alone had to slant opinions against Davy's father.

William knew he must report finding Zelia dead, as soon as possible. He'd say he was just the tenant in the flat, that he'd done odd jobs around the property in lieu of rent. He'd come home late to find the woman at the bottom of the stairs, in the front yard. The tale fell neatly into place in William's mind.

Kirby looked around, noting the dark and deserted street. No lights lit other homes. Everyone slept. Good. He felt sure of no witnesses. He saw no way his claims could be disproved. He phoned for an ambulance. As an afterthought, he phoned the police as well. It had been easy to sound upset.

Before sunrise, DI Grimslade got the call. After routine inspections, ambulance bearers covered Zelia's body on a stretcher and took her away. Lifeless bodies were not emergencies, so no sirens or flashing lights were employed.

William Kirby had been so beside himself in concocting his story, he hadn't given a thought to the motherless boy sleeping upstairs. Grimslade phoned Tim Fun to include him in the investigation.

"Do you want me to attend?" Tim asked.

"No need Tim. You could go in early and man the office though. I've got this covered. The deceased has been removed. I've questioned the person who found the body but we'll bring him in later and record his statement."

"Wait," Tim said, "I remember there's a little kid in that house."

"Damn. That makes it so much worse. The tenant might have mentioned a child, he'd hardly be able to miss there being a kiddie in the house."

"There's a tenant? That was quick. During my surveillance exercise, I actually applied to get that flat myself, but the bloke put me off. He said they'd decided to renovate before offering it for rent."

"Yes there is a tenant, a William Kirby who found the body."

"That doesn't add up." Tim mused.

"How's that?"

"William Kirby is the bloke who showed me around the flat. He's the one I mistook to be the home owner."

"Aha. Now I remember. I knew I'd heard that name somewhere before. But I now know Dulcy Vestige's husband owns the house."

"But the title search turned up the name David Dubois." Tim said.

"That's right Tim. And he is Dulcy's husband. She kept her maiden name."

"So, the couple in the house must rent it from Dulcy's husband."

"Well, Kirby claims himself to be the tenant of the flat." Dougall replied.

"Okay. But he'd said to give him until the weekend because he had to discuss it with his partner, Zelia." Tim added.

"Anything else?"

"He said they had one child. You see, that's why I put the home owners down as being William and Zelia Kirby. I took them to be a family. My mistake. I know. I should have verified everything properly."

"It's entirely possible Kirby and Zelia were friendlier than he'd have me believe."

"It's odd that Kirby distanced himself from a close relationship with the dead woman. He'd given me a very different impression when we first met."

"It is odd and rather telling, Tim." Dougall replied quietly.

On cue, little Davy woke and missed his mother. The child could be heard calling for her. His cries made it plain he was home alone. William Kirby sweated inside the downstairs flat while the detective surveyed the scene. Grimslade called him out.

"Can you go up and comfort that child? He seems to be alone up there, but I assume he must know you. I'd go myself but he'd be frightened by a stranger."

"Christ. I'm sorry. I forgot about Zelia's kid. It's just the shock. You know."

The guilty man hurried up the stairs and inside. Grimslade noted his ease of access through the unlocked front door. William invented a story, telling Davy his Mum had gone for a run. The boy took the lie for granted as Zelia often jogged along the shore early in the morning.

The stand-in father busied himself setting out cereal and milk, but Davy said he wanted a boiled egg. William eyed the boy, wondering if he were old enough to corroborate his vilification of David Dubois. William hustled to boil an egg and began to coach the youngster:

"Davy. You know that man who liked your toy car yesterday? He was big and angry wasn't he?"
"Why?"
"Didn't he make you scared? By all the yelling?"

Davy really thought Will had yelled the most, but didn't say so. He remembered Will ordering him to go inside. Will's harsh voice made the child feel unjustly treated. Davy remembered what happened the day before.

"Mummy said a bad word."
"Did she? When?"
"They was yelling too."

William realised that must have happened after he'd driven off in a bad mood. *Good. Zelia and Dubois must have argued.* He prompted Davy more.

"That big bad man must have upset your Mummy a lot to make her say a bad word."

"A bit. But he said sorry. Hey you know what? He's got a same name like me! David Dubois. That's my proper name." Davy thought that must be a good thing.

Kirby hid his annoyance.

"But, that bad yelling man must have scared you." Will persisted.

"No. I's brave."

"Don't you think he was very nasty for making Mummy say such a bad word?"

"Hmm."

Davy had heard his Mummy use bad words before. Like when he spilt his milk and made a mess on the floor. But Davy did not think himself nasty for making his Mummy say a bad word. He liked the man who shared his name and hadn't considered him to be nasty. It didn't seem a good idea to say so to Will.

Grimslade stayed at the beach cottage until a kindly Child Welfare officer arrived. The woman led Davy from the house and introduced him to some other children waiting in her car.

Davy's close resemblance to Dulcy's husband was noted. Dougall agreed with Opal Bridcombe's assessment of the boy's paternity. The child was a dead ringer for David Dubois.

The welfare officer, appointed to interview the six-year-old while events were fresh in the little boy's mind, specialised in children's trauma management.

Chapter 24

THE SUSPECTS

It's A Soap Opera

Grimslade discussed the incident with Tim Fun back at the office:

"William Kirby is an obvious suspect. He will be brought in for questioning."

"What happens with the little kid?"

"The child goes into protective custody as a ward of the State."

Next, Dougall phoned Dulcy, who'd been surprised at the news.

"What? Zelia dead? How? Was it accidental?"

"A slim chance she fell down the stairs."

"Come on Dougall. What do you really think?"

"It's suspicious Dulcy. I have to ask: Do you know where your husband is?"

"No, I don't, sorry. We argued and I moved out. I'm staying at Damien Cresswicks' place. Remember him?"

"The other half of the Kirkwood Bonn case. How could I forget that one."

Dougall fleetingly revisited the horror that case entailed, not the least being discovery of dismembered human bodies stored as dog food.

"I last heard from David when he messaged to say he would sell that beach house. I didn't reply to him. He's admitted to hiding the existence of his illegitimate child from me. I'm absolutely shell shocked, as you can imagine."

"What will you do?"

"I've requested a transfer back to my old position in Queensland. Though I know you have Tim Fun now."

"I'd love to have you back Dulcy. We need a third anyway."

"Thanks Dougall. Listen, I'll ask around and find out where David is."

A while later, Dulcy phoned back: "David took a short leave and flew back to Queensland. I guess he wanted to handle selling the house in person. I mean, he'd have to inform Zelia...and now...she's found dead? Oh bloody hell. I see." The significance hit home.

"That's it Dulcy. David is under suspicion."

"Oh no. He's trained in army combat but has never been violent domestically."

"No that wouldn't follow, of course army operations are a different kettle of fish." Grimslade agreed.

"I will have to come down there right away."

"Don't Dulcy. You won't be allowed to work this case, given he is your husband."

"I know. Not officially allowed of course, but I'll do what I can."

Dougall shook his head. He'd hoped Dulcy would stay up in The Northern Territory. At the same time, he knew, in her dogged pursuit of truth, she would try to help her husband. Dougall provided her with some hope:

"At least he isn't the only suspect."

"Who else?"

"A tenant in the place or possibly Zelia's live-in boyfriend. We haven't sorted it out yet."

Despite everything, Dulcy feared for David.

"I'm coming back right away. Today." Dulcy declared. "Can you please book me somewhere to stay?"

"Don't you want to stay with Opal and Angus Bridcombe again?"

"Not this time Dougall. Opal has been right all along about David. She hinted strongly that Zelia had a red-haired baby. I'm in no frame of mind to hear her NOT saying '*I told you so*' while it oozes from every pore of her body. I know she means well, but I just couldn't bear it at the moment."

Dougall imagined Dulcy languishing worried and alone in some dreary hotel room.

"Dulcy. You know you could stay at mine. If you like."

"Really? Are you sure I'd be no trouble?"

"No more than usual."

In no mood for banter, Dulcy let Dougall's automatic dig pass.

"Well thanks Dougall. That is so kind. It would take a load off for me."

Dulcy jumped at the invitation to stay with Dougall. Being with the senior detective placed her nearer to the case. Despite being estranged from her husband, she wanted to help find the real culprit. She could never believe David capable of cold blooded murder.

Hastening to clear her absence from work and book an urgent flight, Dulcy quickly explained the situation to Damien Cresswick. As a good friend, he shut up shop and drove her to the airport.

Dougall collected Dulcy at her destination. They hugged warmly on meeting, both glad to see each other.

"It's good to see you Dulcy, although you know I didn't want you to come."

"Don't worry, I won't compromise your professional position. In fact I don't even want to talk about David except as your consultant, and if you see fit."

"Thanks. I've given the situation a lot of thought and can't see anything amiss if we discuss the case together with Tim Fun."

On the drive back to Dougall's house, he attempted to confirm Dulcy's motives in coming back.

"You've left your husband, understandably, in the wake of his actions. So I have to ask, what outcome are you hoping for?"

"I don't want to see David unjustly punished. He has always done what meets his own immediate needs, but harming Zelia wouldn't profit him."

"Have you ruled out sudden rage?"

"No. I can never rule out a rage reaction. I've experienced a moment of near insanity myself, not too long ago either."

"How so Dulcy?"

"I felt like killing David when he confessed. We were in the kitchen. I even looked at the knife rack. I'm sure he read the intent in my face."

"What did he do, if you want to tell me off the record."

"He blustered, more or less saying Zelia tricked him into goodbye sex."

"Goodbye sex?"

"For old times sake. For fun."

Dougall did not reply as he dissected the notion of whether goodbye sex would be better than hello sex. Hello won.

"Let's order takeaway for tonight. What do you fancy?" Dougall asked.

"Oh. Anything. I really appreciate your support, Dougall."

"That's what friends do." he smiled.

Dougall phoned for a delivery from the local Chinese takeaway.

Bogged down with work, Dougall earlier enlisted his daughter's help in airing out the spare bedroom and making up the bed with fresh linen. Isla Birdwhistle worried about her father staying alone in the house since Bella's demise. She liked and respected Dulcy Vestige and hoped the presence of her father's trusted colleague might provide convivial company.

"Dad. I'll leave a few casseroles in the fridge. You'll only have to nuke them."

"You're a gem Isla."

"I know. Also I wouldn't want to subject your guest to salami and pickles too often." she replied.

"Huh. I do eat other stuff you know."

"Like what? Takeaways?"

"Sometimes. The crooks keep me busy you know."

"Is Dulcy coming down to help with a new case?"

"Sort of. But not officially. Listen Isla, keep this under your hat, but this case hits Dulcy very close to home."

"How so?"

"Remember when you mentioned Dulcy's husband buying that beach house from your old landlords?"

"I still cringe for saying that. Obviously Dulcy didn't know or believe it."

"Well, she believes it now. David Dubois admitted buying it. Furthermore, he's been keeping another woman there, an old flame, along with their illegitimate son. And, that child is now six years old."

The injustice angered Isla. In keeping with her feisty personality, she was quick to retort.

"What? The bastard! Not the child, I mean him, David."
"It gets worse. The other woman has been found dead just after Dubois visited her."
"So he might have killed her?"
"Dulcy doesn't think so. That's why she wants to try and help."
"It doesn't look good for her husband though, does it Dad?"
"Nope. To me, it's a suspicious death and he doesn't have a squeaky-clean past given his ongoing deceptions to Dulcy. Then again, he isn't the only suspect."

Personally, Isla considered Dulcy's husband had a strong motive to have done it.

"Poor Dulcy. I hope they get whodunit. But I feel bad for starting this ball rolling."
"How so?"
"Dobbing Dulcy's husband in for buying that house."
"Don't be silly Isla. You weren't to know. It's best Dulcy found out anyway."
"I guess there's always a butterfly effect." Isla mused.
"True. Crimes have far-reaching consequences." Isla's father agreed.

Isla wound up the conversation by inviting Dulcy and Dougall for a meal with her and Aiden, if or when they found time in their busy schedules.
Shown to the spare room in Dougall's house, Dulcy guessed the added touches of fresh flowers and a nicely folded bath towel on the bed, were Isla's kindness.

"Make yourself at home Dulcy. There's a UK whodunit on ABC soon, the food delivery should be here by then."

"I love UK murder mysteries, and ABC is my favourite channel. No ads. I might have a quick shower if that's okay."

"Of course. Here's the delivery now." Dougall replied.

Dulcy returned from her shower wearing a knee length cotton robe over shortie pyjamas, her hair wrapped in a towel. Dougall had missed the fresh scent of a woman smelling of talc and shampoo. It stirred him in a way he'd not thought about for a long time. Covering his secret guilty awakening, Dougall aimed for normality. He busily set out two big bowls on the bench.

"I'll duck in for a quick shower now," he said, "I don't want to miss the start of the show."

"I'll dish up. You go. Where do you keep the chopsticks?"

Chopsticks?

Dougall stared at Dulcy as if she'd grown two heads.

"Joking." she laughed.

Despite the serious errand compelling her presence in Queensland, Dulcy had to laugh at her host's comical reaction. Dougall got that she kidded him and felt his heart lift on that light moment. It had been quite a while since anyone laughed in his home.

When the TV program began, Dougall showed Dulcy to his usual lounge chair. He'd take the one Bella used to sit in, not entirely sure why he did that.

"Put your feet up Dulcy." he shoved a foot stool her way.

"Wow. This is the life." she smiled in thanks.

Dougall supplied cold beers and served the bowls of food on lap trays.

Crossing her bare ankles comfortably on the ottoman, Dulcy's cotton wrap fell open. More inappropriate stirrings bothered Dougall at the sight of her very shapely legs. He'd been glad of the lap tray covering the evidence of his swelling interest.

The lonely man felt terribly disloyal to his dearly departed wife, Bella. He reprimanded himself: *Hell! I'm not long widowed. Dulcy is my junior colleague. Not forgetting she is a married woman! She'll think I'm a dirty old pervert. Besides everything else I look way too old for her.*

Yet, Dougall decided he might access Dulcy's file when next in the office. Just to check her date of birth, out of curiosity. He thought he recalled she was only eight years his junior, though she looked young for her age and he looked old for his. He told himself, knowledge should be no burden.

The pair ate and watched the UK murder mystery in silence, until halfway into the plot, Dulcy asked a question.

"What are you thinking Dougall?"

"Huh?"

He hoped Dulcy could not read minds.

"Whodunit?"

"Oh...um... the oily salesman. You?"

"Nope. I reckon oily salesman is a red herring. Too obvious. I think it's got to be the young barmaid."

"Why?"

"For one thing, she's the least likely, they like to throw in one like that, and I reckon she's had it off with that older man, her boss."

"So?"

"It gives her motive."

"To kill?"

"It's a soap opera Dougall."

Dulcy laughed again over her exacting colleague being forever focused on detective work, even within a fictional television drama mystery. Again, the lilting notes of laughter moved Dougall.

If Dulcy did know where his thoughts dwelt, he would never have guessed.

Chapter 25

INTERROGATIONS

Dubois & Kirby

Following the suspicious death at the seaside cottage, David Dubois was required to attend the police station for questioning. Shown to an austere interview room he faced the senior and junior investigators, Dougall Grimslade and Tim Fun.

A box of tissues, a water jug and a stack of paper cups populated a table that separated the detectives from the subject. All three sat on hard chairs that were not designed for comfort. David kept his hands in his lap. Tim Fun had a diary and seemed poised to take notes. Grimslade activated a recording device placed on a bench against a bare wall.

David Dubois had no idea a third detective, his own wife, looked and listened behind a privacy window. Dulcy could see and hear everything as if she were in the interview room, but nothing could be seen or heard of her presence. As far as David knew, Dulcy remained on duty in Darwin, many miles away up in the Northern Territory.

Dougall Grimslade allowed Dulcy to observe, on condition she didn't intervene. He could not deny his friend's request to be in on the investigation and justified his colleague's presence by the fact she could offer valuable input.

After recording names and times, Grimslade began, confirming David Dubois visited the deceased the day before discovery of her body.

"Why did you visit Zelia Dubois?"
"Zelia Dubois? No that is not her name. She is...or was...Zelia Wild."
"You were unaware she went by your name?"
"If she did, I didn't know. I only just found out she named the child Davy Dubois. The boy confirmed that himself, when he heard me say my own name. Previously, I'd been under the impression Zelia named him Davy Wild."
"What gave you that belief?"
"It is what I'd been told by Zelia herself." David answered truthfully.

Tim Fun wrote that in his notes.

"You refer to the child, Davy, as one you fathered out of wedlock with Zelia Wild or Dubois?"
"Yes. That is correct. Although I knew her as Zelia Wild. We were never in a de facto relationship. We had separate accomodation. We never lived together."
"How did you feel about the child being given your name?"
"I felt surprised because I hadn't known, but I don't have any objections. Actually, I like that Davy has my name. He is a fine lad."

Dulcy caught the pride in her husband's voice.

"How often did you see your son during the six years since his birth?"
"Never. Concerns about damaging my marriage to Dulcy made me stay away to avoid Zelia. I saw Davy once just after his birth but didn't even hold him. I thought it best if I stayed out of his life."

Dougall Grimslade could relate to that sentiment. He and his deceased wife, Bella, had thought it best to stay out of their illegitimate child's life as well, deciding they had no right to disrupt her world.

Initially Bella and Dougall tried to trace where their baby girl went, but ran into red tape with strict privacy laws. Authorities wouldn't divulge her name and they had nothing else to go on. At the time, Dougall had been a new recruit in the police force and Bella just out of re-hab.

Their baby had been dubbed Isla Tickle for a label on a cat box, and spent her entire childhood in institutions. The Grimslades only found out after Isla married Aiden Birdwhistle. Afraid Isla would hate them, Dougall tasked Aiden with telling Isla he and Bella were her birth parents. Initial dramas had been overcome, and a warm family relationship eventuated. [cite The Peckish]

Dulcy Vestige knew all about Dougall discovering Isla. But David Dubois covered his own failings by ignoring his son.

Dulcy helplessly watched her disappointing husband undergo the question session. She admonished him in her inner thoughts: *You damn fool David. It would have been better to face up to it from the start.*

Had David confessed at the earliest, Dulcy might have been more understanding, or at the very least, he'd not have emerged in her estimation as a craven coward. Perhaps they'd have worked it out and stayed together.

Now, finding he had a six-year-old child, Dulcy struggled with those years of her husband's deception.

"Where is Davy now?" David asked.

"Your son is in an approved facility. He is safe."

"But where?"

"We ask the questions Mr. Dubois."

David ran fingers through his thick auburn hair in a frustrated move.

Dulcy felt torn seeing the man she once adored so upset over his son. Yet, envy for him having that child tore her as well. Dulcy began to feel inadequate after he'd accused her of having no maternal instincts. Though owning no pressing aspirations for motherhood, she'd taken for granted they would start a family together when the time was right. That had been part of the grand plan.

Secreted in the observation room, mute witness to her husband's testimony, Dulcy now regarded herself better off being childless. Half siblings would undoubtedly complicate David's furtive evasions of his firstborn. All the same, Dulcy did not believe her husband capable of murder.

Grimslade continued quizzing Dulcy's husband:

"I repeat my original question. Why did you pay the recent visit?"

"I wanted to sell the house. I thought it kinder to tell Zelia in person."

"How did Zelia take it?"

"She wasn't happy. We argued a bit."

"What do you call a bit?"

"We toned it down because our boy could hear us."

Dulcy gasped. David saying 'our boy' stabbed her anew. He shared such an important life event with Zelia. Those two small words cut Dulcy to the quick. She felt even more of an outsider to her husband's life.

"What was said?" Dougall asked.

"I told Zelia I'd support the child another way, with my contributions verified through a solicitor. She accused me of not trusting her."

"Why did you take the step of selling the house and making those changes?"

"My wife found out. I believe you may already be very well aware of that fact, Detective Grimslade."

Grimslade neither confirmed nor denied it. David Dubois glared at his interrogator with ill-disguised animosity.

"You changed arrangements for your wife's sake?"

"Yes. I aimed to cut ties with Zelia for MY WIFE'S sake." David stressed Dulcy's marriage status. "And I sincerely hope she appreciates the pain this has caused."

Stung for being indirectly named causal to the tragedy, and too appalled to shed a tear, Dulcy inhaled a shaky breath. Grimslade realised Dubois' testimony must be rough on his colleague, covertly listening in. Yet the questioning had to continue.

"Mr. Dubois. Did you resolve the issue amicably with Zelia?"

"It was in the air. I suggested her new man might buy the house. He'd obviously done a lot of work on the place. Painting and improving the yard. It added to the kerb appeal and I complimented him on it."

"You know William Kirby?"

"Not really. I met him when I first arrived at the beach house. Zelia was out at the time. I spoke with my boy first. Davy was playing in the front yard. Kirby confronted me and accused me of chatting up a kid."

"So you and Kirby argued."

"Only briefly. He shouted at Davy to get inside. I said not to take it out on the kid. I said I am his father."

"How did he react?"

"He didn't believe me because Zelia claimed to be a widow. But then, I could see it hit him like a ton of bricks when he realised the likeness of Davy to me."

"So your explanation was accepted?"

"I think he accepted it, but he left in a huff when Zelia arrived back home."

"In a huff?"

"He slammed his car door and sped out before Zelia got parked. He didn't speak to her while I was there."

"What then, after Kirby left?"

"That's when my discussions with Zelia went off the rails. As I've said."

"So you and Zelia parted company on an angry note."

"Zelia had reason to be angry. She accused me of leaving her to pick up the pieces. *As usual* is how she put it. Though I suppose she was right about that. I felt terribly sad, not angry."

"And you left at that point?"

"I did. I just hope Dulcy appreciates what I am doing for her." David repeated.

Again, that hope felt like a slap in the face to Dulcy. She'd like to be able to tell David that his efforts were not appreciated in any way, shape or form. Grimslade pushed further partly for Dulcy's benefit.

"So, Mr. Dubois, what did you envisage, going ahead?"

"I just wanted to get my wife back. I love Dulcy. Always have. I would also love to be part of my son's life. Poor little guy, he has no mother now."

David replied woefully, but Dougall thought of another possibility:

"Mr. Dubois. Did you imagine it possible to get your wife back as well as gaining custody of the boy, if his mother were gone?"

David's face reflected horror and disbelief as that insinuation sunk in.

"What? Are you suggesting I wanted Zelia gone?"

"You suggested that yourself, Mr. Dubois."

"I did not! You're putting words in my mouth."

Dulcy wasn't surprised that Grimslade twisted that on him. She'd have done the same herself in a similar situation. Tim Fun wrote extensively into his private notes.

Aghast at how it looked, David felt very afraid. He could see himself being held accountable for Zelia's death. Everything would be lost to him, Dulcy, Davy and his freedom. He aimed to contact his friend Thaddeus Maekris, who had progressed to being a fully-fledged member of his family's law firm. Thaddeus might understand his case better than any other, since they both had Zelia in common.

Grimslade paused the interview to be continued another time. David was not held in custody but told to remain available. Afterwards, while Dougall reviewed the tapes for a third time, Tim and Dulcy put their heads together over a cup of tea in the office.

"Dulcy, I owe you an apology." Tim said.
"Why?"
"I initially muffed my surveillance exercise to find out who owned the beach house. I now know you had a personal stake in the outcome. Grimslade hauled me over the coals for it, quite rightly too."
"Oh dear Tim. Not the dreaded 'jumping to conclusions' lecture?"
"Yep. That's the one."
"Unverified assumptions are Dougall's pet peeve. Look out for spot checks too. He'll bung one in when you least expect it."
"Spot checks?"
"Random conjecture to see if you've been paying attention."
"Thanks for the warning, Dulcy. He sure keeps us on our toes."
"I firmly believe it's his favourite part of the job Tim."

Grimslade's protege and his latest apprentice shared ironic smiles.

Chapter 26

THADDEUS MAEKRIS

Legal Advice

Thaddeus Maekris ushered David Dubois into his impressive private office. He issued instructions to his receptionist before closing the door.

"Please hold my calls Mrs. Frogmorton. Take messages. Say I'm in a meeting and I'll get back to them as soon as possible."

The class divide between the two friends had widened since the surfing holiday when they'd both first met and admired Dulcy Vestige. Thaddeus now wore a tailored suit and dark tie with a crisp white shirt as his everyday business attire. By contrast, David appeared at this meeting in army fatigue pants and a camouflage patterned t-shirt. He hadn't packed many clothes for what was supposed to be a short leave just to advise Zelia he'd be selling the beach house.

"Come in David. I'm abreast of the news so I can guess what this is about."
"I might be in trouble here Thad."
Thaddeus recalled Opal speaking of Zelia having a red-haired baby.
"I take it, you are the father of Zelia's child."
"Guilty of that. But I swear, I didn't kill her."

"You married Dulcy Vestige. Did she know about the baby?"
"No Thaddeus. I kept it from her, but she found out."
Thaddeus tried to lighten the interview to put his friend at ease.
"You would marry a detective, David."
"She also has a senior detective colleague backing her up. I feel behind the eight ball, like he has it in for me."

Bitterness tinged David's reply, but he did not voice his jealous suspicions about Dulcy and Grimslade. Thaddeus leapt on it anyway:

"If you mean Dougall Grimslade, he often testifies in court, so I know who he is. Grumpy faced bugger. He isn't a barrel of laughs. I can't imagine Dulcy going for him if that's a concern for you David."
"No. Of course not. I reckon he fancies his chances with her though."
Thaddeus agreed but kept his opinion to himself, because he fancied Dulcy as well.
"How is Dulcy taking this?"
"She has left me because of it."

David felt himself tearing up. Thaddeus gave him a moment while he made strong coffee from a machine in his office. Thaddeus had remained single. Once upon a time, he entertained the idea of chasing Dulcy since he very liked and admired her. She'd have made a reputable wife worthy of his standing in the family law firm. He knew his parents would approve. Except he would never undercut a mate and everyone knew David claimed Dulcy. Thaddeus felt sure, if he'd won Dulcy Vestige for himself, she'd have become the next Mrs. Maekris. Furthermore, if he had Dulcy, he'd never have stooped to doing the shameful deed with Zelia Wild. As if reading his friend's thoughts, David said:

"I know you took up with Zelia yourself at some stage, Thad."
"Briefly. Something I regret."
"I regret having her as well. Have to feel sorry for poor Zelia, hey."

Both men squirmed with residual guilt for using Zelia.

"I have to ask David, were you unfaithful in your marriage to Dulcy?"

"Yes and no. I had a final fling with Zelia but it happened before we married."

"How long before."

"Not long enough I'm afraid. After that memorable beach holiday disaster, I was lucky to find Dulcy a few years later. I talked her into giving me a second chance. But she'd been cautious and held me off. It was like a no sex trial period for the bad boy. Anyway, at the time, I ran into Zelia again and she'd said how about it for old times sake. Just for fun. You probably know how persuasive Zelia could be."

Thaddeus declined to admit that he knew only too well. He often entertained guilty thoughts of what lusty Zelia did with him.

"Can I assume that final hurrah resulted in your illegitimate child?"

"Yes you can. It had to have happened that last time. I cowardly kept it from Dulcy because I was afraid of losing her."

David did not mention Zelia blackmailed him with the threat of telling Dulcy. He knew it gave him a strong motive to want Zelia gone and would not do his case any good.

"You don't think Dulcy might have been understanding if you'd confessed up front?"

"Dulcy holds high ideals. To my shame, I fell at the first hurdle that tested my control. I'm afraid Dulcy would be only too understanding of the fact I caved so easily to satisfy an urge. I doubted she'd agree to marry me if I told her straight off. I'd almost confessed but then I feared our marriage wouldn't survive without permanent damage."

Privately, Thaddeus thought Dulcy wasted herself on a morally weak player, and if David Dubois had done right by Zelia she might still be alive. It struck Thaddeus to ask his father if a divorced woman could be acceptable as a possible spouse for himself. He would raise the query at the next meeting.

"Is divorce on the cards?"

"It's not impossible, but I hope to get Dulcy back once the dust settles."

Something in Thaddeus's expression got through to David.

"You can't think any less of me than I do of myself, Thad."

"It's a sad state of affairs. No pun intended."

David didn't feel like laughing anyway.

"Can you give me an idea of where I stand legally?"

"Unless you physically hurt Zelia, you've not committed any crime in the eyes of the law, David."

"I swear I didn't touch Zelia. For one thing, our son Davy was there the whole time, watching."

"I believe you David. The onus of proof lies with your accusers, and it seems you are not the only suspect. There is no need to worry at this stage."

"What do I owe you for today?"

"Nothing this time David, I only ask that you please consider us in the future. Our firm specialises in handling divorce proceedings, should you need help."

"Thanks mate. I'll bear that in mind. But I hope not to need it." David said.

Thaddeus would not let the grass grow under his feet in pursuit of Dulcy Vestige, if divorce freed her.

Chapter 27

KIRBY'S GRILLING

Not from the Smell

William Kirby went under the grill next. He'd been picked up from the beach house by a uniformed officer in a squad car. The guilty man would have preferred to drive in his own vehicle, but decided it best not to argue. His cooperation must appear absolute.

Since Tim Fun previously met William Kirby on a surveillance pretext, he'd been required to stay hidden alongside Dulcy Vestige in the sound proof room. Grimslade wanted a nice little surprise for his quarry. He'd give Kirby enough rope to tie himself in knots before springing Tim Fun on him.

Grimslade tried for an unbiased frame of mind towards any suspect, aiming to assume innocence until proven guilty. However, the severe detective took a dim view of the three silver rings piercing Kirby's eyebrow. He considered the fashion trend to be some sort of objection to proper conventions. In Grimslade's personal opinion, tattoos were bad enough without metal bits impaled here and there into random ridiculous places.

Quelling his personal distaste of Kirby's multiple metal and inked adornments, Grimslade began questions fairly:

"Mr. Kirby. Are you a tenant in the flat attached to Zelia Dubois' home?"

"It isn't attached. It's built in under the house. It isn't an extension."

Twerp! The mild correction annoyed Grimslade. He'd enjoy sinking the boot into this one.

"Just answer the question please."

"Yes. I am a tenant."

"You are confirming to be a tenant in the flat under the victim's house."

"Yes."

"How long have you been a tenant in that flat?"

"Three, going on four years or so."

"You must have come to know the landlady quite well in that time."

"Yes I knew Zelia very well, and liked her. It was a terrible shock to find her like that."

"What were your first thoughts?"

"Looked like she'd fallen down the stairs. I called an ambulance."

"Did you touch her at all?"

"Yes. I tried to wake her."

"You believed her to be alive at that stage?"

"Yes. Alive. She felt warm so I was pretty sure she was only knocked out."

"You also called police before the ambulance arrived. Did you deem that necessary for someone whom you thought to be only rendered unconscious due to an accident at home?"

William Kirby blanched, seeing a possible flaw in his fiction. He searched for inspiration, glancing about the room as if an idea might materialise out of thin air.

"Well...I had a sudden thought that she might have been attacked. So I called the police."

"What gave you that *sudden thought?*"

Grimslade liked to mimic a suspect's own choice of words. A sarcastic nuance often rattled them, and he very wished to rattle this one. Kirby embroidered his account:

"A big surly type of bloke dropped by the house that day. I met him because Zelia was out shopping when he turned up. It seemed like he wanted to start a fight with me for some unknown reason. Me! Like I didn't even know him from a bar of soap. Later that night, just after I found Zelia, I had the sudden idea that angry bloke must have hurt her. So that's why I called the police. See?"

To Grimslade, the explanation seemed overdone, hasty and contrived. Kirby toughed it out, drumming his fingers on the table.

"What gave you that *sudden idea?* Describe how the visit with *the big surly type of bloke* went."
"The bloke said he was the kid's father and he had a bone to pick with Zelia. I was minding Davy while Zelia went to the shop. Anyway, I sent the boy inside so he wouldn't hear any more of the bloke's filthy language."

Liar! Dulcy immediately riled at that accusation. She nudged Tim and shook her head in denial. The behaviour Kirby described did not seem like David at all. He wouldn't use obscenities in front of a child. In her mind, that lie put William Kirby as the culprit. She regretted not being allowed to interrogate the man herself. Grimslade deduced Kirby probably embellished the encounter with Dubois to deflect blame.

"What happened when Zelia returned home?"
"The bloke and Zelia started to argue. He was really bad tempered."
"How much did you hear?"
"Not much. Just a lot of four letter words from the bloke."
"Did you try to intervene?"

"No I drove away because it was a domestic. Not my business. See?"
"You didn't think of sticking around since this other man seemed so angry and aggressive?"
"To be honest, I wish I had now."

Grimslade waited for Kirby to relax on his worthy wish. Then he called Tim Fun into the interview room.

"Allow me to introduce my junior colleague, DC Timothy Funicular."
"We have met, haven't we Will." Tim said mildly.

William Kirby's jaw dropped, but he recovered quickly, thinking on his feet.

"Oh. That's right. You're the one who came asking about the flat."
"I did. You told me you and your partner Zelia, had decided to renovate it before letting it out." Tim deadpanned.

Grimslade admired Tim's bland and indifferent stance. He was shaping up well just as Dulcy had done during her inauguration into detective work. Caught in the lie, Kirby bluffed out a contradiction:

"No. I said she might re-let it after I did it up and moved on. See...Zelia let me do renovations, partly in lieu of rent."
"So you planned to move out?" Grimslade asked.
"I was thinking about it." Kirby replied with another lie.

Grimslade hid a smile when Tim Fun adopted a puzzled expression.

"But I recall asking if you had children. You told me you and Zelia had just one youngster. You said he was quiet and well behaved."
"You got it wrong, sorry mate. I said there was just one youngster living there."

Tim Fun silently copied Grimslade's unblinking gaze. William Kirby squirmed. With the man at a disadvantage, Grimslade cut to the chase:

"Mr. Kirby, were you in a sexual relationship with the victim, Zelia Dubois?"

Kirby knew better than to deny it. He'd heard about DNA samples and worried they might be able to prove he'd recently been intimate with the woman. He hoped his blush made himself seem modestly embarrassed, rather than caught lying.

"We had it off sometimes. You know. It was just convenient for both of us."

The detectives made a show of writing notes although the interview was also recorded. They let the man sweat for several minutes. Kirby coughed a bit and cleared his throat. He sat up straighter, removed his elbows from the table and folded his arms.

"That will be all for now, Mr. Kirby. Keep yourself available."
"I know. Don't leave town. Ha ha."
No one laughed.

Dulcy, Dougall and Tim convened after Kirby left the building.

"I think Zelia had been waiting outside the house for Kirby to return. She wasn't dressed for bed. But would she go out and leave the boy alone in the house?"
"What was she wearing?" Dulcy asked.
"Track suit pants and a sports t-shirt."

"I'd wear that to bed if I planned to go out running before breakfast."

"Sure. Sometimes I wear board shorts to bed if I want to catch a wave early." Tim agreed. "Just easier to roll out and not have to change clothes."

"Okay. I must admit, I put my shorts on early in the interests of sports too." Grimslade said.

"Really? I'm intrigued. What sports Dougall?" Dulcy asked.

"All of them. You name it. I peruse all the sports pages. Sometimes the delivery boy misses the porch and I have to fetch the newspapers off the lawn, so I have to be modestly clad."

"And you wouldn't want any random joggers getting a free peek." she laughed.

"I wouldn't even sell them a peek Dulcy."

"Those ten steps out onto the lawn must be like a marathon."

"That grass can be quite chilly in the morning Dulcy."

Tim surveyed his older colleagues. They seemed to have a habit of deviating from the task at hand. Someone had to keep them in line.

"Alright, nothing significant in what she wore, then." Tim said.

"Does David smoke?" Grimslade asked.

"No. He never has." Dulcy replied.

"I found five fresh cigarette butts at the scene."

"Kirby smokes." Tim said. "I could smell it on him."

"Do you know what brand?"

"Not from the smell."

Dulcy hid a smile while Dougall gave Tim a stern look.

"Either or both Kirby and Zelia probably smoked at the scene. I found three butts underneath the stairs and two on the path. I think if Zelia sat on the stairs waiting, she'd drop hers under the stairs. If she smoked three, she might have been waiting for an hour or more."

"What of the other two?"

"Kirby probably smoked those after he found her."

"What does it tell us?" Tim wanted to know.

"Hypothetically, Zelia waited outside for perhaps an hour or more, so she felt nervous about Kirby's return. The ambulance arrived within fifteen minutes of Kirby's call, expecting an emergency. I got there only five minutes later. Kirby might have smoked two cigarettes in that time. Alternatively, he might have smoked them before phoning for help."

The three detectives pictured how it might have been.

"I see Kirby pacing and smoking while he thinks what to do." Dulcy said.

"Were the butts all the same brand?" Tim asked.

"Yes as a matter of fact they were. Why do you ask that Tim?"

"Just covering all possibilities. Not assuming anything that can't be verified. Leaving no stone unturned. Sir."

"Good Tim. Any other thoughts?"

Dulcy gave Tim a little wink. Tim's level of diligence pleased Grimslade.

Tim referred to his extensive notes taken during the interviews:

"Dubois said Kirby drove out as Zelia drove in, but Kirby says he heard them argue. Also, Kirby didn't ask after the child."

"One of them is lying. My money is on Kirby." Dulcy said.

"I'd say the kid is the least of his worries." Dougall mused.

Dulcy fumed her take on it:

"I bet anything Kirby did it. Going so far as to point the finger at someone else. David swears sometimes, but he wouldn't use curse words in front of a child. Also I can't see David picking a fight in that situation. Nothing Kirby said about David sounded authentic to me."

Grimslade was not inclined to be as forgiving of the errant husband, yet he accepted her opinion. Getting to the truth always drove Dulcy.

"Well Dulcy, you know David best." he conceded.

"Kirby has lied for sure." Dulcy repeated her wrath. "I would love to interrogate him myself."

"Well you cannot Dulcy and you know why. It's a pity he's dodged your thrashing. You might have cracked him."

"I'd like to crack him one," she brandished a fist. "One way or another."

Tim pulled a mock terrified face, in jest. Grimslade gave him the benefit of his rather limited experience with women:

"Never underestimate the delicate sensibilities of a woman, Tim."

Dulcy awarded Dougall's sarcasm an ominous frown. Tim opted for no comment and deemed it prudent to get back on track:

"Kirby definitely lied about renting the flat, and what he said to me when I applied to rent it myself."

"Thing is Tim, he could have been big-noting himself pretending to be the home owner. A bit shady but not a crime. We've gone over this before."

"I know," Tim agreed, "but I see it in a different light after what's happened."

"I agree with you both. We're on the same page with this. Kirby is covering up to distance himself from a jealous or angry reaction to David Dubois showing up."

Grimslade's take appeased Dulcy somewhat. He continued:

"We can attempt to chink his composure by finding any discrepancies in his account, however minor, and calling him out on them."

"Is that something like hounding a witness?" Tim asked.

"It's a lot like hounding the witness." Grimslade admitted.

"Sometimes it's like baying for blood." Dulcy added.

"In the business, we call it leaving no turd unstoned." Grimslade said.

"That's interesting. Is there a standard method?"

"Play it by ear. Pick on what rattles them."

"I'd like to have a go at that." Tim said.

"Alright. We'll see what we can do, Tim."

"Won't the little boy be questioned? He might reveal something." Dulcy asked.

"He is only a six-year-old." Tim reminded.

"A highly qualified Child Behavioural Specialist is sounding Davy out as we speak." Dougall said.

Chapter 28

SOCIAL MEDIA

The Peckish

A uniformed officer drove William Kirby home, noting he went upstairs and used his own key to access the main house. This fact had been duly reported back to Grimslade, as per instructions. William Kirby hadn't given a thought to the house key. Full of ideas, he booted up his computer. He had decided to post the tragedy on Facebook, knowing trial-by-media wielded a powerful influence.

The post began with a sorrowful announcement of finding his landlady Zelia hurt. William described how he found her at the bottom of the stairs in the front yard of her home, where, he said, he lived as a tenant in a granny flat on the ground floor.

Kirby claimed Zelia must have died in the ambulance on the way to hospital. She'd been dead on arrival, which would be easy to verify in case anyone cared to check. Fishing for angry feedback, he suggested the young mother may have been set upon by an attacker. Happy snaps attached to the post, depicted Zelia with Davy on the beach. Kirby wrote: *Now this poor little kid has no mother.*

Browsing Facebook, during a quiet interlude in the PI office, Isla Birdwhistle caught William Kirby's post and viewed the photos.

Struck by a memory, Isla exclaimed aloud: "Oh my gosh, I know her! And I think I recognise him too."

Isla checked William Kirby's online profile and studied all his photo albums to be certain he was who she thought. She recognised Zelia and William as a couple whose initial meeting she orchestrated when she'd worked in the supermarket. The former matchmaker immediately phoned the lawman who headed the investigation. He just happened to be her own father:

"Dad. I have to tell you something. I've just seen a post about that tragic young mother. The one that involves Dulcy's husband. I don't know if this is significant, but I recognise the victim and the guy who posted online about finding the body."

"What! It's been posted online? Where is this? Don't tell me the case has already been leaked." Dougall exclaimed in anger.

"Sorry Dad but apparently it has. I'll send you the link." she replied.

Dougall saw Kirby preempted due process by publicly conveying his side of the story. When Dulcy and Tim viewed the post, they agreed Kirby portrayed himself in the best light. Dougall asked more of Isla:

"You knew the victim?"

"Sort of. Not really. She had been among my peckish, and so was he."

"Peckish? What the hell does that mean?"

"Well Dad, I had the idea that if most people weren't actually starving for love, they'd at least be peckish. That's why I began setting up the saddest ones on blind dates."

"I struggle to understand how that fits in, but listen Isla, these people are uppermost in a possible homicide. Your input could be very important. How did you come to know them?"

"In my past as a sneaky matchmaking checkout chick, I thought of the people I sent on blind dates as The Peckish. I actually put those two together."

"You hadn't wanted your so-called peckish to be lonesome, is that it?"

"Well Dad, I commiserated, because at the time, I felt so alone myself. I hadn't met Aiden yet, and no one likes to be lonely. It's only human." Isla explained.

"It's good to know my daughter sees me as human."

Letting on more than he intended with the off-the-cuff replay, Dougall cursed himself for admitting to feeling lonely since he'd lost Bella. He hated self-pity and sped past his lapse of good sense, getting back on topic:

"So Isla, you matched the victim to William Kirby through a blind date."

"Yes, I guess you'd say I tricked them into meeting each other."

"That must have been quite some time ago."

"It would be five years or more. I saw it as one of my best matches too. They seemed really well suited."

"Are you sure it's the same couple?"

"Quite sure. They both had all those tattoos and piercings. I remember she had a little kid in a pram. He's probably the one in the photos. The age seems about right. I guess he might have started school by now."

Grimslade ascertained William Kirby and Zelia had been romantically linked for some time. The timeline shed doubt on the man's version of events.

"He's trying to downplay his close relationship with Zelia." Dulcy said.

"Certainly, their involvement seems deeper than merely off and on casual."

"Does that really matter?" Tim Fun asked.

"It's important because murder is often done by someone closest to the victim, and Kirby contrives to distance himself."

"So it is definitely a homicide case."

"Yes, it is now, and I certainly didn't want that information leaked."

Tim made a note of it in his personal diary. He managed to disguise feeling thrilled for being in on a real murder investigation. Dulcy felt a chill on behalf of her husband. Grimslade explained further:

"According to the coroner's report, just in, Zelia's injuries are consistent with being choked and severely shaken. Cause of death officially declared as cervical fracture."

"So, even if Kirby found her like that, she was probably already dead."

"That's correct. Although a lay person cannot necessarily distinguish between a recent death and a coma. So he can't be held accountable for a mistake."

"But he could really believe she was still alive."

"Exactly. But it doesn't mean he didn't cause her injuries."

"Dead or alive... it hardly makes any difference. Does it?" Tim Fun asked.

"We might clarify that on cross-examination." Dougall replied.

Dulcy felt back to square one in her attempt to exonerate her husband. Dougall felt sorry for his friend's dilemma. He explored another path:

"Isla saw William Kirby's post on social media. Years ago, she had some interaction with that couple but says they wouldn't know her. Therefore, I'm thinking we could get Isla to draw Kirby out by adding comments to his media post."

"Who is Isla?" Tim asked.

"Forget you don't know the history, Tim, but Isla Birdwhistle is my daughter."

"Birdwhistle? Of the private eye firm?"

"That's correct."

"Okay. But mightn't Kirby twig to her name connection to a sleuthing firm?"

"Good point, he might, because he'll be on high alert." Dulcy agreed.

As it turned out, there had been no need to worry. Dougall's daughter kept her original Facebook account in her maiden name. Isla (nee Tickle) relished the task to play along. She added her comments on William Kirby's thread:

Isla: *Oh my god! That's awful. You think your friend was attacked? What happened?*

Kirby: *I don't know for sure, but some big loud mouth angry bloke visited Zelia that day. They argued about her little boy.*

Isla: *How horrible. What did you do?*

Kirby: *I told the kid to go inside so he didn't have to hear the man's obscene swearing. It was obviously a domestic dispute, none of my business, so I left. Wish I'd stuck around now.*

Isla: *You're saying this bloke must have been related to the victim?*

Kirby: *I confronted him at first and he said he was Davy's father. See?*

A few others joined the conversation with results that pleased William Kirby. As he hoped, everyone condemned Davy's father for committing a domestic violence attack. Journalists contacted William Kirby via his social media account. The guilty man obliged, playing his part, answering their questions sadly. An avalanche of footage bounced around cyberspace. William gained public sympathy while implicating David Dubois at the same time.

"He's controlling this!" Dulcy exclaimed angrily.

Grimslade brought Kirby back in. Tim Fun sat in on the second interview but Dulcy had to remain mutely concealed as before.

"Mr. Kirby. We note you have made the event public on social media."

"So? Why shouldn't I? You never said not to." he huffed.

"You've made incriminating suggestions towards another person."

"And? He deserves it. I reckon he did it." William replied.

"It's not up to you to decide that." Grimslade growled.

"Well. You've done nothing that I can see. There isn't even any crime tape around the scene." William accused.

Grimslade smiled to himself. He could not abide his team members jumping to unverified assumptions, but it could be helpful when a suspect fell into the same trap. Clever Tim Fun caught the drift.

"Crime scene? Why are you calling it a crime scene?" Tim asked.

"Because...obviously Zelia was attacked." the man blustered.

"That is pure conjecture on your part Kirby." Grimslade replied.

"You claimed it looked accidental. Like she fell down the stairs." Tim added.

"Well as I've already said, when I thought about it more, I reckon Davy's father attacked her. A lot of people agree with me too."

"A lot of people on social media." Grimslade replied.

William Kirby made an inadvisable retort:
"Anyone with half a brain would come to the same conclusion."

Kirby earned a double set of hawk-eyed stares. Fixated like a rabbit in the headlights, he gulped, afraid he'd gone a step too far. Grimslade wreaked a small revenge by letting him know he'd been under observation.

"You claim to have been only in a casual relationship with the deceased. Yet you have your own key to her house."

"Of course I have a key. Zelia trusted me. I did repairs in her house all the time."

"You were quite close to Zelia I take it? When did you begin dating?"

"Dating? No I only met her when I was looking for a flat to rent."

"We have it on good authority that you met her romantically at least five years ago. You met on a blind date at The Tipsy Turnip Cafe. It was early one Saturday. At 7am to be precise."

Kirby's jaw dropped. He had absolutely no idea how they could possibly know so much. He had no recourse but to continue bluffing:

"So what? I can't even recall when or where I met her. It wasn't romantic, she had a flat to rent. Otherwise I had no reason to be friends with her."

"We have a reliable witness prepared to swear under oath that you met Zelia at that cafe at least five years ago."

Kirby imagined old CCTV footage must still exist, otherwise how could they be sure.

"It could have been five years. Yeah. I think it probably was about that long."

"But mate," Tim Fun adopted his puzzled face again, "Zelia didn't live in that particular beach house five years ago. Did she have another flat to rent somewhere else?"

The questioning deliberately aimed to befuddle Kirby. Zelia had come by that house after they'd met. Yet he had not expected the timing to be a factor. At a loss, seeing his credibility unravel, the man riled up:

"I don't know what she had. And so what anyway? I don't see what that has to do with anything."

"Only that your relationship with the deceased seems to be of a longer duration and perhaps quite a lot closer than you allege."

"We were quite close. I've said that." Kirby's voice rose an octave.

Sitting in exile, Dulcy applauded her colleagues for getting under the subject's skin. She particularly credited Tim Fun's innocent face and needling remarks hitting on specific points of accuracy.

"We find no record of you having paid rent." Tim said smoothly.

"I told you," William shouted, "Zelia waived my rent in lieu of work I did on her house."

"I believe you stated your renovations were *partly* in lieu of rent. Not wholly."

"I did a great deal of work on it. Even installed a new kitchen."

The detectives used Kirby's rise to anger. They'd hit a nerve as intended.

"Yet we know Zelia did not own that house, Mr. Kirby. She was a tenant herself."

The biting remark made William Kirby grit his teeth and slam both fists on the table, though he immediately regretted his loss of composure.

"That strike a chord with you?" Grimslade smiled like a crocodile.

"No. It's just so bloody irritating how you're trying to turn this on me."

Unmoved by Kirby's outburst, Tim asked a question in a chummy tone of voice:

"Hey Will. An idea just occurred to me. Did you think Zelia owned the house and that's why you did so much work on it?"

William Kirby did not reply. His tormentors had arrived at the truth and he saw it boded ill for himself. Grimslade stuck it to him further:

"Mr. Kirby. Were you under the impression Zelia was a widow?"

"It was none of my concern but that is what she told me." he agreed.

They left the interrogation hanging on that note. The troubled suspect was allowed to go home. Dulcy convened with Dougall and Tim afterwards.

"He thought Zelia owned the property." Tim stated the obvious.

"So, he's done all this hard yakka on the place." Dougall added.

"Bet he wouldn't have bothered if he knew David owned it." Dulcy said.

"Nope. I agree. Having David turn up out of the blue, and finding out Zelia lied all along, he'd have to be a tad peed off."

"More than a tad."

"At least two or three tads."

The three mused on it more. Grimslade came to a decision:

"He almost cracked up today. I believe we already have grounds to arrest him on suspicion of causing Zelia's death. But let's lean on him more for a confession. It would save months of court time if he owns up."

"Why string it out? I mean why not do that from the start instead of bringing him in a few times?" Tim asked.

"To see if he changes his tune, Tim. Honest reports remain consistent."

"Couldn't he remember what he'd said beforehand and just fake it anyway?"

"Yes he could. But he might not. It is always worth that gamble. He'll sweat it overnight, thinking what he should have said differently and be trying to adapt it."

Tim wrote that in his personal notes.

"Thanks for the hint, sir."

"It is not a hint Timothy, but a subtle and canny strategy."

Dulcy awarded Tim her own subtle and canny wink. Dougall would be chuffed for being addressed as sir again. She never used that term of respect herself, because he'd said to call him Dougall from the start. The youthful Mr. Fun was indeed shaping up as a promising and diverting team member.

The light moment passed. Dougall sobered getting back to business:

"Meanwhile, before we sit Kirby back in the hot seat, you both need to witness the child's video. I've watched it once. Be warned, you might find it harrowing. I know I did."

Dougall pushed the pack of tissues across the desk.

Chapter 29

DAVY'S ASSESSMENT

He Wants His Mummy

The Child Welfare negotiator provided Davy Wild Dubois' video evidence.

Initial talks with the six-year-old were done within hours of his mother's demise, so events would be clear in the child's mind. A Child Behavioral Specialist Psychologist Dr. Ghaith Ong gently interviewed the boy.

They sat within a relaxed environment in the doctor's own home. Ghaith Ong knew children were more comfortable with an informal name and Davy had been told he could call her Aunty Gong. Apart from Davy, two other youngsters stayed in her home for ongoing counseling, but Davy and Dr. Ong went one-on-one for this important session.

The doctor and Davy knelt on cushions against a low table that held coloured pencils, crayons and drawings. Hidden from view, camera equipment recorded voices and reactions. When the small boy asked where his mother was, he'd been told gently and plainly that she had died.

"I am very sorry Davy, but your Mummy died."

The doctor spoke in clear terms. No platitudes commonly used with adults, such as 'passed away, with God, gone to heaven or with the angels' were used.

Davy's dismayed facial reaction of shocked despair, brought tears to the eyes of even the most hardened of the three detectives on the case. Yet Davy did not cry.

Davy knew something of death, having lost a pet budgerigar named Buddy. That loss at least made the doctor's difficult task slightly easier.

"Buddy died too." Davy said. "We wrapped him in nice paper."

"That is sad. It was good to wrap him up though." Ghaith replied.

"Mummy won't like to be wrapped in paper."

"Oh no that won't happen. Your mummy will be in a beautiful casket."

"Is it like a coffin?"

Davy had viewed funerals on television.

"Yes Davy. It is a coffin." the doctor agreed.

"Will there be flowers?"

"Lots of lovely flowers, Davy."

"And a flag?"

"There can be a flag if that is what you want."

Dr. Ong chose a large drawing to be coloured in. It depicted some people with children in a playground. It showed one little boy sitting alone on a bench.

"I don't think I can do this big picture by myself. I bet you're good at colouring in. Can you help me Davy?"

Davy nodded and took up a blue crayon. He began lightly shading the sky.

"Will said I won't see Buddy again. Never no more, he said."

"Buddy will always be in your memory, Davy. So will your Mummy."

"I *ravver* she was here now." Davy whispered.
"We all rather that, Davy."

Dr. Ghaith Ong privately thought this person called Will must be the insensitive type. She braced herself for the inevitable questions from Davy and did not hurry him.

"Why has Mummy gone deaded?"
"She had a bad accident, Davy."

His face stricken with shock, Davy looked up from colouring the sky.

"Did Mummy fall off the perch?"
"Yes Davy. I'm afraid so."

Davy went back to the picture. Dr. Ong gave him more time to think about it. Her assignment was twofold. Foremost, she had to help the child come to terms with losing his mother. Secondly, she must find whether Davy could cast light on what happened.

"Will said Mummy went for a run." Davy frowned.
Ghaith Ong identified this opening.
"Did you wave goodbye?" she asked.
"No. I was asleep."
"When did you wake up?"
"Breakfast. I had an egg. Will made it."
The doctor hoped Davy remembered the night before.
"Did your Mummy tuck you in when you went to bed?"
"Yes. I had a pill."
"You had a pill? Did it make you feel better?"
"It helps me to go to sleep."
"I see. Did you need help to go to sleep?"
"I was upset. Not much, only a little bit."

Davy repeated what his mother told him at the time, that he must have a pill because he was a little bit upset.

"What upset you, Davy."

"They was yelling. Mummy said a bad word… But I didn't spill my milk."

The lady took up a pink crayon and began colouring flowers in the picture.

"You're doing a nice job on our picture Davy." she said.

"Taa."

"Who was yelling Davy?"

"They all was yelling."

"Were you scared?"

"No. I's brave."

"Did anyone yell at you Davy?"

"Yes. Will yelled at me. Real loud. He said get inside NOW." Davy roared the last word.

"Is that what upset you?"

"…a bit."

Davy took up a red crayon and pressed it hard shading the face of a man in the picture. The crayon broke. The doctor knew the child resented being yelled at by the charming Will. Nonetheless, knowing children had a keen sense of fair play, Davy's reaction may not hold greater significance than he felt unjustly chided.

"That's okay Davy. I've got lots of crayons. Don't worry about it."

Davy carefully placed the broken crayon back in the box. The doctor paused a while to allow the boy to calm down. She did not want anger to drive his response.

"Did you yell too Davy?"

"No. Not me. Just Will and Mummy and the other man."

"Who do you think made Mummy say the bad word?"

"Not me. I didn't."

"That's good. Maybe it was Will or the other man?"

"Not Will. Well, not that time."

"So did the other man make Mummy say a bad word?"

"Um...yes. He said she didn't mean it but."

Aha. The boy's defence showed he had not feared the other man. The good doctor felt to have achieved a small step.

"That was a nice thing for him to say."

"He liked my army truck."

"It must be a good army truck."

"It is. And you know what? He's got the same name like me!"

Davy remembered the fact that seemed most important to himself.

"The man was named Davy too?"

"Not Davy. David Dubois. Like me. That's my proper name."

"It is a nice name. Was he a nice man?"

Davy paused thinking it over, biting his bottom lip and frowning.

"Will don't like him."

"Oh?"

"Will said he is big and scary."

"Did he? When did Will say that Davy?"

"Breakfast. When he made my egg."

"Will made your egg for breakfast this morning. That was good. I like an egg too."

"Sometimes I have porridge." Davy told her.

"So do I." Ghaith said.

"Mummy makes my porridge."

Davy's face wrung with emotion. The doctor knew he'd be thinking of the breakfasts his mother made. Now 'never no more' just as Will had said of his pet budgerigar. Ghaith indicated the drawing, hovering her crayon over the boy sitting alone in the picture.

"Hmm. What colour should I make his hair? What do you think Davy?"
"Sort of brown."
"Can you pick the right colour for me please?"
Davy chose a reddish brown.
"That's a lovely colour. It's a lot like your hair colour, Davy."
"Mmm."
"Why is this little boy sitting all by himself I wonder."
"He wants his Mummy."

Finally, Davy broke down into heart-rending sobs. The kind lady doctor took him into her arms.

"I'm not a sook." Davy gasped.
"No. It's okay to cry, Davy. I'm crying too." Ghaith said.

Davy leaned back and saw the doctor's face streamed with tears.

"There, there." he said, as he patted her back with his chubby little hands.

At the end of the video, all three detectives took long bathroom breaks to splash cold water on their faces. They returned displaying various degrees of sheepishness.

"Ahem. What can we make of that?" Grimslade began.
"William Kirby told Davy his mother had gone for a run." Tim said.
"I guess he had to tell him something."
"Suggesting David was big and scary...sounds like Kirby tried to put that idea into Davy's head." Dulcy opined.

"Yes. I got that impression too." Tim agreed.

"He could have said it to condone any fears Davy felt." Dougall said.

"I don't thing so, because Davy obviously hadn't feared David. If anything, he defended him." Dulcy replied.

The three pondered for some minutes. Grimslade summarised:

"Nothing Davy said disagrees with what we've been told or know, so far."

"Except if Kirby intentionally coached the boy, the motive is important." Dulcy said.

"He was quick to do it." Tim added.

"There is that." Dougall had to concur.

Convinced David didn't kill Zelia, Dulcy hoped they'd allow him to view his son's evidence tape. If the case came to trial, David might get to view it then, but that could take months.

"Dougall, can Davy's interview be shown to David?"

"Hmm. Probably should wait for the outcome."

"He is the boy's father Dougall. And remember Davy requested a flag on the coffin. David might be best placed to organise that."

Grimslade thought about it. Tim asked:

"Do you think a six-year-old would be allowed to attend the funeral?"

"I've seen children at family funerals on television. I can't speak for David, but knowing him, he'd feel duty bound to attend Zelia's funeral himself. I m sure he would want to accompany the boy and lend support." Dulcy replied.

"If Dr. Ong sanctions it, I won't stand in the way. I'll phone her." Dougall said.

Dr. Ghaith Ong considered the father's support would be helpful. She often accompanied children in her care, to funerals, and would go with Davy as well. David Dubois' visits to his son leading up to that sad event, would be overseen by the doctor. At some stage, Davy had to be told David was his true father, an introduction that required some delicacy. Dulcy applauded the professional care put in place towards the ongoing relationship between David and his son.

"Thanks Dougall. But look... I don't want to see David right now and I don't want him to know I've been in on the case...so..."

"You want me to handle it?"

"Yes please. Would you mind? I'd greatly appreciate your help."

"Okay. I'll bring him in again. I was going to anyway to confirm his original account remains the same. He can view Davy's evidence tape while he's here."

David Dubois attended for another recorded interview. Comparing the subject's answers, Grimslade and Tim Fun heard slightly different phraseology but no factual discrepancies with David's original statements.

"Mr. Dubois, we have in our possession footage of a counseling session with your son. Would you like to view it?"

"Yes of course I would!"

David sat forward, eager to view the screen that was turned towards him. He immediately spotted Kirby's attempt to coach Davy.

"That mongrel! Can't you see? He is trying to turn Davy against me!"

"That possibility has been acknowledged, Mr. Dubois." Grimslade replied.

"Oh my God. My poor boy. Where is he? I am entitled to know."

David became tearful, just as everyone did on seeing and hearing the child's reactions. Grimslade believed in the man's innocence and tried to put him at ease:

"Davy is in the care of the child welfare specialist, Dr. Ghaith Ong, who conducted this interview."

"Am I allowed to visit Davy?"

"Yes. The doctor recommends it. Of course, you must speak with her first. She will oversee your visits with Davy before and after the funeral."

"I'll make sure there are plenty of flowers and a big flag draping the coffin. It's what Davy has been led to expect and what he wants. Christ. Zelia's funeral. I never wanted it to end like this."

Overcome, David put his head in his hands. Grimslade continued with a warning:

"Mr. Dubois, need I remind you to stay away from William Kirby. You will very likely see him at the funeral."

"Don't worry. I'm sure Kirby killed Zelia and what I feel like doing to him wouldn't help my case." David replied wretchedly.

"What makes you so sure?" Grimslade asked.

"Because I know for dead certain that I didn't do it."

Grimslade didn't pursue the argument with Dubois. Without being asked, Tim Fun fetched a cup of sweet tea for David. Grimslade raised eyebrows, thinking young Tim could be a bit soft around the edges, though he did not say as much aloud. At the same time, Dulcy's good opinion of the junior recruit soared to new heights.

Chapter 30

IN THE HOT SEAT

You Got That Wrong

William Kirby felt to truly be in the hot seat for his third interrogation. Grimslade began questions. Tim Fun had been prepped to join in if it seemed appropriated.

"You were in a sexual relationship with the deceased, yet lived underneath her house in poor conditions, instead of upstairs in comfort with your lover."

"I told you. It was just an occasional thing with Zelia. We didn't live together."

Tim Fun repeated an earlier observation:

"But Mr. Kirby, from what I ascertained when inquiring to rent that flat, you and the deceased were in a close partnership and had a child."

"No. I already told you. You got that wrong. I said there was a child living there." Kirby flustered.

The two detectives made a show of reviewing their notes on screen and on paper. Beads of sweat formed on Kirby's brow and trickled down. He swiped a hand across his face. On tenterhooks, Dulcy couldn't wait to see her prime suspect lose his cool. Abreast of

Grimslade's methods, she knew he closed in for the kill, and young Tim Fun ably rode shotgun.

"We found no evidence of rent you allegedly paid." Tim frowned.

"I already explained that. I worked on the house in lieu of rent."

"I believe you said your work was partly in lieu of rent. But we find no evidence of even partial payments." Tim reminded.

"I bought heaps of groceries. That's what I mean by saying my renovations were partly in lieu of rent."

"So you shared household groceries even though you rented the flat."

"Yes...because I bought stuff in bulk. See."

"Did Zelia keep records of what you contributed in lieu of rent?" Grimslade asked.

"Not that I know of. As I said, she trusted me. We trusted each other."

"Did you keep receipts yourself, in support of your renovation work?"

William breathed in relief. He had kept receipts which he felt backed up his claims.

"Yes! I do have all the hardware receipts. And I can tell you, that kitchen makeover alone came to over twenty thousand dollars."

"Goodness. On top of your labour, it seems you grossly overpaid for your rent on that dingy flat." Grimslade said.

"Wow. That's harsh." Tim marvelled.

William Kirby resented giving so much to the conniving Zelia, and that it was all a complete loss. He knew he had Buckley's Chance of recompense from David Dubois, and that recent bitter knowledge stuck in his craw.

"I overpaid for sure." he grumbled.

"When did you understand you'd been overpaying?" Grimslade asked.

Kirby understood the question aimed at him having a motive to hurt Zelia after Dubois turned up. He declined to answer promptly. In the interval, Tim prodded with another jibe:

"Sounds like you were well and truly suckered Mr. Kirby. Big time."
"Seems that woman took unfair advantage." Grimslade crocodiled his smile.
"She played you. You got royally ripped off." Tim chortled.

Grimslade and Tim Fun sniggered together to provoke the subject.

"It's no laughing matter." Kirby cried.
"Come on mate, it is more than a little amusing." Tim smirked.
"And the jokes on you Mr. Kirby." Grimslade taunted.

William Kirby's angst escalated. These smug bastards were making him out to be a prize mug and a fool, just as Zelia had done. His anger boiled over.

"No one could blame me!" Kirby shouted gruffly.
"For what?" Tim asked.
"Did you kill Zelia Dubois?" Grimslade asked at that crucial point.

William raised his head indignantly and replied quietly.

"I throttled the lying bitch. But I didn't mean to kill her."
"Yet you ended her life whether you meant to or not." Grimslade said.
"She had it coming. You've both agreed she did."

Neither Grimslade nor Tim Fun replied. Kirby was charged, handcuffed and taken into Queensland Corrective Services custody.

Chapter 31

STILL SHINING

After Death

Dulcy Vestige breathed a sigh of relief hearing William Kirby's confession. Her husband was off the hook for Zelia's death, yet he remained unforgiven for his years of deception.

Duty bound, Dulcy returned to the Northern Territory. She continued boarding with Damien Cresswick while awaiting transfer back to Queensland.

David Dubois did not return to Robertson Barracks. Granted compassionate leave from the army, David gained legal custody of Davy after presenting DNA proof of his paternity.

Rather than sell the beach house, David occupied it with his son. Little Davy never asked why Will disappeared. He seemed untroubled by that change, taking it in his stride. He welcomed the fact that David Dubois replaced Will as man of the house. The child's only anxiety had been that this might not last, since nothing had been forever in his short life.

"Aunty Gong, is he really my proper Daddy?"

"Yes Davy. He really is. He is your proper father. You could call him Daddy if you wanted to."

"He likes my army truck." Davy repeated his positive impression.

"That's because your father was a soldier in the army, Davy. But he wants to take care of you, so the army said he can leave to do that."

On the next supervised visit, David hugged his son for the first time.

"Aunty Gong says I can call you Daddy."

"I'd like that very much."

"Dominic says Dad is better than Daddy for a soldier."

"I don't mind, Dad or Daddy. Both are good. You're my little soldier Davy."

Davy often spoke of his best friend, Dominic Chiron. The adults knew the boy held Dominic's opinion in high regard. Adamant it would benefit Davy to return to the home he knew and attend school with his same mates; Dr. Ghaith Ong facilitated the connection between father and son.

In first grade at the local primary school, Davy Dubois' best friend heard the gossip doing the rounds at the surf club frequented by his mother, Chantel. Dominic knew Davy's Mum had died and Davy got to go to her funeral. Dominic envied him for that until reminded it cost him by losing his mother.

"Oh yeah. Now he can't do that again no more." Dominic replied philosophically.

" Nevermind. You've always got my funeral to look forward to." Chantel said.

"Can I bring Davy too?"

"We'll see."

The next time Dominic saw Davy, he remarked in conversation that it must be a bummer losing your Mum.

"It's a bummer alright." Davy replied.
"I found a Christmas beetle. Do you want to see her?"
"Yep."

Dominic delved into his pocket and produced a matchbox, opening it carefully to reveal an iridescent insect, shimmering gold and green and with tiny black spots. Impressed by the sight, Davy said:

"Wow. She's a beauty."
"She's got freckles like you." Dominic pointed out.

He carefully closed the box and put it back in his pocket.

"Will she get out?" Davy asked.
"Nope. She's dead, but she's still shining, hey."

The children didn't dwell on it for long. For some reason Davy felt encouraged by that Christmas beetle, still shining after death.

Dr. Ong's joint counseling of father and son continued as necessary. Pleased with progress, sessions became fewer and less frequent.

Chapter 32

POPPY GOES TO PRISON

Visiting

Sentenced to ten years jail for manslaughter, William Kirby avoided the more serious charge of murder. Deemed to have acted under extreme provocation, in an instance of diminished responsibility, he got off lightly for causing the young mother's death.

During Kirby's incarceration, the naive young woman he'd misled at work with fake amorous overtures, made it her mission to see William again. Unsure how to apply for a prison visit, Poppy Papadopoulas, sought advice from a family friend in the legal field, Thaddeus Maekris.

Thaddeus and Poppy had attended the same large Greek family gatherings since childhood but hadn't spent any time together. As a tall gawky boy, ridiculously full of his own importance, young Thaddeus ignored sooky little kids like Poppy.

Poppy shyly fronted the legal office front desk. The receptionist, heavy with child, struggled to stand.

"I'll show you in." she said.

"Oh no. I can see you are near due so please don't get up. I can knock on Thaddeus's door myself."

"Thank you dear. I owe it to the firm to come in when they're busy. By rights I should be at home with my feet up. I'll let Mr. Maekris know you've arrived and buzz you in."

Poppy knocked politely, before timidly opening Thaddeus's office door.

"Come in Poppy. You're looking well. What can I do for you?"

"Thank you Mr. Maekris...um Thaddeus." Poppy blushed. "This is awkward, but I want your advice on how I might gain permission to visit a prisoner."

"Goodness. Anyone I know?"

"His name is William Kirby."

"Not the man convicted over that domestic violence death?"

Thaddeus declined to mention he had known the victim well. He had no wish to recount his brief fling with Zelia.

"Yes. He is that William Kirby. But, I feel desperately sorry for him."

"But Poppy...alright. Can you enlighten me more? How do you know of him?"

"We both worked at the same place and Will used to be my boyfriend, at least until he met that woman."

"That woman whose life he took." Thaddeus made his concerns clear.

"I know how it looked. But Will never showed any aggression towards me."

Thaddeus felt Poppy should not make that visit, yet aware she could easily obtain permission he reluctantly gave her standard advice.

"Prisoners are allowed various visits from friends or family. I can tell you the requirements and help fill out the forms for submission, if necessary."

"I feel you are against me doing this. But I thank you for your help Thaddeus."

"You're welcome Poppy. But you are correct, I would not like to see a sweet young woman such as yourself wasted on an unworthy man. And I don't say that lightly."

Miffed by Thaddeus's comment, but determined to go her own way, Poppy stood up to leave.

"I will see your receptionist about settling my account."

"Please don't be offended by my concerns, Poppy. May I take you to lunch to make it up to you?"

"Perhaps some other time, thanks Thaddeus. I have used up my lunch hour for this visit, and now I must to get back to work."

Thaddeus attended the evening roundup meeting with his father.

"I see you had an appointment with Miss Poppy Papadopoulas today."

"Yes father. Poppy only wanted basic advice. I did not charge any fee."

"Hmmm. I have given much thought to your *hypothetical* question on whether a divorced woman would be considered a suitable choice for someone in this firm."

Thaddeus realised his father knew the question had been personal.

"I admit to having someone in mind for myself, but she has not sought a divorce. Yet."

"Thaddeus, I find it difficult to comprehend how a handsome, well mannered, successful law-abiding young man as yourself, is not inundated with eminently suitable females chasing after you. Surely you would have your pick of many."

"I also find it difficult to comprehend, father."

"Do you make any effort?"

"Yes. Only this morning I asked Poppy Papadopoulas to lunch but she had to get back to work."

"Hmmm. Miss Papadopoulas would be ideal for you Thaddeus. Do you find her attractive?"

"I suppose she is quite pretty."

Thaddeus only asked Poppy to lunch to make up for offending her. Privately, he rated his father's choice as a bland alternative to Dulcy Vestige. Poppy lacked the exciting verve and athleticism he admired in the policewoman.

"So. Will you pursue the possibility with Miss Papadopoulas?"

"Her heart is set on someone else, father. Also, I don't think Poppy likes me in that way. Story of my life."

Back at work, with her matronly boss still out to lunch, Poppy accessed William Kirby's confidential employment file to check on his birth date. She had finished knitting his jumper and decided it would be a nice birthday gift.

The record of entries in William's file were embellished with frequent red ticks inside heart shapes, which mystified Poppy. She could not know those marks represented days he supplied extra services to their lady boss, usually performed across the sturdy office desk, or between the filing cabinets where Poppy now stood. About to close the file, Poppy turned around to find her irate employer tapping a foot and glaring in anger.

"What the hell are you doing in my private office Poppy?"

"Sorry. I just wanted to check William's birthday because I have a gift for him."

William had sworn his interest in Poppy to be only a smoke screen. Yet the girl's doe-eyed simpering over the macho mechanic, had been a constant irritation. The older woman supposed her personal icons commemorating special toyboy events would be blatantly clear to almost anybody. A goody-goody like the snooping office girl might miss the gist, but it was reason enough to get rid of her.

"You're fired Poppy. Get out. And don't come back."

"What? Why?" Poppy exclaimed, shocked.

"I could call it industrial espionage." her irate boss spat.

Poppy had no idea if taking a sneak peek at William's file amounted to industrial espionage. Scared witless, she immediately sought Thaddeus Maekris' advice.

Poppy entered the business foyer only to find the front desk unattended, and Thaddeus' office door ajar.

"Please take a seat." he called out from within. "I'll be with you in a minute."

"It's only me again. Poppy."

"Ah. Poppy come in. As you can see, I'm in a tizz this afternoon. Mrs. Frogmorton had an episode with her tadpole."

"Oh, a problem with her pregnancy?"

"Not guilty." Thaddeus said.

"Pardon?"

"Um. Sorry. Ignore that. It's just one of my inane automatic responses."

"Oh. Well, I hope the lady and her baby are alright."

"Her dam broke during a loo break. Her husband came in and drove her to hospital. Their tadpole is a healthy girl by the way. Apparently all well. What a day! Anyway, have you reconsidered anything Poppy?"

Poppy sat down and inhaled a shaky breath.

"I just got fired from my job because I looked up William Kirby's file. I only wanted to check his birthday because I have a gift for him. But the boss says it's industrial espionage."

"Did you see anything that could be construed as such?"

"No. I only took a quick peek anyway. There were notations made on some days but I don't know what they meant."

"What sort of notations?"

"Red hearts with ticks."

"Hmmm. Describe your boss."

"She's a tough woman. No one ever talks back if they want to stay employed."

"Do you know her age?"

"I remember when she turned sixty, but she doesn't look that old. Her husband gave her a fancy new car with 60 in the number plate and she wasn't pleased about everyone knowing her age."

"I see." Thaddeus felt sure he did indeed see what red hearts and ticks on Kirby's file probably signified. "You could have a case for unfair dismissal Poppy."

As they spoke the phone in reception rang repeatedly. Poppy knew by the several lights on Thaddeus desk console, there were multiple incoming calls. She couldn't abide an unanswered phone so dared to make an offer:

"I could stand in if you like Thaddeus. I know how to work that phone system."

"Would you Poppy? I'd be most thankful."

Poppy manned the reception desk for the rest of the day. She fielded calls, handled appointments and had no problem managing Eftpos payments. Thaddeus considered her ability a godsend, plus she was in need of a job.

"Poppy. This receptionist position is yours if you want it."

"What about Mrs. Frogmorton?"

"Froggy gave notice a while ago and was only filling in until I found someone as efficient as she. You fill the bill admirably. You've been amazing today." Thaddeus smiled, genuinely grateful.

"Goodness. Thank you so much Thaddeus. I don't think I'll bother with that other workplace problem now."

"Perhaps I will just send a letter to your past employer Poppy. I believe you are owed compensation."

"I will trust your advice on that." Poppy smiled.

That evening, Thaddeus attended the usual summary meeting with his father.

"I hired a replacement for Mrs. Frogmorton this morning."

"Well done. Big shoes to fill but I hope the new one is at least half as good."

"She stood in all morning and managed everything magnificently. I was so impressed, I hired her on the spot."

"Does this paragon have a name?"

"You already know her. Poppy Papadopoulas."

"Hmmm. That is pleasing news son, however, you know our constitution strictly forbids fraternisation with the staff."

"I am aware of that father."

"As CEO, I will waive that rule in this instance."

"Thank you father. But as I have mentioned, Miss Papadopoulas does have her heart set on another."

Within the week, the matronly workshop employer quaked on receiving a registered letter from the prominent law firm. The blistering contents delivered innuendos and threats to prosecute for unfair dismissal on behalf of their client. With no desire for publicity, a substantial settlement was paid to Miss Poppy Papadopoulas out of court.

In pursuit of a romantic experience, Poppy visited William Kirby in prison. She'd had her hair salon styled the day before and wore her prettiest frock.

"Thank you for coming Poppy. On a Sunday too." William said.
"I skipped church for once, because I had to see you Will. I am so sorry for what happened to put you in here."
"So am I Poppy. Zelia was so beautiful. I wish I'd done what she wanted and got a home loan to buy that beach house. She spun a lot of lies to me but I shouldn't have lost my temper. I didn't mean to kill her."
"Of course you didn't mean it, Will."
"You know, the detectives agreed she deserved it." William said.
"No! Did they say so?"
"They said she played me for a fool, and I got royally shafted."
"Perhaps they took a dim view of her lying and leading you on?"
"They did. But in a way, that was part of Zelia's attraction. She was always feisty and forward. I loved all her tattoos and piercings. She really turned me on."
"Is that so." Poppy said shortly.

Poppy had gone to great lengths to acquire permission to visit William in prison, and to look her best. She didn't appreciate him talking about Zelia so much. Or at all. Due to her visit, William knew he still had the young girl enthralled.

"You look very pretty Poppy. Is that a new dress?"
"This old thing? Well it is cool and comfortable so I threw it on."
"I wish we'd had more time together Poppy. But you realise how I stupidly got sucked in by Zelia."
"Perhaps you were bewitched, Will."
"I was bewitched. You are very understanding Poppy."
"Thank you Will. I can see it from your point of view. There are two sides to every story. I think perhaps you were led up the garden path?"

"Exactly. I could kick myself for not choosing a nice girl like yourself."

"Well. You won't be in here forever, Will."

Poppy could hardly breathe. Will wished he'd chosen her. This was going far better than she dared hope.

"I hope you will keep visiting me Poppy."

"Of course. If you want me to. Look Will, I don't want to give you false hopes, but I have a very clever legal friend who might act on your behalf to acquire early parole."

William realised Poppy could be useful in many ways. Her dreamy eyed expression encouraged him to think she'd be easily manipulated.

"I say Poppy, we might be allowed conjugal visits. How about it?"

"Oh Will. Really? You would marry me? Goodness. I'm not sure how that can be achieved but I will certainly ask advice of my legal friend tomorrow. I didn't expect this to happen on my first visit to you, but I feel ever so excited."

William Kirby definitely hadn't intended to propose marriage. But what the hell. If he got what he wanted, it needn't be permanent.

"It can be very exciting Poppy. So, how do you feel about getting a few tattoos and piercings? I especially loved the clit ring Zelia had. Maybe you could get the same? For me? And maybe have my name inked somewhere really naughty too? Zelia had my name on her left butt cheek. I used to joke about who owned the other side." he laughed.

Confronted with William's great expectations, Poppy's dream plummeted to despair. She felt the carpet had been pulled out from under her feet. Disappointed and appalled on many levels, the girl somehow managed a sarcastic reply:

"Would you like me to get some nipple rings as well? Maybe a big one for my nose too?"

"That'd be fantastic Poppy. Wow! I don't know why, but I always thought you were kind of dull. Hey, don't look like that. I meant dull in a good way. Like...um...anyway not in a bad way. Good luck with your legal eagle tomorrow. And, next time you visit, could you bring me some of that nice flaky cake stuff you make?"

That Sunday night, Poppy unraveled the jumper she'd knitted for William's birthday. She found the exercise liberating. The wool would be remade into something else, perhaps a blanket for the cat basket. Monday morning, Poppy attended her new position in Thaddeus's office. She'd been crying all night. He couldn't miss her tear stained face.

" Are you Okay Poppy?"

"I visited William Kirby in prison yesterday."

"Ah. I guess that would be upsetting."

"Upsetting? He offered to marry me so we could have conjugal visits."

"Goodness. I hope you aren't...I mean...so are you going to do it?"

"Well Thaddeus. What do you think of his proposal depending on me getting a few tattoos in naughty places and a ring pierced through my clit like Zelia had?"

"What? She didn't..." *oops* he almost blabbed to having sex with Zelia himself; by saying she didn't have it when he bonked her.

"Yes, it shocked me as well, Thaddeus. But, according to Will, Zelia had one of those obscene things and it turned him on no end."

Thaddeus wished he'd been a fly on the wall for that conversation. He dearly wanted to hear Poppy's reaction.

"I can't imagine what you would have said to him after that awful demand."

"I said how about I get my nipples pierced and a big ring for my nose. And William thought I meant it! Seriously! Really Thaddeus, can you imagine me with a clit ring?"

Thaddeus even had trouble digesting that the words *clit ring* fell so easily from the sweet rosebud lips of the demure Poppy. His imagination worked overtime. His pretty employee prattled on:

"I have made baklava for our morning tea, I hope you like it Thaddeus."

"I do. Very much. That slice is my absolute all-time favourite cake. Thank you Poppy."

That night, Thaddeus could think of nothing else but Poppy mentioning her private body part and his favourite traditional Greek slice in almost the same breath. He tossed and turned with fervent dreams. The tall guy managed to wait a frustrated few days before asking Poppy out on a date. He was soon to discover his new receptionist possessed unexpected hidden depths of passion. They began to make use of the classic chaise lounge in his office during lunch hours. Following a remarkably short engagement, they married. Over the years, Poppy and Thaddeus enlarged the Maekris family by half a dozen natural increases.

Thaddeus Maekris only kept one well guarded secret from his beloved wife. Poppy would never learn he'd known Zelia in the biblical sense. If anyone let on, he'd be prepared to deny everything and sue the snitch.

William Kirby might have spent the next ten years contemplating where he'd gone wrong with silly little Poppy Papadopoulas, but he soon forgot her.

Chapter 33

THE SLEEPOVER

Game On

More than another year passed before Dougall Grimslade welcomed Dulcy Vestige back to Queensland. His chief investigative squad regrouped as a formidable force to be reckoned with. The team of three included the clever and mild-mannered Tim Fun, who added a different flavour to the mix.

Avoiding any more unpleasantness, Dulcy had no intention of contacting her estranged husband again. She had not proceeded with divorce for no other reason than she couldn't be bothered putting herself out over David anymore.

Needing to rejuvenate, Dulcy began swimming in the sea before work, when she'd meet up with Dougall's daughter Isla. One Saturday morning, by chance David Dubois and his son were on the beach.

"Hey. Isn't that David?" Isla pointed him out.

"Bugger! He's the last person I wanted to run into." Dulcy swore.

"He's seen you now. Tough it out. You'll be okay Dulcy." Isla replied.

"Dulcy!" David exclaimed in delight, running to her. "How good to see you."

David admired his wife's well-rounded figure in her clingy wet swimsuit. Dulcy set eyes on David's cute red-haired son in person for the first time. There could be no mistaking paternity, though Davy's face had a sprinkling of freckles, a legacy from Zelia. Having mixed feelings, Dulcy didn't know how to react. Isla walked up the beach and stepped under the outdoor shower, to give them privacy.

"This is Davy. He is my son." David proudly introduced the boy.
"I can see he is. Hello Davy."

Davy said hi politely, then ran off to play with some other children on the beach. David remarked on his boy's quick departure:

"You'd think he'd see enough of that bunch of imps at school."
"So you have custody? That's good for you, and the boy."
"I take it you're back with Grimslade."
"I am back working in my old job. Yes."

David looked out to sea, an assortment of emotions flitted across his handsome features.

"Can we talk seriously Dulcy?"
"What is there to say David? I'm glad it worked out for you."
"It can work out for all of us."
"How."
"We could be a family. I'm still your husband. Before you say it, I know that isn't necessarily set in stone, but you're still mine. Dulcy, I love you. I want you back."

Dulcy got that he asked her to be a surrogate mother to his son in that deal.

"Sorry David. I can't." she replied cautiously.
"Davy is a good kid. No trouble."
"I am sure he is. You can be proud of your son. It's not about him though."

"What? Are you still miffed about me and Zelia? You must know she got murdered by another guy she tricked."

"William Kirby got off on manslaughter. Not murder." Dulcy corrected.

"So you followed the case. Of course you did. You've always been in with bloody old Grimslade."

David's retort held bitterness. Up until lately, David's jealousy always left Dulcy feeling at fault. Now, since she'd given up on their marriage, Dulcy's unspoken attraction to Dougall felt guilt free. At least she could grant David a concession.

"I more than followed the case, I watched the interviews. By the way, I never believed you killed her. I stuck up for you."

"Did you? I very appreciate that Dulcy. Surely it means you still have strong feelings for me. Doesn't it?"

"I had some very strong feelings at the time. I heard you hoped I appreciated all you were doing for MY sake."

"I did hope that. Obviously, we share loyalty to each other. We could make it work Dulcy."

Dulcy assessed her true feelings as she regarded her husband. David's handsome face and beautiful fit toned body no longer did anything for her. All she could see were his flaws and all she could feel amounted to disappointment in him.

"No. Sorry. I couldn't make it work. Not after your years of deception. Your love child never had anything to do with me except to keep me in the dark. Despite what you've accused me of in the past, I don't resent you for having your son, David."

"Do you resent Davy because of his mother?"

"Why on earth would I hold any resentment towards your Davy? He seems a nice boy. As I've said, it's not about the child."

"But you won't even give him a chance." David persisted.

David's refusal to see her side, exasperated Dulcy.

"Are you listening to what I am saying? I could never trust you again David. Simply put, you are not who I thought you were. Furthermore, I did not appreciate being made a factor in Zelia's death either."

"What? A factor? How did you arrive at that daft idea?"

"Your statement David. Your decision to sell the house for MY sake."

"It was for your sake Dulcy. I was doing it so you'd see I cut ties with Zelia."

"Another mistake, David."

"I didn't know it would get her killed."

"I meant another mistake thinking selling the house would make any difference to me or change my perceptions."

Isla toweled off, watching the argument intensify between the estranged couple. Never a wilting violet herself, Isla called out:

"You alright Dulcy?"

"Yes *I* am." Dulcy stressed the 'I' as a parting barb to David.

After exchanging words on the beach, David sadly watched his wife walk away, and felt bereft that Zelia's death, albeit not of his doing, had been for nothing.

Another onlooker, Chantel Chiron, watched the mini drama, less sadly, from outside the surf club. Saturdays, Chantel volunteered at the surf club canteen. Having finished the morning set up, she took a coffee break, sitting outdoors in the fresh sea air.

From under the Pandanus trees, Chantel observed the confrontation. She could tell David begged and Dulcy gave him the flick. She knew very well who they were, and much about their situation from local gossip. Chantel smiled thinking - *looks like trouble in Paradise.*

Chantel called her son back from playing with other kids on the beach.

"Dominic, would you like a glass of milk? Run and ask your friend Davy if he'd like one too."

Davy and Dominic sat drinking milk and enthusing over a new *Bob the Builder* video game, blissfully unaware of any developments with the grownups.

"Missus Chiron, can Dominic come over to see my new video game?"

"That would be very nice Davy. Maybe he could have a sleepover at your house tonight. But only if your dad says yes."

"Wow. Thanks."

Young Davy raced back to his father, his school friend Dominic in tow. Chantel followed at a slower pace.

"Dad! Can Dominic have a sleepover at our house? I want to show him my new *Bob the Builder* game. Can he? Please."

"I guess so, if his mother says it's okay."

Chantel sauntered over and greeted David. He never forgot the sultry young mother giving him the come-on at that wedding breakfast in the surf club.

"Chantel isn't it?"

"That's me."

"Do we agree to a sleepover?" David asked.

"I'd love a sleepover." Chantel replied with an alluring come-hither grin.

David did not miss the blatant proposition in her message.

"Cat got your tongue?" Chantel laughed.

David stuttered:

"I..I...I'll order pizzas."

"Yummy."

David could not believe his good fortune. The yummy mummy appeared just when he needed her most. Chantel confirmed she'd be coming for the sleepover by saying what she'd contribute.

"I'll bring popsicles. I like something to suck on for afters."
"I could really go a popsicle." David said, without meaning a popsicle.

Chantel knew what he meant. She could really go one herself.

"My Dad says yes and we're getting pizza and popsicles." Davy yelled.
"My Mum says yes too." Dominic air-punched in triumph.

The boys ran around whooping happily. Saturday night didn't get much better than *Bob the Builder*, pizza and ice lollies.

"Tonight's the night then." Chantel winked.
"Game on." David replied.

David couldn't wait. He temporarily shelved missing his prickly wife in anticipation of the night ahead.

An immediate outcome ensued from changes at the beach house. Tim Fun approached the new landlord, David Dubois, and began renting the flat from him. Newly painted and with a nice little kitchenette installed, the flat was even better than when Tim first viewed it with the capable handyman, William Kirby.

Chapter 34

FOOD FOR THOUGHT

The Matchmaker

The Saturday morning after bandying words with David on the beach, Dulcy went back to Isla's place for lunch.

"Aiden won't be home until tonight, so I'm just having a cheese sandwich and a cup of tea. I don't want to eat alone, so you must come up."

"I could murder a cup of tea." Dulcy replied thankfully.

Dulcy picked up bananas and grapes from a weekend fruit stall near the beach.

"I got green grapes and black muscatels. I didn't know what you prefer, Isla."

"I love both. Grapes still seem exotic to me. You know, I never tasted a grape or a fresh pear until I left the orphanage." Isla replied conversationally.

"You're kidding? But you had fruit didn't you?"

"Oh sure. I didn't go without healthy food. But fruit meant apples usually, and sometimes bananas or oranges. Apart from tinned, that is."

Reminded of Isla's institutionalised upbringing, Dulcy ventured to say:

"I'm so happy you and the Grimslades found each other."

"Thanks Dulcy. I can't believe it's nearly two years since we lost my Mum."

Isla grieved for her lost birth mother, but had never known Bella Grimslade in the maternal role, as they'd not met until Isla married. They'd hit it off more as girlfriends than mother and daughter, and got along famously from the start.

During their first meeting on the beach, Isla and Bella walked down to the shore, leaving their husbands, Aiden and Dougall, sitting under the beach umbrella.

For more reasons than one, Isla had disliked DI Dougall Grimslade. She'd thought him beyond rude, incensed at the way he stared her down when they first came face to face. Mortified by the knowledge he must have viewed her in compromising situations, did not endear the man to her either.

Dougall knew Isla scorned him. He'd said as much to Bella after discovering Isla to be their long-lost offspring. During the first meeting of parents and daughter, Bella defended Dougall for nailing her when she'd been only fourteen years old.

"If anyone needs to be blamed, that would be me." Bella said.

"But you were so young!" Isla argued.

"I passed for at least seventeen and he didn't know my age. I chased him and set him up. Your see, I planned to boogie with Doogie because he was so dead gorgeous, good-looking and famous."

"Famous! You're kidding. Was he?"

"Nope. Only in my silly teeny bopper head because he sang in a pop band."

"Goodness. I can't imagine that at all. Him singing? Was he talented?"

"Put it this way... lucky he had a day job."

Dougall possessed a pleasant singing voice, but mother and daughter bonded with a shared laugh at his expense. They walked back to the men, who guessed they were the topic of conversation. Isla remarked:

"Anyway, bet he was easy."

"He was." Bella winked.

"So was Aiden." Isla chortled.

Bella and Isla enjoyed a teasing laugh over how easily they'd seduced their men – *like candy from a baby* – their shared catchphrase.

The scandal of the young teenager putting it over her upright goody-goody father, rather appealed to the daughter. Suffice to say, the duplicated echo of her mother went more than skin deep for Isla.

Chatting over tea and sandwiches, Isla and Dulcy discussed ongoing issues that shaped their lives:

"Bella and you could have been taken for sisters." Dulcy replied.

"I know. Every second of our short time together had been happy. I can only imagine what it must be like for my Dad now."

"At least Dougall is kept busy with work and having a new recruit to train. I think that helps. He likes to teach."

"Oh yes. He calls it his Tim Fun Run." Isla laughed.

"Tim is lucky to have such a good mentor. I might add, Tim will soon be officially DC Anwei Timothy Funicular."

"Is that his proper name?"

"Yes, his file is tagged as F.A.T. For Funicular - Anwei Timothy. Before we met him, Dougall and I wondered if he'd be fat. However, he is anything but. And is adamant about being called Tim Fun."

"Maybe his name had been ridiculed before. Kids can be cruel. I copped it in the orphanage at times and got into strife for fighting back too."

"Your Dad says you were an unruly child, by all accounts."

"I was for sure. Aiden reckons that doesn't surprise him in the least." Dulcy nodded. It did not surprise her either.

"Dougall is very proud of you Isla. I'm glad you got past your negative feeling for him."

"You and Dad get along well. You've got that whodunit thing in common."

"True. I've benefited by his expertise, just as Tim has. Your Dad is a genius at getting to the crux. He doodles thought processes, impossible to decode. Just numbers, arrows, crosses and ticks with a cryptic word here and there."

"I feel guilty about disliking Dad, in the beginning. Until I found out he...um...anyway enough about me." Isla said. "We need to discuss your set-to with David this morning. That's more important right now."

Dulcy knew exactly what Isla almost blabbed. DI Dougall Grimslade had risked much to protect his only child. A certain yacht containing embarrassing evidence exploded into smithereens one dark night. It was no mystery to Dulcy 'whodunit' but she would never let on to anyone.

Isla and Dulcy veered their conversation onto the more recent showdown on the beach:

"He wants me to be in a cosy family of three. Me, him and the boy. I told him it would never work. It wasn't about the child by the way, but he took it to be."

"You stopped trusting David. That's the real reason isn't it." Isla guessed.

"He lost my trust. Also, his subterfuge struck me as cowardly. You see, I held him dear as my brave soldier."

"What if he'd owned up for putting Zelia up the duff from the start?"

"I don't know to be honest, Isla. Admit I'm rather strait-laced."

"Dad is the same. I guess that's another reason you two get along so well."

"Yes we do see eye to eye... You know, perhaps I shouldn't mention this, but David has always been crazy jealous of your Dad."

Isla found that interesting. She hadn't seen her father as a contender in that way.

"Crazy jealous? Why?"

"Because we worked closely together on cases. David riled up when I laughed during phone calls with Dougall. You see, your Dad resorts to black humour at times, but he can be very funny. I'm guilty of encouraging him by laughing."

"I know you and Dad have to deal with some horrible stuff and his off jokes are a coping strategy."

"Oh you get that. Thank goodness. A lot of people wouldn't. Including David."

It dawned on Isla that a certain magnetism existed between her Dad and Dulcy Vestige. Privately, she imagined they might even act on it, given time. If that ever came about, Isla would be glad, as her father's loneliness tore at her heart.

Dougall's daughter could never imagine her staid parent making a first move. Dulcy admitted to being conservative too. A gentle shove might be in order. They were both alone and her father widowed. Isla's previous form as a matchmaker came to the fore. She mused on the idea: *What harm could it do?*

Convinced Dulcy would never get back with David after the recent altercation on the beach, Isla worked on a strategy:

"Say Dulcy, could you drop a casserole off at Dad's place on your way?"

"Sure. I guess he'll be at home. There was nothing urgent at the office."

"He'll be at home for sure. Dad never goes out except for work. He mostly eats in from of TV and watches whodunits. It's a bit sad really." Isla said.

Dulcy shied off admitting she'd do the same.

"You're a good daughter, cooking for him."

"Actually, Aiden does most of the cooking, he's better at it than I am. But if I didn't send meals for Dad now and then, he'd live on unhealthy takeaways."

Dulcy identified, it's what she'd do. Swerving off the subject, she replied:

"You're so lucky. Have to love a man who cooks."
"I know. Aiden is a darling. I love being Mrs. Birdwhistle."

Isla wrapped a big casserole dish in a cotton tablecloth. The generous meal contained more than enough for two, and the schemer felt certain her Dad would invite Dulcy to share. Now all Isla had to do was explain to Aiden why she'd given their dinner away.

Since losing his wife, Dougall Grimslade spent much of his loneliest two years sitting outdoors in the evenings. During those hours, he scanned the sky for shooting stars, remembering fond notions Bella embraced.

To Dougall's pragmatic mind, shooting stars were meteors that burned up on entering Earth's atmosphere, trailing fiery tails of light. Bella preferred romantic legends and myths of blessed celestial messages sent from the spirit world. The lonely widower, however hard-headed, doted on seeing shooting stars, hoping in vain to experience some connection to Bella.

Dougall faced another desolate weekend, moping about aimlessly. Even a call to investigate some crime or other would have made a welcome diversion. Having no appetite for food, he avoided thinking about his supper. Instead, he'd sat outside watching the sun set, waiting for something interesting to come on TV. Dulcy couldn't knock on the door with her hands full carrying the big tureen, so she called out aloud.

"Knock knock. Are you there Dougall? It's only me."

Dougall's heart lifted on hearing his favourite colleague's familiar voice.

"Dulcy! Come in."

"Isla asked me to drop off this casserole on my way."

Dougall took the heavy bowl and placed it on the kitchen bench.

"Crikey. What's in this thing? Half a rhinoceros?"

He lifted the lid and looked to see what Isla had sent.

"Chicken and cashew nuts with button mushrooms. Mmmm. You have to stay and share this with me Dulcy."
"It does smell delicious."
"I insist."
"That would be really nice, thanks Dougall."

Lodging with Opal and Angus Bridcombe, mealtimes could be loud, chaotic and messy with their three boisterous young children. Only yesterday, Dulcy had to swipe scrambled egg out of her hair. The day before, it had been tomato sauce on her clean shirt.
After the upset of the morning, having crossed swords with her errant husband on the beach, a quiet meal with Dougall seemed just the ticket.

Chapter 35

YOU DON'T KNOW ME

Now You Do

Dulcy messaged Opal to say she wouldn't be back for tea. Her friend replied briefly with a thumbs-up emoji. Dougall put the food in the oven to reheat.

"There's a UK murder mystery coming on TV early."

"Wonderful. The Bridcombe children are often still up at 7.30, and they aren't allowed to view murder shows, so I'd miss that time slot at Opal's."

"How's it working out for you there?"

"Not too bad. It's only temporary until I got sorted. I've just been too busy or too lacking in motivation to find somewhere else. I feel a bit of a gooseberry at times, so I must pull myself together and make an effort."

Dougall considered what Dulcy might do, knowing her estranged husband had moved nearby.

"So... I know David has taken up residence in his beach house. Will you get back with him now?"

"Not bloody likely." Dulcy replied.

"Oh?"

Dulcy outlined how it went meeting David by chance, on the beach that morning.

"Sounds like you could use a stiff drink." Dougall reached for the Johnny Walker.
"Thanks anyway. Better not. I'm driving."
"Stay the night. I've got spare pyjamas. No problems."
"Really? That is kind of you, and I'd love a scotch. I'll message Opal again."

Hi again Opal, sorry won't be home tonight. Something came up.
Opal sent her return text: *Okay. Take care Dulcy. See you tomorrow then.* The flippant reply did not match what Opal said to her husband:

"Bloody hell Angus. I hope Dulcy isn't getting back with damn David."
"Why do you think she might do that?"
"Says she won't be home tonight."

Angus liked Dulcy but also liked having the privacy of their home to themselves.

"Woo hoo. Early to bed for us then."
"Seriously Angus! Is that all you ever think about?"
"Maybe Dulcy is thinking about it too. Maybe she misses David." Angus said.
"No way. She's smart enough to know he'd be just using her again."
"He's probably really missing Dulcy. She is his wife after all."
"And he needs a mother figure for the surprise kid he's sprung on her."

Opal could not imagine Dulcy swapping her career or knuckling under to play Mums and Dads with David's illegitimate son, but that could happen. Angus added a thought:

"Of course, she might resent the boy for being Zelia's child."

"Hmmm. I can't see it working out. I mean, Dulcy is good with our brats, but I reckon she's ever so glad when they go to bed."

"I'm ever so glad when our brats go to bed too." Angus grinned.

Opal let that comment pass, her mind on Dulcy's dilemma.

"Apparently David accused Dulcy of having no maternal instincts."

"That's a low blow. He compared her to Zelia by saying that." Angus replied.

"David Dubois is a low bastard, Angus. I've never liked him. God, I hope Dulcy doesn't end up going back with that cheat."

"She's a big girl and can make up her own mind. You wouldn't want your best friend to spend her life alone, would you?"

"Of course not. But I'd rather see her with any other single man apart from David Dubois."

"Even someone like old Grimslade? He's single."

"Dougall Grimslade isn't that old, and he actually has a certain rugged appeal."

"You'd do him would you? If you weren't extremely lucky enough to have me."

"Now there's a cosy thought I can amuse myself with." Opal teased.

Opal did consider Dougall to be ruggedly manly and rather handsome when he wasn't scowling, but Angus hooted at her assessment:

"Grimslade is rugged alright. He looks about twenty years older than Dulcy. Not that she's anyone's ideal candidate as a main squeeze."

"Hasn't stopped you ogling her big tits when she's walked around bra-less."

"What? I never have!" Angus fibbed.

"You almost salivate."

It hadn't proved easy living with another woman in the house, but Opal could not accuse her best friend of dressing seductively. Dulcy's usual leisure wear consisted of a big police club t-shirt and rather baggy old track pants.

"I think you're jealous." Angus smirked.
"Only of Dulcy's big tits."
"Ouch. That hurts. You're a vicious woman Opal."
"Vicious? I'll show you vicious white boy." she replied.
"Show no mercy." he laughed.
"You say that now Angus. Wait till you see what I have in store for you, and you'd better not wake the kids with your screams of agony."

Opal grabbed Angus by his shirtfront and pulled him in for a preliminary kiss before nipping him on his chin. Her hulking heavyweight policeman husband, descendant of Vikings, squealed:
"Eek."

Dougall Grimslade's lonely Saturday improved immensely having Dulcy turn up, out of the blue. Even better, Dulcy agreed to dinner, watching a UK murder mystery with him, and staying overnight so she could enjoy a drink.

"How do you like your dram Dulcy?"
"Preferably with rocks. If you've got some."
"I've got rocks. You can have first shower while I fix our drinks."

Dougall presented his guest with a neatly folded pair of men's brown plaid pyjamas and a fresh towel. The PJ top reached to Dulcy's thighs, and she had to pull the drawstring of the bottoms in by several inches. Dulcy reappeared in the roomy checkered outfit, the sleeves and legs turned up to fit. Dougall's mood had so lifted, he made a playful comment:

"Are you comfy in those? I worried they might be tight on you."
"Go soak your head Dougall. While you're in the bathroom I'll serve up the food, and turn the TV on."

Dougall worried Dulcy might turn more than the TV on. He'd chosen those plain pyjamas imagining she could not possibly look sexy in them. He'd been wrong. His lady colleague looked impossibly cute.

They settled in to eat in front of the television and watch the whodunit. Feet bare, Dulcy crossed her ankles on the ottoman. The glimpse of smooth skin engrossed Dougall. He tried hard to concentrate on the program.

Dulcy gauged murder mysteries on degree of difficulty in guessing the culprit. Narrowing it down to at least two obsessed her.

"Who's doing it for you Dougall?"
"Pardon?"
"Is the killer the creepy bell ringer or the femme fatale?"
"Huh? Um. Oh. My minds been on the enchantress." he replied truthfully.

The TV show murderer remained a mystery since a second episode only went to air the following week.

"Oh no. I hate when they do that. It's so frustrating." Dulcy exclaimed.

"How about a nightcap, just another wee dram to stave off frustration. I like to enjoy the fresh air out on the back verandah on these mild nights."
"Perfect."
"Why don't you choose some background music from my rather dated but wide collection."
"Alright. Hmm. I see you're into the golden oldies."

"You mightn't like older types."
"You don't know me."
"That's one of my all time favourites. I play it often."

Dougall referred to the song title *You Don't Know Me.* Dulcy meant it another way. She put the Ray Charles rendition on to repeat-play. Picking up a few bars of the lyrics, Dougall crooned the part about being just a friend. He often played those lines in his head since they resonated deeply within him. He'd not felt like breaking into song for a long time, but the present company raised his spirits.

"You have a beautiful soulful singing voice Dougall."
"Aw, thank you."

Dulcy relaxed to the music, enjoying the familiar and solid company of her most admired man, in such a beautiful setting. The elevated location spanned a view across treetops to the distant ocean, aglow under a full moon.

"The air out here is intoxicating," Dulcy sighed, accepting her drink, "part native bush scents and part sea salt."
"It's a good place to unwind." her host agreed.
"It's so peaceful."
"Compared to the busy Bridcombe household?"
"Well. Yes. It can be hectic at Opal's. Though I very appreciate them having me stay there. As I said, it's only temporary until I sort myself out."

Throughout the TV show, Dougall tossed over asking Dulcy to move into his home. He had plenty of space. It seemed only polite to suggest it.

"Dulcy, just a thought...you'd be welcome to lodge here. I mean, if you wanted somewhere quiet and handy to work."

Dulcy took so long answering, he began to think he'd been out of order. She replied only after giving the idea due consideration.

"It's very good of you to offer. Only... I envisage some tensions with that."
Dougall had some tensions already.
"Not with my daughter."
"No, not with Isla. I actually suspect she set us up to dine together tonight."
"Aha! Of course she did! I see that clearly now. Isla already has my freezer well stocked with home cooked single meals ready to nuke. There was no need to task you with delivering such an enormous casserole. She knew I'd ask you to share it with me."
"Cripes. Bet she gave us their own dinner! Poor Aiden might get beans on toast tonight."

They shared a guilty wince over enjoying Aiden's gourmet meal. Dougall pursued the topic of Dulcy moving in, with the idea her estranged husband figured in the mix:

"So...do you envisage tensions with David if you were to lodge here?"
"Too bad if it sticks in David's craw. I no longer give a toss what he thinks."

Dougall gave nothing away, yet his inner being performed a happy dance.

"So not Isla and not David."
"And not Opal either, though she'd love to run my entire life."

Dougall almost hit on the truth when he ventured a comment.

"Correct me if I'm wrong, Dulcy. You fear I'd want to take advantage...me being a man and you being a woman."
"You're wrong."

"You're not a woman?" he joked.
"I am definitely a woman. I'm glad if you noticed."
"I noticed." he gulped.

Aware her comment sounded loaded, Dulcy left it at that. To say more would be begging. Dulcy sipped her whiskey, eyeing him over the rim of her glass, saying nothing. Dougall's joking mood sobered.

"So... you DON T fear I'd want to take advantage?" he ventured.
"No. That is not what I fear."
"What then?"
"I fear you would NOT want to take advantage." Dulcy confessed.

Lyrics of the song playing in the background echoed Dougall's amazement. Stunned, he could hardly speak, his heart was beating so. Dulcy returned his gaze, evenly and honestly. Now she'd braved saying what she desperately wanted, there was no going back.

The detective's brain explored Dulcy's startling statement. If he heard correctly, she feared he would NOT want to take advantage. He knew it was very unlikely his level-headed colleague would embark on an ego trip or be fishing for assurances. He told himself not to jump to conclusions and searched for other shades of meaning apart from the obvious.

Dougall matched Dulcy's honesty with his own, supposing he could turn it into another lame joke if he had misread her intent. He dared to say:

"I'd milk it to the full, Dulcy."

Wow. Milk it to the full. So he does have rocks. Dulcy thought. She'd secretly yearned to be with this man for years, with no hope of having him, until now. Knowing it could happen soon, this very night, her inner heat built like molten lava. Dulcy strove to keep her voice cool.

"When could I move in?"

"Well...you're here now." he replied, reasonably. Hoping beyond hope.

"I am. That is true."

"So here we are then."

"I believe we have established that fact."

Accustomed to holding her feelings in check, Dulcy waited for the man to make a move. He didn't rush into it. She imagined DI Grimslade doodling a crime scene with crosses, ticks and cryptic words, like the method he habitually used working out complex crime events.

The couple faced each other, deliberating. Dougall did not want to make a fool of himself. He framed his leading question in a way that provided an escape route, in case he had misconstrued the situation.

"Could I alleviate your concerns?" he asked, politely.

"Yes please."

"Does that mean yes please to moving in?"

"It simply means yes please. Whether I move in or not, Dougall."

Surely she meant what he most wanted. He asked himself *what else could it mean?* No other answer came to mind. The man dredged up every ounce of logic he could muster to temper his wishful speculation.

Dulcy waited for her colleague's astute detective brain to analyse it - *Cripes he's solved murders quicker than this.* Yet, his poised stance emulated closing in for the kill on a suspect.

His suspect's face appeared even more beautiful in the moonlight. Her enigmatic smile portrayed some secret knowledge. Perhaps he might crack the mystery if he played this scene right.

Taking the crystal tumbler from her hand, Dougall carefully placed it beside his own on the wide verandah railing.

It had been a very long time since the lonely man practiced the delicate art of seduction. During his youth singing in a boy band, his finesse with girls had been likened to a bulldozer. Turned out it hadn't been a compliment. Who knew? At least he learnt charging in like a rabid bull might go wrong.

Stage fright had never bothered Dougall until now. Pressure impelled him to make a move or miss his chance. If these days a man still had to ask some sort of permission, he didn't know how to best go about it, or what to say.

Ray Charles sung *You Don't Know Me* in the background. The lyrics of longing to kiss helped the befuddled widower form a declaration:

"Dulcy, there's something you should know about me. I'm like it says in the song."

"You're just a friend?"

"I'd like to be more than just a friend. The longing part is me. I want what it says about longing. With you. Now."

Dulcy gave her hand to him. They laced fingers. Dougall pulled her closer and gently stroked her cheek. When she murmured her pleasure, he threw caution aside. DI Grimslade knew about clues.

Their lips met in a lingering kiss that filled their hearts with joy. Cradling a hand behind his head, Dulcy drew herself nearer and allowed his body to touch hers intimately.

When she stretched up on tiptoe to deepen the kiss, the over-sized men's pyjama bottoms slid down to the floor. Wrinkled in loose folds around her bare feet, she stepped out of the pants neatly without breaking that first long kiss.

The verse about walking away with the lucky guy always made Dougall feel like the one who watched her walk away. This time, he really, really needed to be the lucky guy.

On the brink of changing the nature of their relationship forever, Dougall hesitated. He was pretty sure the glib - *how about it* - used in his youth wouldn't sit well with Dulcy. She beat him to the draw anyway.

"I want more. I want you Dougall."

Her surrender inflamed him. In his mind, the slow tempo of the love song accelerated to a lively upbeat. In sudden hasty purpose, Dougall clutched Dulcy's hand and towed her further along the verandah to the open door of his bedroom.

Gaining the darkened bedroom, intense need replaced all semblance of romantic gestures. In a fever of arousal, Dougall ripped his shirt off over his head with one hand and began fumbling Dulcy's buttons undone with the other. The loose pyjama coat could have easily slipped over her head, but Dulcy relished having him undress her so frantically.

Finally the jacket fell away from Dulcy's smooth shoulders. Dougall ran his hands over his younger colleague's warm skin. He bent to kiss the side of her neck and felt the quickening pulse there with his lips. His deep growl as he kneaded her ample breasts, exhilarated Dulcy beyond measure.

"Definitely a woman." his voice roughened with desire.

The definite woman eased his shorts down over the impressive member that had nudged her impatiently during their first passionate kiss.

"Are you licensed to carry that weapon?"
"I'll be gentle." he lied.
"Don't be."

Sinking together onto the bed, Dougall thrilled to Dulcy's keen response. He explored her body further, running hands over her hips, puzzled to find her bare from the waist down.

"When did that happen?"
"My pants fell down as soon as you kissed me."
"Well, I'll be blowed. Then I've still got it."
"You never lost it."
Never lost it?

Dougall would muse over that particular comment later, but his most urgent priority possessed him.

He took Dulcy lustily, hoping she truly meant *don't be gentle*, since at that point he'd been incapable of any gentlemanly pretence.

The earth moved like never before for Dulcy. Having desired this man for so long, her planet shifted off its axis.

Dougall's exquisite pleasure multiplied for knowing without a doubt, he'd delivered the same result for Dulcy.

Chapter 36

SHOOTING STAR

Double Bluff

Niggling guilt for taking Dulcy in the same bedroom shared with Bella for twenty years, played on the widower's mind. Dougall prayed, if his late wife existed in some heavenly realm, she would wish for him to find happiness again.

Waking in the witching hours of that night, Dougall quietly eased from his bed to close the shutters against a chill mist seeping in from the sea. The starlit sky remained clear above a massive cloud shelf roiling in, darkening the ocean. For some moments, he stood mesmerised in awe of the natural spectacle.

About to return to bed, Dougall stopped in his tracks. The brightest shooting star he'd ever encountered, streaked across the heavens and shattered into a myriad of spangles. He had spent two years observing meteor displays, because Bella believed shooting stars represented divine messages and new beginnings. None compared to this phenomenal vision. He'd never seen any as dazzling.

Transfixed by the luminous spectacle, a magical balm of peace, as tangible as a physical caress, settled in the widower's heart. Somehow, he completely understood Bella blessed his union with Dulcy. Never again would he question romantic notions of myths and legends of yore. Hand on his heart and his head in the clouds, Dougall returned to bed.

Dougall snuggled into Dulcy's warmth and wrapped an arm tightly around her, wholeheartedly claiming his new woman. He kissed the back of her neck.

"I never want to let you go Dulcy." he whispered.

"Mmm that is so nice." she murmured sleepily, "but I'm sorry to say, you just might have to."

Removing his hand from her breast and his arm from her body, Dulcy swung her legs over the side of the bed. Dougall fell to earth with a rude jolt. She was going! He could not believe his newfound lover did not want to stay with him.

"No way! Now just look here, Dulcy, and hear me out. I could not care less if you are still married. I don't even want to know if you are. How can you leave me after tonight? Our connection is so special. You know it is. Tonight has been amazing. I reckon I did alright. Unless I'm a complete idiot, I think you thoroughly enjoyed a skirmish with me. As much as I did with you."

Skirmish?

"Furthermore Dulcy, I think I'm in love with you. No. I not only think it. I know for sure. I am in love with you. Can you come up with even one good reason why you're going?"

"Yes, and I only have the one."

"I'm listening. What is it then?"

"I have to pee." she replied, matter-of-factly.

In the dark, he could not see the broad grin on her face, as she wandered towards the bathroom. Dulcy managed to stem an urge to laugh out loud, which would have been too unkind.

Dougall's outburst surprised her. Perhaps only he could be so objective as to mix skirmish and love together. It struck her as strange he imagined she considered leaving. *Wait.* Dulcy cautioned herself. She detected a ruse.

His little speech could be a spot check to see if she recognised some premise. *Aha.* He tested if she held some unproven preconceived ideas. She had no idea what those ideas could be. But the dreaded *'leaping to unverified assumptions'* lecture had always been his strictest lesson. The place and timing almost put her off. *Nice try Dougall you crafty fox.*

At least her reply called his bluff since she really did need to pee. Dulcy congratulated herself on winning that round although some show of after-sex romance instead of talking shop would have been nice. Dulcy sighed *oh well can't have everything.*

Dougall's face blushed scarlet learning Dulcy only needed a loo break. He'd spent much of his career lecturing others about verifying facts rather than jumping to conclusions. Yet he not only committed the ultimate amateur mistake himself, he bloody did it with his star protégé.

The embarrassed man thought: *Even worse, she will think I'm ridiculously needy for going on and on like that. I am a complete and utter idiot.* He'd gone and done it now and kicked himself. The blunder had made his throat go parched as well. When Dulcy re-entered the bedroom, Dougall aimed to minimise his lapse of judgement and put the situation back on an even keel.

"While you're up, could I trouble you to bring me a drink of water?" he asked.
"Of course. No trouble at all." she replied politely.
"Thank you."
"Not at all. And by the way Dougall, I'm in love with you too."

That statement delighted DI Grimslade. He replied with his usual moderated response when agreeing on a case particular with his younger colleague.

"Good. Good. Very good Dulcy. We're on the same page then."

Alert to another trick question, Dulcy parsed Dougall's request for a drink. She must not assume anything. He'd not specified any particular vessel or type of water.

"Glass or cup? Tap water or cold? I know you have both plain and sparkling bottled water in the fridge. Or do you prefer warm water with or without a splash of lemon?"
"I'm dying of thirst here Dulcy."

His past pupil seemed to be particularly pedantic. Serve her right if he changed his mind and demanded something completely different and more trouble.

"You know, it's almost dawn. I think I'd really rather have a nice cup of tea."
"Billy, Earl Grey, English Breakfast or herbal?"
"Earl Grey, no sugar, exactly two drops of milk. No more no less. Full cream. Thanks."

Dulcy returned from the kitchen with two cups of tea on a small round tin tray.

"I chose china cups and saucers Dougall. Only a Philistine would serve best Earl Grey in earthenware mugs."
"Well done Dulcy." he approved.

So, it had been a test. Dulcy commended herself once more for picking up on Dougall's lurk. He chose a strange time and place to impose it, obviously a canny ploy to catch her off guard.

Dougall took the tea tray from her and placed it on his lap.

Modestly covered with a sheet, the couple sat up in bed, sipping their brews in the pale light of dawn, thinking their separate thoughts. To justify his ridiculous tirade earlier, the man spoke first:

"Sometimes we can over think it." he began.

"It's an occupational hazard," she agreed, "but I tried to cover every possibility. I only flew by the seat of my pants with the cups and saucers, because of your excellent brand of Earl Grey."

"Oh yes, your major production over my drink of water. A sneaking doubt has crept in that you may have been pulling my leg."

"When I pull any of your appendages, Dougall, it will be well and truly pulled to perfection, leaving you in no doubt at all."

Dulcy's risqué reply triggered an unbidden reaction. The tin tray bucked on Dougall's lap, rattling the fine bone china saucers and silver teaspoons.

"Ooh. That piqued your interest." Dulcy giggled.

He counter-attacked: "You are a brazen hussy Dulcy."

Dulcy rescued the tray and said: "I'm ever so glad it's Sunday. I hope Tim Fun deals with any other police issues that pop up. I've got this one covered."

"Blimey. I rather like your brazen side." Dougall grinned.

Over a late breakfast, the couple discussed their newfound level of unity as they would a crime scene.

"You called me brazen, Dougall. I do feel terribly brazen, daring to seduce you, at long last."

"At long last?"

"I've wanted you for an indecently long time, Dougall."

"For an indecently long time or indecently for a long time?"

"Both."

"Okay. Both is good. Except...I seduced you Dulcy."

"Nope. I lured you in. Otherwise you'd never have made a move."

"I plied you with alcohol."

"I allowed it."

"I invited you to move in here with me."

"I accepted."

"No you did not. When I asked if I could alleviate your concerns, I can absolutely quote you as saying: *yes please whether I move in or not*. That statement is burnt into my memory for evermore."

"I hope it's a fond memory."

"Earth moving. And I don't mean like with a bulldozer."

"You have such a way with words Dougall."

"I'm not just a pretty face." he replied.

"Do you still want me to move in?"

"More than anything in the world Dulcy."

That Sunday evening, Dulcy returned to the Opal's home to collect her few belongings. It did not take long, everything fitted back into her two suitcases. She gave thank you gifts of sweets and movie dvds to the Bridcombe family.

"I can never thank you two enough for putting up with me these past weeks."

"So you've found somewhere else?" Opal replied cautiously.

"I know what you're worried about. Just get it off your chest, Opal."

"Okay. David doesn't deserve your loyalty in my opinion. Just saying."

Opal had her hands on her hips, prepared to argue. Trying to lighten the atmosphere, Angus weighed in:

"Opal would rather see you with anyone else, even old Grimslade."
"That is provident then." Dulcy smiled.
"How so? No! Don't tell me. You're moving in with Grimslade?"
"Yes I am. Dougall asked if I'd like to share his house. It seemed logical since we work together and he has plenty of room."
"Well, I think you'd be safe with him." Opal replied.
"Do you see it as permanent?" Angus asked.
"Yes again. I don't see why not." Dulcy smiled.

Opal explored the idea, searching for some downside she could pick on.

"Are you going to be happy there? I mean you see each other all the time at work. It might be sort of like taking your work home with you."
"I've always done so anyway Opal. Dougall and I speak on the phone nearly every night when we're on a case. It's not like the crime dramas can be switched off after hours."
"Really? You spoke on the phone every night? How did David take that?" Angus asked.
"It brought out a jealous streak in him. He reckoned I had thing for Dougall."
"As if. How ridiculous." Opal retorted. "But Dulcy...what if Grimslade starts to feel his Uncle Toby's? I mean with you walking about his house...without a...I mean, like, dressed casually."

Opal meant bra-less. Angus knew it. His gaze flitted over Dulcy's full figure, thinking: *Grimslade would have to be nuts if he didn't try.* Too late, Angus saw eagle-eyed Opal clocked his ogling. He repeated yesterdays response to his wife's scowl:

"Eek."

Dulcy laughed: "Eek Angus? I'm not afraid of Dougall you know."

That was good for another lecture from Opal: "Seriously Dulcy. Of course you're not afraid of him. But what if he does try it on? I mean living in the same house every night is different to speaking on the phone."

"Then I will try to be gentle with him."

Dulcy's reply came with a cheeky wink to Angus. He blushed scarlet thinking Opal must disclose some very personal details in girl talk with her best friend. Otherwise the lady sleuth had not missed much. Not knowing what to say, he resorted to his well-worn rejoinder.

"Double eek."

"Double? Why say double Angus?" Opal demanded.

"Because...it's just a saying. You know. Like, poor old Grimslade will have both you and Dulcy on his case. Double trouble."

"Angus, you can't fool me. I know you better than you think..."

Dulcy left quietly while Opal read her personal version of the riot act to her tolerant long-suffering husband.

Chapter 37

Sordid Combat

Pulling Rank

Less than twenty-four hours since consummating their relationship, Dougall and Dulcy were sharing a house. They'd never been thrown together in a domestic situation with a view to continuity. Negotiating unknown territory presented a few teething problems.

Dougall grabbed Dulcy's luggage, a suitcase in each hand, as soon as she arrived back that Sunday afternoon.

After rushing about in the steamy weather for most of the day, Dulcy felt sticky, whiffy and irritable from the heat. She'd been glad he hadn't gone in for a close embrace before she freshened up.

The man carried her suitcases into his house and placed them in the spare bedroom. Over the moon to have his new love move in, Dougall made a magnanimous offer.

"This is your private space, just for you Dulcy. I won't ever come in here. So you can always escape my sordid combat whenever you like." he said.

Sordid combat! Could he think of a less romantic way to describe making love to me?

"Thanks Dougall. That's a sweet deal. Alright. I'll sleep in here from now on."

Dougall stared at Dulcy's stiffened back as she began to unpack, unsure if he'd made some faux pas. It occurred to him perhaps she expected a hello kiss before he grabbed her suitcases. Or maybe as an independent career woman, she wanted to carry her own bags. He feared his flawless generosity may have backfired.

Dulcy began unpacking her wrinkle-proof business clothes. Chosen for ease of laundering, the outfits went straight onto coat hangers in the wardrobe.

Dougall analysed what he'd said that apparently put her back up. He wished for a pen and paper to clarify the process. He wondered if by saying her room was her own, she thought he wanted to keep his own space off limits. He'd have to knock that idea on the head because he wanted this woman beside him all night, every night. She seemed to be miffed so he decided to give her time to settle down.

"Let me know if you need more coat hangers. Or anything." he said.

"Oh. Are you still here?"

"Sorry. Okay. I'll leave you get on with it."

Dougall's thoughts went in circles as he made his way to the kitchen to nuke something for the evening meal. Giving her a hello kiss now seemed too late because the right moment had passed. At least he could set a proper tea table instead of eating from trays in front of the box. He told himself women liked that sort of crap.

His new lodger appeared, fresh after her shower. She looked cool, calm and collected in a summery nightdress. High humidity made for a very warm evening, and after the previous night of naked bedroom action Dulcy deemed it false modesty to add a robe.

Standing in the open doorway of the back verandah, Dulcy hoped to catch a breeze off the ocean, though not a breath existed in the becalmed weather. In the last light of day, the sight of her curvy figure silhouetted through fine cotton left little to the imagination.

Seeing her like that, Dougall determined to put his foot down about where she'd be sleeping. For the time being, he decided to play it cool by making mundane conversation.

"Spaghetti and meatballs okay? This is one of Isla's gourmet contributions. I'm not sure what the herby bits are."

"Basil and oregano. It smells delicious. I'm quite hungry now."

"In honour of your first dinner here since you've *really* moved in properly, I've set the dining table."

"It looks lovely. Thanks for taking the trouble, Dougall."

"Sorry I couldn't find any candles."

"That's okay. It feels too warm for candles anyway. But I'll get some next time I grocery shop. I'll plan some meals to cook too. We shouldn't keep taking advantage of Isla's generosity now that I'm here."

Encouraged by Dulcy's better mood, Dougall added another incentive.

"I'll do my fair share too Dulcy. Isla thinks I exist on takeaways, but I do cook sometimes." Dougall said.

"Really? Do you have a favourite dish?"

"No, I just grab one of those earthenware plates off the dresser. They're supposed to be heat proof, but I found they crack if you try heating them on the stove top."

Dulcy couldn't be sure if he was serious.

"Okaaay...but what do you like to cook Dougall? What are you good at?"

"Toast."

"Toast?"

"Yep. You name it, I do it. Bread, crumpets, English muffins. Admittedly, I triggered the smoke alarm once. I'm proud to say I've since mastered the intricacies of cooking raisin bread."

Unfamiliar with the domesticated version of Dougall, Dulcy suspected he was having a go.

"Are you practising your poker face now Dougall?"

"Huh? Do you doubt my ability? I can do you a buttered toast right now to go with the spag."

"No that's okay. The spaghetti is plenty. Thanks anyway."

Dougall made a show of pulling Dulcy's chair out. He'd seen movies where waiters did it. On top of his culinary expertise, he felt being so well house trained had to impress. He congratulated himself when Dulcy smiled her approval.

"We can watch the box later though. There's a rerun of Vera on."

"Wonderful."

Dougall poured light ales and they sat down to dine.

"Pass the parmesan please."

"There you go."

"Thank you."

Apart from polite small talk, they ate in silence. The night ahead featured uppermost in both their minds. The lawman decided to lay down the law, to make sure they were on the same page:

"Ahem. Dulcy, we need to talk. I just want to straighten something out. In case I gave you a wrong impression."

Dulcy smiled to herself. She'd been waiting for this.

"Have you something important on your mind Dougall?"

"Well, as you know Dulcy, I don't like pulling rank. Not with you anyway."

Pulling rank? Has he absolutely no idea at all?

"I feel a *but* coming on." she said
"But..."
"And there it is. Yes?"
"... I stand by what I said, the spare room is your private domain in this house, however..."
"However?"
"... you will be sharing my bed with me. Every night." he declared.
Dulcy returned his gaze. Her expression gave nothing away.
"Yes sir."

Surprised Dulcy caved so meekly, and for the first time ever, actually called him *sir*, Dougall scanned her face.

"Are you practising your poker face now Dulcy?"
"Maybe. How am I doing?"

Dougall twigged to a sham. She'd had him tap dancing madly for a while thinking they'd be sleeping apart.

"You can do the dishes." he said.
"I was going to anyway." she replied.
"I'll wipe." he compromised.
The domestic task only took five minutes.
"Would you like cocoa or coffee while we watch TV?" Dulcy asked sweetly.
"No thanks. It's way too hot for that. I like a drink of cold milk before bed in this type of weather."
"Okay. I'll bring it in to you...glass or..."

"Either in a cup or a glass, thanks. Plain full cream white milk. Not flavoured. I will leave the choice of vessel to your vivid imagination Dulcy."

"Good." she smiled.

"Not an eggcup."

"Spoilsport."

They watched television for an hour enjoying the UK murder program. Throughout, Dougall had half his mind on Dulcy's teasing, while he formulated a pay back to even the score. After all, they had to work together. He had to uphold his senior status and male superiority.

"Would you like to go for a nice stroll on the beach before bed, Dulcy?"

Surprised he made such an unexpected romantic suggestion, Dulcy enthused:

"Oh. I'd really love that Dougall. Yes. Okay. I'll put my sand shoes on."

"Lock up when you get back in." Dougall yawned. "I'm turning in."

Dulcy was not amused. Not to be outdone, she walked outside and shut the front door. Hard. Dougall sighed, followed her out and found her sitting on the porch bench.

"What are you doing?"

"Putting my sand shoes on. Why?"

"Come on Dulcy. You can't seriously be going walking alone at night."

"It was your idea."

"Guilty as charged. Happy now? What will it take to make you come back in?"

"You could always _pull rank_ and order me to obey. Sir."

"Okay. Granted I used a bad choice of words before. I didn't mean to sound controlling."

"Don't wait up." she huffed.

Dougall tried appealing to her practical side:

"Anyway, there's a storm brewing, and you can't go anywhere wearing nothing but that skimpy nightdress."

"How do you know what I'm wearing under my nightie?"

"I'm a detective."

"A detective who jumped to an unverified assumption." Dulcy crowed.

Dougall stepped in closer, ran his hands up and under her nightdress, and felt what he fully expected. No underwear.

"Verified as assumed. Now kick those damn shoes off, scoot your sassy arse inside and bloody well plonk it in bed beside me."

"Gee. And I thought you were devoid of poetic phrases."

"Dulcy, it's getting late. I want you to come inside. Please."

"Why? Do you want another SKIRMISH? A bit more SORDID COMBAT with me?"

"That's the idea." he said. "Wait. Okay I get it. I suppose that didn't strike you as a particularly sensitive way of putting it."

"Well done Dougall."

"You'd better come in, just look at that lightning."

"I will come inside when _I_ am good and ready. Not when _you_ tell me to."

Dougall realised Dulcy adhered to a principal of eschewing subservience. *Bloody women.* Betting she'd just wait outside for a while, he went inside and got into bed. The man smiled smugly as an ocean squall gusted in, pinging small hail stones against the bedroom window.

After waiting for what seemed ages, more lightning flashed, and icy rain began blowing into the open porch. Chilled to the bone, with the hem of her nightdress dripping down her cold bare legs into her canvas footwear, Dulcy hurried inside. Forcing the door shut against outside pressure, she locked up and discarded her wet shoes and nightie.

Dougall feigned sleep when Dulcy slid shivering into bed beside him, though her freezing hands and feet made it almost impossible. Refusing to flinch, Dougall gritted his teeth waiting for her to warm up. Pretending to wake, he mimicked words she used earlier to bother him:

"Are you still here?"

"Obviously."

"I thought you were keen to take a walk."

"I've been and done that. Thanks for thinking up such a lovely idea for me."

"I'm always thinking of you." Dougall said. "So how was your walk?"

"Brief and bracing."

"I see you ditched the nightdress."

"It got wet."

"On your walk in the rain."

"Hey. You should be a detective Dougall."

"Yet your hair feels dry." the skilled police investigator observed.

"I wore a hat."

"Not my good old yellow sou'wester?"

Dulcy had never taken any notice of the several hats hanging in the porch, but she flew with the handy suggestion.

"Yep. Your good old yellow rain hat came in useful." she fibbed.

"That's funny. That old yellow sou'wester blew away in the cyclone last year. I guess it blew right back into the porch. Maybe it's a homing sou'wester."

Dulcy cringed. He'd caught her out after she'd crowed over an alleged unverified assumption.

"Is that another of your canny and subtle interrogation strategies?"
"Admit it Dulcy. It worked a charm and I cracked your evidence."
he chuckled.
"I bet you imagine it got you nearer to some end goal."

Dammit. Dougall cursed his obsessive penchant for detecting flaws
in statements.

"I'll just shut up shall I?" he said.
"Yes please do. Sir."
"If you keep calling me 'sir' I'm going to be calling you ma'am."
"You win."
"Pardon? Say that again. Can I have it in writing?"

They lay apart in comparative silence, until a sonic boom of thunder
split the ambiance and broke the impasse. Dulcy yelped and startled
in fright. Opal would call it a white girl moment. Dougall drew his
terror-struck woman close and kissed her brow.

"It's alright my love, don't be afraid, you're safe with me." he
crooned.

Instantly, Dougall's clumsy foibles were totally forgiven. His caring
sentiment reinforced Dulcy's devoted allegiance. She loved and trusted
this man. Apart from sleety rain lashing the window, the storm passed
over.

"You almost hit the ceiling then."
"That was just an involuntary physical reaction. I wasn't scared"
"Does anything scare you?"
"I'm scared you plan to talk all night."

"I'll shut up after you tell me how much you love me."
"Deal. Okay. I love you more than a bushel and a peck."
"Is that all?"
"I said more than."
"And you say I lack poetry."
"You're hard to please."
"I'm making that my motto." he smirked.
"How about – I am so in love with you it hurts."
"Well, I did say I'd be gentle, but you...."
"Don't spoil the moment Dougall."

Snuggling warmly together as weather cooled the atmosphere, Dulcy stroked Dougall's broad chest and crept her hand down to his belly.

"Oh yeah." he groaned. "So how about it Dulcy."
"Has that line ever worked for you before?"
"At least once."

Dulcy loved how desire deepened the timbre of his voice. She really, really wanted him.

"I think I'm having another involuntary physical reaction." she said.
"I'm having a voluntary one. I'm stoked you came back to me when you felt good and ready."
"Yes. On my own terms."
"Now I'm feeling good and ready too." he admitted.
"I could stand some of your sordid attentions."
"Just as well." he replied.
"Why?"
"It's the only sort I have."

Chapter 38

GAMES PEOPLE PLAY

Tim Fun Twigs

The boys and their parents enjoyed the *Bob the Builder* sleepover so much, eventually it gained permanence. Chantel and Dominic moved into the beach house.

Occasionally when David and Chantel went out at night, they trusted the tenant Tim Fun to stay and mind the boys. It became obvious to Tim that Chantel and her son had moved in with his landlord.

If only having Chantel in the picture inflamed Dulcy's jealousy, David would have rubbed it in on her. Instead, he accurately foresaw his wife's total indifference to what he did and with whom.

David enjoyed Chantel's passion and company, but he did not love her as he loved Dulcy. He forever regretted burning his bridges and nursed a bruised ego knowing the outcome. Abreast of local gossip, Chantel made sure to keep David informed. She relished reporting that Dulcy moved in with Dougall Grimslade.

More than anything, it irked David learning Grimslade ended up with Dulcy. Embittered, David told himself that had always been on the cards, and considered himself hard-done-by. A recurring dream of seeing her walk away with the lucky guy haunted David.

Tim Fun reported information back to Grimslade, saying David Dubois seemed to be sharing upstairs of the beach house with Chantel Chiron from the surf club. Smart enough to employ tact, Tim surmised more than he let on.

"I didn't know if that news might be significant in any way." Tim said.
"Well Tim, it could be significant. But keep it under your hat."

Dougall imagined Chantel may not endure. Women were often more intuitively aware of goings on than given credit for, and surely Dubois would be trying to win his lovely wife back.

Dulcy had never mentioned divorce, leaving Dougall forever curious whether she remained married to Dubois. He would not ask her outright, telling himself it didn't matter.

Continuing her morning swims in the surf with Isla, Dulcy often glimpsed David on the beach. He must have seen her as well, though he now avoided meeting.
David hoped his deal with Chantel was not common knowledge and didn't want to get into that conversation with Dulcy. At the same time, the old adage *pigs might fly* bothered him with the thought bloody Grimslade was flying high with Dulcy.

Yet David could not let go of a shred of hope. He won hands down in the looks department against grumpy old Grimslade. Surely Dulcy would come to her senses once she got her catty retaliation act out of her system. David fantasised over Dulcy begging to come back.

Chapter 39

Shopping

Big Girls Do Cry

As in the past, Vestige and Grimslade worked the worst cases together. After attending a shocking domestic violence incident, they returned home exhausted.

Having reached the troubled home before uniformed officers, they chased the wife basher who'd made a sudden bid to run. Dulcy tackled the man to the hard bitumen road, ripping her shirt sleeve, just before Dougall caught up to cuff him. Fortunately, the backup squad sped in and took over.

"I didn't know I had a fast sprint left in me." Dougall puffed. "Hey you're bleeding!"
"Just scraped my elbow. It's nothing."

The incident victim suffered serious and personal injuries. Dulcy had the onerous duty of witnessing her medical examination at the hospital, while Dougall completed the arrest and paperwork. Home at last, Dougall gratefully shut the front door.

"I wish I could close the door on what happened there today."
"The romance had really gone out of that relationship."

"Let me see your elbow. And you're limping too."

"It's just a gravel rash. They put iodine on it at the hospital. I'll get over the limp, with a few more swims in the sea."

"You're tired out Dulcy. Why don't you turn in early and I'll cook tonight."

"Toast?"

"Sure. And I'll nuke some soup to go with it."

"That's the most romantic thing I've heard for a long time, Dougall."

"Romance is pretty important, hey."

"More to some than others."

Romance wasn't Dougall's strong suit. Aware he deprived her of it he said:

"You know that time I duped you into thinking I wanted a walk on the beach?"

"I know it well."

"Maybe we could do it for real some time."

"That's okay. I get that you don't want to make any public display of our personal lives."

Dulcy replied so wearily, he felt chastened watching her limp to the bathroom.

"I'm not ashamed..." he began to say, but she had already left the room.

Dougall carefully scraped the charred bits off the toast and burnt his fingers on the microwaved soup, thinking *she's worth it*.

He carried Dulcy's supper tray into the bedroom, only to find her fast asleep.

She wore his over-sized brown plaid pyjamas, evoking his fond memories. Famished, Dougall finished off all the toast and soup himself, vowing he'd bring her a breakfast tray in the morning to make up for it.

Tired as he was, Dougall went back outside to the front porch to make a quick phone call to his daughter. Isla picked up.

"Dad. Hello. All okay?"

"Hard day at the office. But I'm not calling about that. I need your help with something. It will be quite a project I'm afraid. Just say if it freaks you out, Isla."

He gave her a bare outline.

"Wow. Dad. I love it."

"Thanks. I hoped you'd take it well. I'll get back to you with more details this week. Just wanted to forewarn you."

Later, he caught himself searching online for how to boil the perfect egg, as if he needed any more proof that he truly loved Dulcy Vestige.

Dulcy's limp improved with a few more swims in the sea. Salt water stung her grazed elbow. The laceration began to heal but still needed a gauze dressing.

Isla emerged from the surf and prattled on cheerfully:

"Hey Dulcy. Guess what. Tiff wants us to go shopping to help her choose what to wear to the charity ball."

"You're kidding. As if Tiffany needs fashion advice. But I'm in. I have so few clothes now. Everything I own fits into two suitcases."

Tiffany Birdwhistle, nee Dellapinto, enjoyed renown as a local TV celebrity. She featured in a beach soap opera and worked as a local news weather girl. Clothes shopping with Tiff received special treatment at every store. Isla and Tiffany loved to shop and seemed just as obsessed with finding the right outfit for Dulcy.

"Have you got a strapless bra Dulcy?"
"Nope."

Isla just happened to have one in her bag.

"We're about the same size."
"Um. Do you actually carry a spare?"
"No I brought it in case I tried on something off the shoulder."
"Aren't they uncomfortable to wear?"
"Torturous."

Envious of the well-endowed, Tiffany sang - *Big Girls Do Cry.*

"It will be too warm for long sleeves, but I have to cover this damn elbow bandage. Please don't say to wear long gloves because I won't."

Dulcy slipped her casual flatties off to step into the many expensive gowns brought to her booth. Tiffany tried the shoes on for size.

"I'm an eight as well. You've got to come back to my place and try on some of my heels. You can borrow whatever you like."
"Thanks Tiff but I could buy something at a shoe store."
"Not as good as mine, and I have at least fifty pairs. Italian."
"Dulcy, it'd be great to try the shoes on with the dress, and you can do that at Tiff's place."
"You're both being so kind to me."
"Well, Dad told us about your hard day at the office, injured in the course of duty and all, so we want to give you a treat anyway. Plus we can have lunch at Tiff's as well."
"Do you always go to this much trouble clothes shopping?"
"It's like a fatal attraction." Tiffany said.

Dulcy lost count of the outfits she stepped in and out of. She liked many that her younger friends rejected. Finally, Tiffany squealed with delight. She'd found a dark blue one-sleeved gown that covered Dulcy's elbow but bared the other shoulder in a diagonal style. The snug bodice flared softly off the hips to just below the knee.

"You've got to get this one Dulcy. It's perfect."

Back at Tiffany's place, they found the ideal pair of shoes to complement the elegant dress.

"The outfit doesn't need a lot of bling. Just wear those good pearl stud earrings you've got Dulcy."

"I'll take your advice. Thanks girls. I can't believe how the nice shoes improve the effect."

"It helps that you've got great legs too. You look absolutely lovely."

Dulcy actually felt pretty for the first time since learning she wasn't good enough to keep David from straying.

The Birdwhistle sisters-in-law had prepared a light lunch in the apartment that had once been Aiden's bachelor flat. Ethan and Tiffany took it over when they married. Isla surveyed Tiffany's living room with some nostalgia.

"This room is where I first seduced Aiden. It just took a good bottle of wine; he was a complete pushover."

"Ooh. We want to hear all the scandalous details." Tiffany said.

Isla entertained them with her hot unedited version.

"You were a very naughty girl Isla! But I can't talk. Chantel and I competed for Ethan because he was the choicest pick of the lifeguards. Still is too. Anyway, I won. My old school uniform still fits me, so sometimes I wear it to remind him of our first time."

"What? You were still at school Tiffany?" Dulcy exclaimed.

"Yep. Ethan said I was his first virgin. Perhaps not his last because we split for a while when I went to uni. We both played the field. It was understood between us. Anyway, Ethan didn't know I was only fifteen when he rescued me from drowning in the surf. That day, I wore an itsy bitsy teeny weeny yellow polka dot bikini. On purpose of course."

"You're such a strong swimmer too Tiffany." Isla laughed.

The girls looked at Dulcy expectantly as if she had an interesting story to tell. Shaking her head, she gave them a one-word answer:

"Taboo."

"Taboo?" Tiffany laughed. "Oh I get it. If you plan on having your wicked way with Isla's daddy, you can't say so in front of her."

"Less of the in-depth interviewing Tiffany."

"Isla, you sounded like Ethan then. He says that a lot. Everyone's afraid I'll say something inappropriate."

"There is a reason for that." Isla laughed.

Dulcy had no problem engaging in provocative girl talk with Opal and the *poked club* gang. In this instance, Tiffany hit the nail on the head. Describing Dougall's lovemaking to his daughter seemed obscene.

Chapter 40

ONLY YOU

Destiny

The following week, everyone had tickets to the charity ball run by the police club. The major event on the social calendar had long been dubbed The Whodunit Thing.

Dougall and Dulcy attended, but not as an obvious couple. She wore her new dress, her pearl stud earrings and Tiffany's expensive shoes. Dougall told her, in his own words, she looked beautiful before they left home.

"Wow. You scrub up well."
"Thanks Dougall. You're alright yourself. The shade of blue in my dress exactly matches your tie. Is it new?"
"What? This old thing." he said.
"I'll just snip the price tag off it, shall I?"
"Goodness. How long has that been there?"

They shared a long dining table set for nine, with the four Birdwhistles, Opal and Angus Bridcombe, and Tim Fun. After the meal, those at their table divided into men at one end and women at the other. The male end often erupted with laughter over ribald jokes they felt unsuitable for female ears. The women had some raunchy topics of their own which the men never suspected.

Several energetic dancers gyrated their stuff to popular tunes, though none from the nine at their table got up. As the hour grew later, the DJ announced a change of pace:

"I'll dim the lights and set a little mood music. Grab your honeys for a cuddle shuffle."

Several couples moved to slow dance under the revolving lights of a mirrored disco ball. Two numbers into the segment, the DJ piped up again.

"I have an earlier request for *Only You by The Platters*. I'm old enough to remember this one myself. I kid you not. I really am." he waffled.

Dougall rose, straightened his tie, and to Dulcy's great surprise, approached her with purpose. He bowed slightly before taking her by the hand to lead her onto the dance floor. The DJ remembered to add:

"Oh yes. This one is dedicated to Dulcy from Dougall."

The chosen song announced Dougall's feelings for Dulcy publicly. Fingers entwined, he turned her once to the music then drew her close.

"Dougall, everyone is watching us."
"Good."

Slow dancing cheek to cheek, Dougall crooned the loving lyrics close to her ear. The gist of the song declared her to be his dream come true and his destiny. Nothing so beautifully romantic had ever happened to Dulcy. At the end of the song, Dougall kissed emotional tears from her wet cheeks.

"Dulcy, I mean every word of that for you, from the bottom of my heart. I'd go down on bended knee, but I mightn't be able to get up again. Also, I've just had this suit dry cleaned."

Dougall took her hands in his.

"My love, will you marry me?"

Laughing and crying at the same time, Dulcy nodded yes.

The DJ fired up: "I'd say that's a yes!"

Unaware the spotlight had been focused on them, the blushing couple suddenly knew themselves to be the centre of attention. Applause, wolf whistles and a few cheers ensued from the audience. Some at their table gaped, speechless. Aiden caught Isla and Tiffany sharing a triumphant high-five.

"I bet you've had a hand in this Isla. Did you and Tiffany set them up?"
"Maybe."
"For once I'll have juicy gossip to tell Chantel." Tiffany smiled.
"I bet your hot line will be buzzing tonight, Tiff." Ethan said.
Opal exclaimed: "Apparently Dulcy and Grimslade have been a thing for a while. How come I didn't know about this? Who else knew?"
"I knew." Tim Fun said.
"How so?"
"I'm a detective."
"Dougall actually sung all the words to her. I am so jealous." Opal said.
"Why?" Angus asked.
"Grimslade was my plan B for when you dump me." she joked.
"Behave!" Angus said.
"What did you say?"

"I said, behave yourself Opal."

Opal stared at her big gentle husband. The reprimand was the first he'd ever given her.

Encouraged, Angus added: "Or else."

"Eek." she said.

Elated and relieved for nailing the high notes pitch perfect, Dougall completely forgot to present Dulcy with a gift. The costly necklace of freshwater pearls rattled in his pocket.

"Dad. You forgot the pearls!" Isla hissed.

Cripes I knew I'd stuff this up. I'm supposed to say something flowery Isla dreamed up. How did it go? I should have written it down.

"Just do it now Dad."

Borrowing from Aiden's ideal proposal speech to herself...*I'd love to give you the moon and the stars*...Isla had carefully tutored her father on what to say when presenting the gift. Dougall gave it his best shot:

"Dulcy, I'd love to give you the planets..."

Isla mouthed MOON.

"...and a moon."

The other menfolk fell about laughing.

"Anyway, if you don't like these beads, Dulcy, I'm getting my money back."

He clipped the beautiful pearl necklace around Dulcy's neck and kissed her full on the lips. Everyone showered congratulations upon them. Isla and Tiffany wore smug smiles when Dulcy chided them.

"Oh, you two bad girls! I was completely taken in with your charade."

"Welcome to the family."

Dulcy hugged Opal and whispered in her ear: "Darling Opal, you were right all along..."

"Nevermind about that. I'm happy we've both got good strong men now."

Angus yelled, "Now let's see you give her a moon Dougall."

"Of course. They aren't perfect." Opal shrugged.

Dougall put his arm around Dulcy's waist. "I'm taking my woman home now. We fancy a walk on the beach. Enjoy the rest of your evenings."

Unsure if Dulcy remained married to David Dubois hadn't prevented Dougall making his intentions known to all. During a romantic barefoot moonlight walk on the beach he asked:

"When can we make it official?"

"As soon as the paperwork goes through. Decree absolute takes one month and one day after decree nisi. I thought you knew..."

"I didn't like to assume. You know. Without verification. So will you keep your own surname?"

"Do you want me to?"

"No."

"I love you so much Dougall Grimslade, taking your name will be a great honour."

Since Dulcy did not take her first husband's name, Dougall felt to be given his ultimate reward.

Chapter 41

SHUFFLING THE DECK

Life Goes On

Dulcy Vestige finally divorced David Dubois, married the true love of her life and officially changed her name to Mrs. Dulcy Grimslade.

Avoiding pressure to marry his live-in lover, David Dubois failed to mention his divorce to Chantel Chiron. She knew of it from Tiffany anyway but never let on. Chantel liked to keep her options open as well.

David did not see the divorce as final. Absolutely certain Dulcy had always helplessly thrilled to his touch he imagined she must long for him still. Admittedly he'd done wrong by her. Of course she'd need time to get over it. He resolved to forgive her for Grimslade in the circumstances and take her back. It seemed only a matter of time.

Nevertheless, David and Chantel made the most of their union. Chantel remained living in the beach house, making up a family of four. Both were lenient parents, raising their sons as brothers. Largely allowed free rein, the boys grew up to be tearaway larrikins.

In the wake of being childhood fans of *Bob the Builder*, Davy Dubois and Dominic Chiron gained tradie work in the building industry. As teenagers with healthy disposable incomes, the pair got up to all sorts of mischief, partying, drinking and smoking pot.

Hormones raging, Davy and Dominic moved out of the beach house into a flat of their own. When the pair pursued risky entertainments with obliging girlfriends, they all landed in hot water. [*cite A Fair Crack*]

Life chugged along predictably with all the friends and families, who managed to avert too much drama for several years.

Sand hit the fan when all three of the Bridcombe teenaged daughters, Xanthe, Lirah and Kinta, set their sights on the same unassuming bachelor. They'd first met the young detective at a Whodunit Thing they attended with their parents.

As a surf club member, their heart throb did not fit the traditional image of an Australian surfer, being neither blond nor brawny. However, if he was anything like his name, he promised to be FUN.

Never a dull moment ensued on that picturesque Australian coastline.

Chapter 42

HEAVEN SENT

Choices

On his retirement, Dougall and Dulcy Grimslade ventured northwards on a sight-seeing tour.

Dulcy wanted Dougall to meet her much valued friend, Damien Cresswick, of the Kirkwood Bonn murder case.

Happy to know Dulcy married a good man, Damien invited them to stay at his place for as long as they liked: "Mi casa su casa."

One fine day, the Grimslade couple fronted up to *The Brilliant Health Clinic and Wellness Centre* where they planned to spend a few days with Damien.

After meetings and greetings, they settled into Damien's comfortable living room for pre-lunch snacks and aperitifs. Damien brought up the past tragedy that had bonded his friendship with Dulcy.

"I believe you worked together to find Kirkwood's killer. And I thank you both for the exceptional effort you made to discover the truth at last. The outcome remains incredible, yet I have reason to no longer doubt it." Damien said.

"In the long run, we had to accept it as true. Though we'd been skeptical ourselves." Dulcy said.

"We turned it inside out. Because, of course, finding the victim and his killer to be full blood brothers, had been difficult to grasp." Dougall added.

With the most awkward subject aired, they moved to the dining area, where Damien provided a lavish luncheon.

"You're looking very well Damien." Dulcy commented.

"A lot has changed for me. I've achieved some semblance of closure after losing the love of my life. Albeit, it has taken eighteen years."

"I am glad for you." Dulcy said.

"We arrive at closure in various ways. It can take years." Dougall ventured.

Dougall recalled the spectacular shooting star display that enabled his closure on losing Bella. He wondered, without asking, if Damien had undergone anything similar to his celestial experience.

Damien did have an experience of his own to relate:

"Kirkwood's presence has only recently been restored to me. By chance, I hired a junior assistant, who turns out to be Kirkwood's nephew."

Dulcy put two and two together. Surprise lit her features.

"Kirkwood's nephew! Do you mean Alba Jenkins' baby?"

"I do. He is a teenager now. His name is Kirk Jenkins. Alba named him Kirk because that is the name she'd been given by the man who pretended to be my Kirkwood."

"Of course his father had to be the criminal."

Damien forestalled the hated name of the killer being mentioned.

"Yes. That's correct Dulcy. And young Kirk's family resemblance to my dear Kirkwood is uncanny."

Dulcy had trouble imagining Damien hiring a lad who'd been sired by Kirkwood's murderer. It seemed inconceivable that he would want to. As if reading her thoughts, Damien added:

"I realise hiring that boy might seem a strange choice. I struggled with the concept at first. But I could not blame the innocent offspring, who had nothing to do with any of it."

"And now you work together."

"Yes. Happily. And it's as if I have Kirkwood back working with me. Amazingly, Kirk Jenkins is as near to a reincarnation as...to be a cloned replica of him. I could hardly breathe when I first saw the boy. My heart raced so fast, I feared having a stroke. It was electrifying."

"The impact must have been enormous."

"It still is Dulcy. I am constantly astounded. The lad's appearance, the tone of his voice, turn of phrase, everything about him. On top of it all, he shares the same birthday as me and Kirkwood. When that came to light, I think my hair stood on end. It still gives me goosebumps."

"That is truly extraordinary, Damien."

Damien smiled. He felt closer to Dulcy than to any other adult and expanded on his deeply personal story.

"I know it sounds airy, but I really feel to have part of Kirkwood returned to me. As if Kirk Jenkins has been sent...or is truly a message from...heaven...for want of a better explanation. At any rate, I can't explain it any better, but I feel more at peace now. It's as if dying isn't the absolute end, and we might be connected with our loved ones on some higher plane."

Damien Cresswick paused to sip his drink. He acknowledged his take might seem arty-farty to a staid older police detective like Dougall Grimslade who no doubt had his feet firmly planted in reality.

"There I go pontificating. Sorry for going on and on." Damien said.

Dougall replied to put the gentle man at ease: "No need to apologise, Damien. Having a positive outlook makes life worth living."

Years ago, transfixed by the luminous shooting star episode, Dougall perceived it as Bella's blessing for his union with Dulcy. He had played it repeatedly in his mind and still felt it to be real. Hearing Damien's account, Dougall suspected anew there had to be more to life after death.

Once upon a time, the dour detective would have ridiculed such an idea as wishy-washy frivolous codswallop. Yet, the heaven-sent message enabled the widower to take Dulcy wholeheartedly as his new woman, with no self-reproach.

Dulcy loved that Dougall took such an understanding view, and felt blessed to have Damien share his innermost feelings with them both. She had hoped the two men she held dear would get along, and they did. Her thoughts reeled back to her first meetings with Alba Jenkins, leading her to ask:

"Is Alba Jenkins still going alright?"
"Yes. Gladly Alba survives with no apparent ill will towards anyone. As you might recall, her slow wit made her a target of snarky gossip around town. I dare to say, the woman is as nutty as a fruitcake, to be frank. Though she is harmless. Kirk loves her dearly despite being a source of embarrassment for him. He resides in the old homestead with Alba and an older guardian he calls Bob."

Dulcy recalled the backward woman getting pregnant as a result of a one-night-stand with Kirkwood's killer. Alba had imbued her baby's sire with all manner of surreal illusions.

"I remember Alba imagined that man had been sent on a spiritual mission to give her a baby. My view had been, if it prevented her resenting the child, those fantasies served a useful purpose."

"Young Kirk realises he wasn't found under a cabbage leaf, but he must never learn the whole truth. You see, I feel extremely protective towards the lad. Fatherly, if you will."

"It would not do him any good to know."

"I certainly would never tell him. I've been careful to keep all the photos of Kirkwood secured in my private suite...the awkward thing is, young Kirk found an old newspaper article at home. For some reason his mother hung onto it."

"I can imagine Alba doing that."

"So he's seen several good likenesses of Kirkwood there, and read the missing person story. It mentions this clinic and myself and Kirkwood as proprietors. It also remarks on the new female investigator heading the search. That's you of course, as Dulcy Vestige back then."

Memories of her first important case in NT flooded back to Dulcy.

"Some cases just keep cropping up."

"It's the butterfly effect." Dougall said.

"Well, apparently Alba and the old guardian Bob won't say more than it's best forgotten. So, Kirk brought the paper in to ask me about it. I understand his curiosity of course. And I know he is smart enough to figure a connection to himself."

Dulcy recalled some case details.

"The missing person angle had wide coverage but withheld the homicide aspect. How did Kirk handle the news article and seeing the photographs?"

"I had to tell him he is closely related to the missing person. He hasn't asked, but he must know by now the nature of the relationship I shared with Kirkwood."

Dulcy felt sure the teenager would strive to learn more.

"And...is the young Kirk fitting in with your wellness centre here?"
"He is fitting in wonderfully. Kirk is proving the godsend he represents. The lad did well at school and is exceptionally smart. I introduced crystal therapy, to refresh the business, and he picked up straight off that it can only have a placebo effect. Yet, he agrees that can assist some people."
"Though I never met Kirkwood, it sounds like young Kirk Jenkins takes after his uncle and not so much after his mother, or any other." Dulcy said.
"I know what you mean, Dulcy. It's hard to believe Alba Jenkins produced such a personable and clever young man." Damien replied.

They all mused on the fall of the dice in the genetic gamble.

The Grimslades met Kirk Jenkins when he showed up on the final day of their stay. The teenager's mannerisms seemed oddly old fashioned and quite endearing.

"This visit has been wonderful, and we thank you Damien for your hospitality. If you can get away to Queensland in the future we hope you'll stay at ours. Both of you. Dulcy and I have to hit the road though my back is still stiff from the journey up." Dougall said.
"Before you take off, I have a therapeutic application that should help ease that back tightness. Don't worry it's a proven remedy, nothing to do with gem stones."

Damien insisted on giving Dougall a heat treatment and massage in the clinic.   Kirk Jenkins took the opportunity of being alone with Dulcy to speak privately. Having noted her fairly unusual name he asked if she'd been the investigator mentioned in the old newspaper article.

"Yes Kirk. It was my first big responsibility as a police detective."

"I see. So Mrs. Grimslade, I hope you won't think me too forward. But I am eaten up with needing to know why I look exactly like the missing person."

"Kirk, I understand from Damien you are closely related to the late Kirkwood Bonn. If that helps."

"I realise you may be sworn to confidentiality in your private and professional capacity. But please enlighten me if you can. Obviously my boss Mr. Cresswick and Kirkwood Bonn had a special relationship. I am not that way inclined by the way. Not that there is anything wrong with it."

"I am subject to certain ethics." Dulcy hedged.

"Please bear with me if you will. Allow me to cut to the chase Mrs. Grimslade. Was Kirkwood Bonn my actual father? I know that would make him bi-sexual of course."

"I can only confirm off the record that you share DNA."

"Thank you kindly Mrs. Grimslade. It is just as I thought then."

Dulcy may have misled young Kirk on his true lineage. She chose the prevarication as providing the murder's son a better self-image than the real truth.

Arriving home after their holiday, Dougall tentatively brought up the topic of everlasting life.

"What did you make of that visit with Damien Cresswick, Dulcy?"

"On the surface of it, Damien feels blessed to have a part of Kirkwood Bonn back in his life. It's almost as if young Kirk Jenkins is their child, his and Kirkwood's, since he admitted to fatherly feelings towards the lad."

"I suppose if it helps him come to terms there is no harm in believing what he wants to. Sort of like the placebo effect he spoke of with his gem therapy."

"That's what I decided when Alba Jenkins announced her pregnancy to the criminal. At first I couldn't understand how she could be happy about it. Bruce Luck lied, took advantage, robbed her and turned out to be a heartless murdering scoundrel."

"Though she never begrudged bearing his child." Dougall replied.

"On the contrary. Alba believed she'd been especially chosen. She elevated the sperm donor to some sort of spiritual hero whose arrival out of a dust storm had been magic. I guess being rather witless worked in her favour and benefited her baby."

Dougall nodded.

"Stranger things happen. I'm led to wonder if certain outcomes aren't part of some grand master plan."

"You are being particularly philosophical today, my love."

He patted Dulcy's knee, affectionately. Dulcy kissed his cheek. She enjoyed the rare occasions they shared deep and meaningful conversations.

"Something plays on my mind Dulcy. I think about you and me. How we got together. It took a tangled roundabout turn of life-changing events."

"I've contemplated the *what ifs* too. I mean, what if the terrible tragedies hadn't happened. And what if David hadn't deceived me.

Then if I go way back to my childhood...what if I hadn't been so obsessed with solving mysteries."

"And what if you hadn't joined the police force."

"True. The old butterfly effect did its thing."

"Sometimes I imagine we're a match made in heaven, and you were especially chosen for me, Dulcy."

"Well, my darling Doogie, perhaps that is the case."

"You called me Doogie."

"Did I?"

Dougall never spoke of his farewell with Bella. It did not sit well with his pragmatic outlook, nor with his bent for logical explanations. Yet he came to firmly believe Dulcy had been especially chosen for him. His reply homed in on both his dearly loved wives.

"Very Good. We are all on the same page with that then."

The End

GLOSSARY

<u>Theme credits:</u>

You Don't Know Me [Ray Charles – 1962] Written by Cindy Walker & Eddy Arnold recorded 1956.

Only You [The Platters - 1954] written by Buck Ram & Andre Rand.

Song lyrics cannot be reproduced here due to copyright laws. Artists videos and lyrics are readily available online.

<u>Colloquialisms:</u>

Give a moon – Mooning is the act of displaying one's bare buttocks by removing clothing, e.g., by lowering the backside of one's trousers and underpants, usually bending over, and also potentially exposing the anus and genitals.

Having a go at someone – kidding them

Pull a leg – deceive someone in a humorous or playful way

www.ingramcontent.com/pod-product-compliance
Lightning Source LLC
Chambersburg PA
CBHW070432170726
48291CB00002B/465